MURDER IN YIDDISH

MURDER IN YIDDISH

BY

ISIDORE HAIBLUM

ST. MARTIN'S PRESS
NEW YORK

Design by Jaya Dayal

Library of Congress Cataloging-in-Publication Data

Haiblum, Isidore.
  Murder in Yiddish.

  "A Thomas Dunne book."
  I. Title.
PS3558.A324M79   1988   813'.54   87-28608
ISBN 0-312-01482-1

First Edition

10 9 8 7 6 5 4 3 2 1

For Tomar,
my guardian angel,
with love and kisses

CHAPTER 1

I'D ALREADY FED MY PAL, THE GRAY MOUSE, AND HE'D BEAT IT back to his hole or wherever he hung out. I ignored the roaches; they'd have to fend for themselves. The spiders and I had a deal. They'd been here longer, so if they let me alone, I was willing to return the favor.

The lights were doused. I'd planted myself in the battered easy chair by the window; it was a bit short on stuffing, but there were always the springs to prop me up. I could stand some propping. Outside, murky night pressed down on the row of tenements like some huge black hand. A few lit windows made feeble swipes at the darkness, but the rest had tossed in the towel. The entire neighborhood seemed blighted by fatigue, myself included.

I sat glassy-eyed, gazing across the scraggly back yard at Keller's digs. The guy was still awake. I knew this for two irrefutable reasons: first off, I could see him, or at least part of his sloping back and right shoulder—I had a pretty good view through his rear window; secondly, I was getting an earful of his dumb TV. It was coming in loud and clear. About a month ago, during Keller's absence, I'd rigged a pair of spike mikes in his flat. They looked like tiny nail holes and were stuck in his living room and bedroom ceilings. The sending equipment, no bigger than a cigarette pack, was buried under a floorboard. The whole thing was sound-activated. I didn't get street noise, but anything above a certain decibel was picked up and broadcast to a recorder at my elbow. By keeping the volume up I could catch all the nifty goings-on in Keller's place while they actually happened, which meant listening in on four, five hours of TV most weeknights. On weekends the guy made an extensive tour of the local bars and got home too late and too plastered to turn on the tube. Don't think I wasn't grateful.

I'd spent the day trailing after him. He'd taken me on a merry jaunt to the local OTB parlor, where he put in a tough five hours playing the ponies; a couple of seedy bars, either to celebrate or recuperate; a candy store, where he shelled out for a batch of Lotto tickets; and McDonald's, his eatery of choice. In between we trudged through the gray, dismal streets. This Keller, without a doubt, led the dullest life on record.

Mendelssohn's E minor quartet drifted over WNYC on my bedside radio, blending with Keller's TV. I turned Keller down to a suitable murmur, gave my attention to Mendelssohn. My mood began to shift. The creaky house, deadbeat tenants, and assorted vermin faded into a distant corner of my mind, one that didn't count. I soared away with the maestro's quartet. As always, it brought peace and calm, put things in their right order, made me feel whole and centered again. He'd knocked off the E minor while still a mere kid. The least I could do was get through another day, right?

At eleven fifteen the TV finally shut up, and five minutes later Keller's window mercifully went dark.

"Night, deadhead," I muttered.

I stood up, yawned, peeled off my blue T-shirt, jeans, and shorts, kicked off my New Balance running shoes, climbed into a pair of bright green pajamas, and fell into bed like a certified cadaver. I'd done nothing all day but drag after this nerd and here I was dead tired. The mattress—it had come with the territory—felt hard and lumpy and about two inches thick, which may have been one inch too many. A thin slice of moon gleamed coldly through one of the grimy windows. I could hear the rumble of distant traffic on Second Avenue. Haydn took over from Mendelssohn. I listened awhile, but my thoughts kept creeping back to the jerk across the yard. I killed the radio, rolled over onto my side, pulled the blanket up over my head, and went to sleep. I'd had my fill of Keller. Enough was enough—only it wasn't.

In the dream, Keller's head floated in midair like a small, ugly, flesh-colored balloon. He had thin lips, a long nose, graying hair. His eyes were black and staring. The guy was yakking away a mile a minute, but with the voice of a young girl. That surprised me. I tried to catch his words—I knew they were important—but they made no sense, came tumbling out in one long endless sentence that was pure gibberish.

Then I was running along a deserted street, dark, squat houses on both sides of me. Keller's crazy high-pitched girl's voice was screaming behind me. I twisted around, peering back over my shoulder, but saw nothing. I kept running. Ahead, a lone figure stood next to a streetlamp. It was Keller. He wore a pin-striped three-piece business suit, a narrow red tie. The screams came from his mouth. I tried to turn, to run away—I knew I shouldn't meet this guy—but some force dragged me toward him. Now there were two voices screaming, his and mine.

I opened my eyes.

The room was dark. The luminous dials on my clock read 1:20. So far, so good. Everything shipshape, nothing to complain about. Except maybe for one very small item: the screams. I could still hear them. I lay there and wondered vaguely how they'd managed to escape from my dream. Some trick. I waited for the noise to stop, for sanity and sweet reason to reassert themselves. My patience was rewarded. Silence reclaimed the darkness.

The damn quiet did what the screams couldn't do: rolled me out of bed, as if a thick finger were prodding me in the ribs. I fumbled for my robe, got the lights on all at the same time. In this dump the tenants were either doddering oldsters or welfare mothers. If someone was in trouble, I wasn't merely their best bet, I was their only one—an honor I needed like a hernia.

A few steps carried me out of my bedroom into my catchall living room. An antique stove, a holdover from the horse-and-buggy era, and a beat-up kitchen table sagged against one wall, all but wheezed; a chipped bathtub and sink leaned against the other. One of the rusty faucets gave off its usual irritating drip.

I got to the door, worked the double locks, turned the knob. In the hall, dim light from a single naked thirty-watter splashed over crooked stairs and peeling walls. My bare feet scraped against the splintery floor; I'd neglected to put on my slippers. That made it perfect. I stood stock still, cocked an ear. Nothing. Not even a peep. For a brief second I wondered if I'd imagined the whole thing, if tailing Keller on his dopey errands hadn't finally rotted my brain. Then I was racing up the stairs toward the fourth floor. The screams had seemed to come from somewhere above me.

Four apartments to a floor. No lights under any doors, no voices raised in alarm, as though the building had long been vacated for demolition and I was the only tenant left in the place.

I stopped again, straining my ears. Nothing doing. For all I knew, screams here were a regular occurrence, the work of some hophead or wino, old hat for the other tenants, who didn't give them a second thought anymore. I was starting to feel silly, as though I'd been caught playing hide-and-seek all by myself.

One floor left. I climbed the stairs more slowly now, doubt putting a crimp in my legs. The stairs seemed to groan under each step I took, the walls to veer away at my touch. If this dump were a horse, they'd have shot it long ago. I reached the last landing. Three doors were dark on the fifth floor; faint light came from under the fourth. I could hardly believe it.

Two steps brought me to the door. My knuckles pounded on the wood panel. I waited, trying to remember who lived here. Miss Sachs? That wasn't right. It wasn't old man Lipsky, either. "Mrs. Kazmir," I said hopefully, "you okay?"

Instantly, the door came open.

Jackpot!

Jackpot ended right there.

She was short, stooped, her face a maze of wrinkles, her long white hair in disarray. She wore a worn brown robe over a faded flannel nightgown. The bent finger she held up to her lips shook. She motioned me in wordlessly with a twitch of her head. That twitch would have sent most men running for their lives, but I was too groggy to be sensible.

I stepped in and the door swung shut. Kazmir turned the lock, fastened the chain. She was taking no chances. All of her was shaking, I saw, not just her hands.

I glanced around the flat: a junky table, a couple of mismatched chairs, a rusted sink, bathtub, ancient stove, and four peeling walls. Just like home. If there was anything wrong here, I couldn't spot it.

"What is it, Mrs. Kazmir?" I asked.

She turned from the door; her finger darted up to her thin lips. Her head wagged at the right wall. She stared at me. In the silence, I stared back.

An unpleasant thought began crawling through my mind: this Mrs. Kazmir had slipped her moorings, landed back in second childhood. Here was my midnight screamer in the flesh, every last wrinkled inch of her. My headlong charge up the stairs hadn't been a stroke of genius to start with; now it began to look like an outright act of idiocy. Playing nursemaid to this fossil wasn't precisely my idea of how to spend the night.

I made my voice low, comforting. "Don't be afraid, Mrs. Kazmir. Tell me what happened."

"I not know it you, Mr. Gordon. I think it them."

"Them?" I said.

5

"Two men come next door," she whispered. "Beat Mrs. Silbert. I hear through wall."

I looked from the old girl to the wall and back again. Neither was an uplifting sight.

She wagged her head some more. "Put ear to wall. You hear, maybe."

I put my ear against the wall and listened. A lot of stony silence greeted me. I hadn't expected anything else. I turned to Kazmir. "It's pretty quiet," I told her. The understatement of the year.

"They there," she whispered. "Do terrible things to Mrs. Silbert."

I nodded, but it was only to humor the old crone, not out of any sense of conviction. Conviction had flown the coop long ago; you could see it kicking up its heels down the road. Silbert was a drab gray-haired lady in her late sixties, I seemed to recall, who worked in a bakery. Imagining anyone in his right mind wanting to do terrible things to her was no cinch. It required a lot more effort than I was willing to put out just now.

"Police! Run! Bring police!" Kazmir hissed at me.

Run, yet. I shook my head sadly. Someone had been having a bit of a nightmare, either poor old broken-down Kazmir, or Silbert. The kind of help they needed didn't come from cops. Lord knows where it *did* come from. But it sure as hell wasn't my problem.

"We'll see," I said. I moved toward the door.

"Where you go?"

"Next door."

"No! They hurt you, Mr. Gordon—"

"I'll be fine," I assured her.

She dodged in front of me. "Not go, Mr. Gordon."

I put a hand on her shoulder, gently shoved her aside. "Trust me," I said.

I unlocked the door and went back into the dim hallway. The odor of damp plaster, rotting walls, dried urine assailed my nostrils. I didn't waste any time. I stepped over to 5C, knocked. "Mrs. Silbert," I called. "It's me, Gordon from downstairs. You okay?"

My words drifted off in the empty hallway like stray birds. The silence that followed seemed to bunch up around my shoulders. I had the very creepy feeling I was back in my dream.

"Mrs. Silbert," I called, this time louder. My hand went to the knob, turned it. I pushed, and the door swung slowly open. How about that?

Dark inside. And dead quiet. The smell of boiled fish and cabbage, Lysol and stale air washed over me, making my stomach cringe. My stomach had the right idea.

A step took me into the flat. "Mrs. Silbert."

My hand groped for the light switch. It clicked on, but no light came. Great. Defective wiring, broken switches, burned out bulbs were the rule in this joint, not the exception.

Pale light from the hall seeped through the doorway, showing me a kitchen–living room that was just like all the others. I was on familiar ground. I went toward the bedroom. In my mind I pictured a rumpled, stewed Mrs. Silbert snoring away in her bed. My mission would be complete then, another triumph of stupidity.

I opened the bedroom door.

A half sliver of light shone through a window and slanted across both walls. I saw Silbert sprawled on her bed, motionless. I saw a dark blur of movement behind the door reflected in the dresser mirror. I saw enough.

I threw myelf left, away from the movement, tumbling to the floor. A shape detached itself from the wall and dived at me.

No time to get to my feet. I sank a fist into the shape's crotch. It grunted, fell away. Another took its place, this one shorter, broader. It kicked at me. An error.

I caught its shoe in both my hands and twisted. The shape joined me on the floor, became a thick-nosed man who stank

7

of whiskey and needed a shave. I drove a fist into his face. His head thumped against the floorboards, a neat, satisfying sound. He rolled away.

I got to one knee. A shoe came out of the darkness, catching me high on the cheekbone. I went down again like a nearsighted oldster hunting a lost coin. Dust filled my nostrils. I tasted blood in my mouth.

A tall thin man, who belonged to the shoe I'd grabbed, landed on me. Another error. The guy was a lightweight. I was still alive. He shot his fist into my face, smacked me again. I didn't like that. I put my elbow in his throat, then sliced hard at his neck with my open hand. He twitched. I slammed him in the jaw. He went limp. I flicked him off me like a piece of lint and scrambled to my feet.

Shorty was already there to greet me, his fingers curled around a thick sap. He swung it at me, a nice wide arc. I stepped in close, blocked it with my right forearm, sank a left into his belly. He doubled over. I snapped his head back with a right and he stumbled against the bed.

Sugar Ray never moved faster. I forgot about the guy behind me: he was supposed to be safely out for the count. Guess again. *My* error this time—I only got to make one. Something very solid crashed against the back of my head, rocking me right down to my toes. The room lurched sideways and began to spin frantically.

I lost track of the bout, stopped caring about poor old Silbert, whom I hardly knew anyway. The world was twilight. With a blinding clarity I seemed suddenly to understand the whole of Ludwig Wittgenstein. This was peculiar, because so far I'd only managed to get through two and a half pages of his work.

Another whack seemed to split my skull into lots of tiny unruly splinters. A dark wave rose out of the night, started to carry me away with it. I didn't mind. By then I was more than ready to go.

CHAPTER 2

THE NOISE CAME FROM A LONG WAY OFF. IT WAS AN ANNOYING sound that had nothing to do with me. I lay very still, hoping it would go away. I got my wish. Darkness covered me again like a warm, cozy quilt.

I don't know how long I lay there.

Cold air nudged me. I heard the sound again; it seemed closer this time. I moved my head. No wisdom in that. I stopped moving, and whoever was hammering spikes into my cranium stopped too. That left the nausea. I thought I might live with it, just barely, for a very short while.

By now any notion I'd had of grabbing another forty winks had gone by the boards. I was awake, and worried. My memory had sprung a fatal leak. Something *bad* had happened, but I couldn't for the life of me remember what. Or even to whom. I played possum for a while, waiting for enlightenment. Time crawled by like a badly crippled spider. Enlightenment didn't follow. This could be a long wait, I realized. Very slowly I pried open an eyelid.

My left cheek was using the floor as a pillow. A dark shape hovered above me: the bed. Instantly I recalled where I was and what had happened, and wished I hadn't.

I heard the sound again and this time knew what it was: a groan. At least it wasn't mine.

In slow motion, making very sure not to move my head, I

raised one hand, then the other, to the edge of the bed and began to lever myself up. It took some doing. My knees were made of cheap cardboard and my stomach was busy trying to crawl up my windpipe.

I stood swaying on lifeless legs, trying to ignore the room, which was doing cartwheels around me, and looked down at Silbert. I'd seen prettier sights. My two pals had worked her over plenty. Both eyes were blacked; bruises covered cheeks and chin. There was blood on her forehead. The old girl was still breathing, but how long that would last was anyone's guess.

My eyes searched the room. No phone, of course; that would make things too simple. The window leading to the fire escape was wide open. The chill air that had goaded me awake had come from there. The pair of goons had probably used the fire escape to make their exit. I wished them lots of speed.

I sighed. Time to get a move on. This life of ease could ruin a man's character. Silbert needed help pronto, and I wasn't feeling so hot myself. All I had to do was make it down the stairs to my flat and the phone. All was plenty.

I took a deep breath, turned, and slowly started for the door. It figured to be a long, depressing haul.

A sound that could have been a word came from behind me, bringing me up short. Another sound, half word, half gurgle followed it.

I wiped sweat from my forehead and did a careful about-face, as if a large, bulky weight were precariously balanced on my shoulders. Tom-toms pounded in my head, and fireflies were dong a hoedown in front of my eyes. A little more entertainment of this sort and I'd be all set to claim my wings and halo. Through the haze, I saw Silbert. She was awake, her eyes open. She was trying to speak.

I held up a shaky hand. "Take it easy," I told her in a voice I didn't recognize. "Lie still. I'll call an ambulance."

Silbert rolled her head. Something that sounded like *No* came through her puffy lips.

I looked at the old girl. *No* was the wrong word. She was hardly in shape to be left alone. Even if she didn't want an ambulance, there was always me to consider. Any humanitarian would. I was a prime candidate for the medics if ever there was one.

I whispered, "Listen—"

Silbert opened her mouth. Maybe what she said made perfect sense to her. All I got was a number of disconnected syllables and more of a headache, if that was possible.

"Hold it," I whispered. I gauged the distance between me and the bed. True grit would find a way. Putting one foot in front of the other, as though I were walking a shaky tightrope, I started back. This being a Good Samaritan could have its drawbacks, I saw.

Reaching the bed, I rested. I thought of leaning over but gave it up as a lousy idea. "Okay," I mumbled at her, "shoot. But go slow. You're tough to follow just now."

"Book," Mrs. Silbert said.

"Uh-huh," I said. I'd finally made out a word. But it hadn't exactly brought enlightenment.

"Bookcase," she whispered.

"Yeah?" I said.

"By door."

"Go on."

"Eight book. Left. Bottom shelf."

"What about it?" I asked. It seemed a reasonable question.

"Take."

"Take," I said.

"Please."

"Mrs. Silbert," I began.

"Take! Must take!" She started to cough.

"Okay," I told her, "easy does it. I'll take. Then I'm going for help."

"Yes."

I shuffled off on my errand. That was the simple part; reaching the bottom shelf was another matter. My head wanted no part of bending. I finally lowered myself to the floor and perched there like a sitting hen—it was either that or keel over.

I counted eight books from the left and removed a faded green volume, which turned out to be a cookbook. Naturally. Now we could whip up a small soufflé while the oven was free. Silbert was raving, but I couldn't blame her; I was headed down the same route myself.

Clutching my find, I used the bookcase to hoist myself back onto my feet. I waved the book at her. "This?" I said.

Her voice was very weak. "Open."

It was no time for arguments. I opened.

The sealed envelope was between the cover and the last page. There was no address on it. I was too beat to be startled, or even interested.

"What do I do with this?" I asked.

"Keep."

"You want me to open it?"

"Keep."

"You're the boss, lady."

I wobbled toward the door. A babble of words came after me. It took me a second to realize they were in Yiddish. That's all I needed in my confused state: to be plunked back into my childhood. I turned. She was breathing heavily, her eyes closed, her lips moving. I recognized enough of the words to know she was going over the whole thing again. I don't think she even knew I was in the room.

I went out into the hall. All the doors were shut tight, including Kazmir's. I was on my own again.

I used the railing to help me down the stairs. My mind kept flicking on and off like a shorted light bulb. I stopped half a dozen times to keep from passing out, unaware of how long it was taking me. I finally reached my floor and made it through the door to my apartment.

My bugging device, the recorder-receiver, was out in full view, a real eyesore if I was going to have visitors. I yanked the plug from its wall socket. The gizmo worked on batteries too. I thumbed them on. The whole thing was no bigger than a shoe box. I chucked it into the closet. For good measure, I tossed the letter after it, managing to drop a blanket over both. The workout left me gasping.

I dialed 911—police emergency—and gave them the address and apartment numbers.

"What is it?" a female voice wanted to know.

I was certainly going to tell her, but my mouth suddenly felt as though somebody had stuffed a mattress into it. That made me think of sleep. All on its own, the phone drifted out of my hand. I heard it land far away, too far to worry about.

I tossed in the sponge . . . and dived after it.

CHAPTER 3

I OPENED MY EYES.

I was in a hospital ward, or something enough like one to be its twin brother. Long rows of beds were on either side of me and across the aisle. I got an eyeful of their occupants; they didn't look like world-beaters. There were plenty of casts and bandages, a lot of moans and groans. Half of these guys had tubes sticking in them, attached to overhead, glop-filled bottles. I shifted my gaze and saw that I had one too. I lay there breathing hard and fighting the shakes, just like any other seven-year-old. I'd had my tonsils out around then and made a vow never to land in another hospital as long as I lived. What good was a man if he couldn't keep his word? Daylight shone through a couple of large windows. I smelled medication, antiseptic, pine-scented cleanser, and a lot of disgusting odors I couldn't and didn't want to place.

I moved my head. The results weren't encouraging. A nurse hustled by and I tried waving at her; it wasn't to make a pass. She ignored me. I went back to sleep. It seemed the smart thing to do.

The next time I awoke the tube was gone from my arm. The sun was way over in the west, its rays just catching part of one windowsill. I was snoozing my way around the clock, just like the idle rich, but probably enjoying it less.

I managed to sit up. It only took a couple of tries. My bed

pals, I saw, looked no better than before. Worse, if anything. Last time I'd missed the dried blood on their bandages. I'd hit rock bottom, all right. To be with this crew, I was probably at death's door.

A young guy in a wrinkled white jacket with a stethoscope dangling from around his neck was making the rounds. He had sunken cheeks and black lines under his eyes, and looked only a tad healthier than his charges. He didn't inspire confidence. I managed to get his attention. After a while he actually came over. Score one for the disabled.

"Hi," I said.

"How do you feel?" he asked.

"Like I went ten rounds with the champ and lost each one."

"You've got a concussion," he told me, "somewhere between minor and middling. A little more force and you'd've landed in our intensive care unit."

"How bad is it?" I wanted to know.

"You'll live."

"Thank God. Where am I?"

"Metropolitan Hospital."

"How long do I stay here?"

"Another night."

"That's all?" I was surprised.

"It should do," he said.

"I'm on the mend, eh?"

"We need the bed."

The intern poked around awhile, listened to my heart, took my pulse, peeked under my eyelids, nodded, and went away. I still felt rotten. A little later a short brown-haired nurse showed up with something that was supposed to be dinner. It didn't look any happier being eaten than I was eating it. A tasteless custard pudding passed for dessert. Next time, I decided, I'd think twice before letting someone bash my brains in if this was going to be the payoff.

Eating had worn me out. I closed my eyes, intent on a quiet doze; I had one coming. I slept.

"Mr. Gordon," a voice said. It was a mellow, musical baritone. But why should Robert Merrill want to visit *me?* My eyes came open.

Dark shadows peered in through the windows. The sun had disappeared. Another day down the hatch. Easy come, easy go.

The man above me, I saw instantly, was no sawbones. He was six foot three, a heavyset party in a rumpled gray business suit, blue and purple striped tie loose at his neck. His face was broad, his nose and lips full, his graying black hair combed straight back with a part in the center. His jaw gleamed blue-black; here was a guy who'd always need a shave. An unlit cigar sticking out of one corner of his mouth wagged at me.

"I know someone taller than you," I told him.

"Who, the Jolly Green Giant?"

"Skip it. What can I do for you, Mr. . . . ?"

"Danker. Detective Danker." The guy flashed a buzzer.

"Danker means 'thinker' in German," I told him. "You know that?"

"Yeah. In Dutch, too. Up to having a word with me, Mr. Gordon?"

"Are you kidding? A guy in my condition? Gimme a break. I'd be signing my death warrant."

"You've been doing pretty well so far," he said.

"Last gallant effort," I told him.

Danker pulled up a chair and seated himself heavily, grinning at me and bobbing his cigar in my face. "I'd light this thing but the smell might kill some of the patients."

"You'd be doing them a favor," I said. "Want my story, eh?"

"That's what I want, Mr. Gordon. Your story."

I sat up slowly, as a man might whose body had spitefully turned to rubber, and fooled with the pillows behind my head. Traffic sounded from outside. It seemed a long way off, probably on another world—a better one, I hoped, although I had my doubts. The ward was crawling with a variety of sounds, most of them unpleasant: a jumble of hoarse murmurs, whispers, an occasional moan. A couple of TV sets were going full tilt somewhere in the corridors, each tuned to a different channel. No one seemed to mind. Except me. There's a sorehead in every crowd. I said, "I hit the sack around eleven fifteen. Screams roused me."

"About one thirty?"

"One twenty. I checked."

He nodded. "Half the building heard those screams. Some of the tenants even thought of doing something—they say."

"Nice of them."

"At least they didn't get in your way."

"Yeah. Gordon, the one-man rescue squad. Well, I jumped out of bed like the good citizen I am, beat it up the stairs, had a powwow with Mrs. Kazmir, who directed me to the right place, and went barging in. Lucky me."

"Had a key?"

"Door wasn't locked."

"You and Mrs. Silbert close?"

"Best friend I ever had. Sometimes I even remembered to nod at her in the hall."

"You're a real wit, Mr. Gordon. Go on."

"Mrs. Silbert was on her bed, only she wasn't napping. Two guys were there, tried to jump me. If there was any justice, they'd be here instead of me. They almost were, too. I was holding my own pretty good, till one of them got behind me. When I came to, they were gone. The old lady was all banged up."

"She say anything?"

"Groaned a couple times. I said I'd bring help. I managed to get back to my place and called the cops. Then I blacked out again. I woke up in here."

"Think you can describe the pair?"

"I can try."

Danker got out a pad and pencil from his inside jacket pocket. The pencil had teeth marks on it, as if someone had mistaken it for a snack. I gave him what I had, which wasn't a whole lot; the place had been too dark for fine details. He wrote it all down carefully, as if what I told him might actually be of some help. This Danker was an optimist. "Any idea what it's all about, Mr. Gordon?"

"Search me," I said. "I just happened along. Ask Mrs. Silbert?"

"Can't."

"Still out, eh?"

"Dead, Mr. Gordon."

"*Jesus!*"

"Yeah. Old dame never woke up. Went into a coma early this morning and died three hours later. Internal injuries. You're lucky, Mr. Gordon. You got off easy."

"Charmed life," I said.

"Sure. How long you been a tenant there?"

"Me?"

"Not the guy behind you."

"About a month. Why?"

"Where'd you live before that?"

I looked at him. The damn question had come out of left field. I all but turned a nice shade of brick red. If I'd been in better shape maybe I'd have come up with something smart. But my shape was as out of whack as a squashed banana. I heard myself say, "Upper West Side." Not one of my better lines.

"Got an address?"

"One sixty West Seventy-seventh Street."

Danker nodded. His notebook was still out; the address went down on a fresh page.

I said, "Figure I knocked off Silbert, then brained myself?"

"Perish the thought, Mr. Gordon. The old lady, Kazmir, backs you up. You're aces with me. A damn hero, in fact."

"So what's the beef?"

Danker chewed his cigar. "Tell me something, Mr. Gordon."

"Yeah?"

"What's a healthy young guy like you doing in that rattrap?"

"Jeez," I said, "it's not a flophouse."

"Maybe. It's not the Ritz either. Or the West Seventies, for that matter." He grinned at me good-naturedly.

"Okay," I admitted, "I kinda miss the old neighborhood. But since when's it a crime to go broke?"

"No crime," Danker said. "What happened?"

"I got canned."

"Your job was what?"

"Sales."

"Anything special?"

"Industrial tools."

"And you can't find work?" Slowly, Danker placed his cigar on my nightstand. "I'm surprised."

"Why?"

"Ought to be lots of opportunities," he said, "for an experienced hand."

"These were drilling tools," I told him.

He smiled. "Oil wells?"

"Uh-uh. For machines. Mostly small ones."

Danker eyed me silently.

"Look," I said, "I was with Clinton Tools."

"Where's that?"

"Down on Canal."

"Go on."

"Shop's one of a kind. No competition in Manhattan. Nearest rival's way off in Jersey City."

"Nice place, Jersey City."

"Maybe. But they're full up. And there's not much carry-over to other fields."

"Tough."

"Could be worse," I said. "And probably will be."

"Let's hope not," Danker said. "Why were you laid off, Mr. Gordon? Trouble?"

"Uh-huh. For Clinton, not for me."

"Bad year, I suppose?"

"They've seen a lot better."

"Sure, and someone had to get fired."

"*Jesus*," I said. "What're you digging for, Danker?"

"Nothing, really. Just curious, Mr. Gordon."

"Yeah, nothing. Look, I'd been with Clinton maybe six years. The other guys were twenty-year men, had put in their time. When the crunch came, I got the ax. What's so hard to understand? It happens every day—even to cops, I'd bet." I glared at him. "Satisfied, Detective Danker?"

He picked up his cigar, eyed it sourly and rose. "I'll let you know, Mr. Gordon."

CHAPTER 4

I'D LOUSED UP MY SHARE OF DEALS ALL RIGHT, BLOWN SOME whoppers, but never anything quite like this. If they came out with a special award for screwups this year, I was the odds-on favorite.

Of course, there were extenuating circumstances: the blow to my head had turned my brains to eggplant; I'd thoughtlessly forgotten my Boy Scout motto and been unprepared; I was too busy being a patient to pay attention to my job. Yeah, I had lots of excuses—some real doozies, in fact—and they all led straight to the breadline.

I don't know whether I nodded off for just a moment or a couple of hours. Next time I looked the night was a solid black sheet against the windows. No clocks decorated the white walls, since the natives in these parts had better things to worry about than the passing of time. But time was suddenly important to me.

Only one nurse to the floor. She went scooting by like nobody's business and vanished through a door at the rear of the ward. I was left alone with the groaners and moaners. There were plenty of them just now, and they were working overtime. That was all the encouragement I needed.

I pushed back the blanket. When it came to blankets, I was a whiz. That left the rest of it. Slowly, as though my bones had turned to chalk, I swung out of bed and planted my feet on the cold floor. Not too bad. But a long way from good.

I sat there for a while, breathing hard, as if I'd just climbed a very high mountain and wasn't quite sure how to get down. Then I stood up. My stomach launched itself skyward and my legs turned to pulp. If what I had was only a minor concussion, I didn't want to think about the major kind.

My off-white gown, a real pacesetter in 1902, felt damp and drafty, as if I'd just come in out of a rainstorm. No sign of any pajamas. But some nice person had left my maroon robe neatly folded on the bottom shelf of my nightstand. Thank God for nice persons. I managed to snag it with two fingers, bending only my knees and keeping my head and waist perfectly straight. Perfection is hard to achieve, but I had the proper incentive. I got the robe on, knotted the belt, and was all set for action—that is, I shuffled off down the aisle on bare feet, hoping I wouldn't conk out.

I found the duty nurse in a small, doorless cubbyhole at the end of the ward. She was a bulging, overweight customer in her mid fifties with a squarish, no-nonsense face and a gravelly voice to match. She looked a little like a boxcar. She told me to get back into bed. I said I had to use the phone. She told me it was against regulations at this hour. This hour was only eight thirty, I saw by her wristwatch. I explained that to stay out of hock, I had to take care of a few small matters. In the morning, she told me. The morning, I said, was too late. I pointed out how I was a genuine hero who'd gotten his lumps fighting for a lady and whose business would now go down the chutes if I didn't get to a phone. She said I couldn't tie up the line on her desk. I figured maybe I was making progress. I asked if a pay phone was handy. She said in the hall. I asked if she'd lend me a couple of quarters. We tossed that around for a while. It took a good eight minutes before she coughed up the change. I've never had to work so hard for half a buck in my life.

I grinned at her, clutching my prize. "You're not as tough as you think."

"Don't you believe it," she said. I didn't.

I tottered out into the hallway and made my call. The phone rang three times before it was picked up. A woman's voice said hello. I asked to speak to Mr. Neely.

I stood in the hall between wards, glumly eyeing the dirt brown walls and waiting to pass out. I wanted to sit down on the floor but the phone cord didn't reach that far. Naturally.

A man's scratchy voice said "Yeah?" in the earpiece.

"It's me," I said.

"*Christ!*"

"Something's happened," I told him. "Get to the phone."

"Shit!"

The line went dead.

I put the receiver back in its cradle, eased myself down on the staircase, and sat around for a while. My thoughts weren't exactly uplifting. When I figured five minutes had slipped by, I got up and used my last quarter. A half ring this time.

"Shaw!" Neely bawled into my ear. "What the fuck's going on? You *crazy?*"

"It's like this—" I began.

"Christ, you ain't never supposed to call me at home. *Never!* Never! What the fuck's *wrong* with you, Shaw?"

I pictured Neely in the phone booth we'd picked two blocks from his Queens house and hoped it was at least cold, damp, and lonely in there. Maybe the sucker would get himself mugged. Or a large hole open up under him. This Neely was a bony, nervous, fiftyish squirt with a narrow, lined kisser and beaky nose who lived with a cigarette permanently stuck in his mouth. At best he was a real pain to work for. At worst he was an out-and-out shithead.

"Simmer down," I told him, "our secret's still safe."

Neely coughed his smoker's cough but fell short of hemorrhaging into the receiver. "So why couldn't this wait till

Thursday?" Thursday, eleven P.M., was our regular check-in time.

"Because," I said reaonably enough, "by then it might not be a secret anymore."

"If you put this project in jeopardy—"

"Do me a favor," I said, "shut up."

"*Listen* Shaw—"

"You listen, pal. I'm at Metropolitan Hospital."

"Keller's been hurt?"

"Not Keller. *Me.*"

"You?" The creep sounded dumbfounded.

"That's what I've been trying to tell you. I've just become a patient here."

"You in an accident, Shaw?"

"In a manner of speaking. Some old lady in the building where I have the stakeout was getting the hell beat out of her. Perhaps I wasn't thinking too clearly. What I should've done, probably, was mind my own business. I didn't."

"Shaw," Neely said, "you're getting top dollar for this job."

"I know that."

"And you let some foolishness distract you?"

"They killed her," I said. "There were two guys, and they beat her to death."

"I'm sorry. But this has nothing to do with what I'm paying you for."

"Sure. But I got sapped when I put my two cents in, sapped hard enough to land in here. Know a cop named Danker?"

"Yes."

"Well, he just visited me."

"Ah, *Christ!*"

"He hasn't tumbled to anything yet," I said, "but he can smell something."

"This is your responsibility, Shaw."

"Right. But I'm sort of handicapped just now. I've got a concussion, I may be laid up a day or two. Everything's back at the flat. I had to borrow two bits just to make this call. I gave Danker a story, but it won't hold up if he checks—" The quarter clicked in the box. "Hell. Take this down," I told Neely, and rattled off the number.

He didn't waste any time calling back. "Jesus Christ, you brought the cops into this! You fuckin' moron! This is the dumbest stunt I ever heard of. You sunk us, Shaw, knifed us in the back, butchered us—"

"Cool it, pal," I cut in, "no harm's done yet—"

"You brought the cops in!" Any second the guy would break into tears. Either him or me.

"You're not listening, Neely. I can't stand here chewing the fat all night; I haven't got the strength. And you'll run out of quarters. Just listen. If we cover a few items, we're home clear. I gave Clinton Tools as a job reference. That's okay. I know old man Clinton, used to date his daughter. All I've got to do is talk to him; he'll play ball. My landlord may be a bit tougher."

Neely's voice held all the warmth of an ice cube. "You gave your real address?"

It was cold in the hallway, but not for me. I was sweating like a polar bear stuck in a Florida zoo. My story sounded dumb even to me, and I was the most sympathetic party likely to hear it. A guy with a story like that ought to be hawking pencils and shoelaces on street corners, not wasting a client's money. "Had to," I told him. "This job didn't call for a phony background. Simple surveillance. So there was nothing to fall back on. My place was the best I could do on short notice. Listen, the building's run by Ajax Management. I'm on a first-name basis with a couple of their folks. I can fix it so that Stuart Gordon used to live there."

"You *better* fix it."

"Yeah, well, that's the problem."

"Problem?" He made it sound like the plague.

"Uh-huh. I may not be able to get around for a while, and this thing needs taking care of right now."

Neely's voice was deadly. "Any suggestions, Mr. Shaw?"

"We've got to bring my partner into this, have him pinch-hit till I get back on my feet. There's no other way."

"That beating, Shaw, must've scrambled your fucking brains. I hired you to do a job, not give me orders. This is your mess; you get yourself outta it. I don't want anyone involved but you. That was our deal."

"You're a real sweetheart, Neely."

"Who told you to get your brains beat out, wise guy? I'll be here Thursday. I better hear you got this thing under control."

"I'll do my best."

"You better do better than that, fuckup."

The line went *click*. I was left standing alone in the drafty hall with my king-size headache, damp scratchy hospital gown, and cold feet. It wasn't one of my finer moments, that was for sure. Actually, I knew, there was nothing to be hysterical about—not yet. I was merely getting in some practice.

I went back and haggled the hard-faced nurse out of another half buck. It only took ten minutes and made my chat with Neely seem like child's play. I used the hall phone again and got Harry Canfield on the first ring.

"Harry? Jim."

"Ah," Harry said, "a voice from the void."

"Just about. I've had a little accident."

"Fell off the wagon, huh?"

"That was last year's accident. I'm in Metropolitan Hospital."

"You kidding?"

"I should be so lucky. Know where it is?"

"Sure."

"What's the soonest you can get here?"

"Half hour; forty-five minutes, tops."

"Okay, I'll meet you by the parking lot entrance. Bring some slippers and an overcoat. Got that?"

"Yeah."

"See you."

I forked a quarter back to the nurse, thanked her, asked directions for the men's room.

"Through the ward on your left," she said, "but you should use your bedpan, Mr. Gordon. You need rest."

"Who doesn't? But I need my dignity more."

I padded off to the men's room, where I laid low for a while. No one bothered me. Once I took a squint in the mirror. A face that seemed vaguely familiar stared back at me. It wasn't quite the face I knew and loved or could address on a first-name basis. This face had seen better days. It was the type they usually put on cans of weed killer and Flit. I splashed water on the damn thing but couldn't wash out the purple patches under the eyes, the pinched look around the mouth, the greenish tinge of the skin. I was starting to feel sorry for that face. I couldn't afford the distraction. I gave it the cold shoulder from then on.

Some thirty-five minutes later I used the stairs to creep down to the ground floor. Only five floors, but it seemed more like a few dozen. I hung on to the dumb bannister as if it were a life preserver, stopping every few steps to catch my breath. Sweat made my gown cling to me like a sex-starved lover. Here was a first-class preview of decrepitude, and I hated every second of it. I met no one on my way down.

Leaning against the wall by the double doors that led out to the lobby, I waited till the coast was clear. I was breathing hard and fast, as though I'd just run the New York Marathon and come in last. When no one was looking, I made my play: I stepped into the lobby and stumbled toward the nearest exit.

The street was cold and dark. An icy blast of air all but sent me sprawling. My bare feet were ready to take root and freeze me to the spot. If my concussion didn't get me, pneumonia would. I tightened my robe around me and went hunting for the parking lot.

Streetlamps made bright ovals in the darkness. A few pedestrians gave me the eye but kept on going. A well-trained bunch. I felt as if I'd just busted out of the state pen, when all I'd really done was taken leave of my senses.

I rounded the corner and there was the parking lot, a concrete isle surrounded by a wire fence. Harry's '68 blue Ford was parked by the gate.

I waved a feeble arm, which went unnoticed, and ended up hiking the distance. I rapped on the window. Harry's round boyish face with its mop of blond hair turned; he peered through the pane. The car door popped open and I tumbled in. Nothing to it.

He said, "Hi. You look awful. Should I take you back to the hospital?"

"To a funeral parlor," I told him. "Why bother with the middleman?"

Harry nodded cheerfully, gunned the motor, and we sailed off into the night.

CHAPTER 5

I MANAGED TO WIGGLE INTO THE COAT AND FIT MY FEET INTO the soft slippers Harry had brought along. I stuck my hands into the wide coat pockets, sighed, and waited to get warm. I felt almost human; all it took was the right getup and the sight of Metropolitan Hospital fading into the background. Almost, however, wasn't quite enough.

Outside, the night streamed by in a dim, cheerless streak. Empty, weedy lots, and crumbling tenements competed for space with high-rise towers still under construction. The area looked as if it were ravaged by a time warp, half yesterday, half tomorrow, with no in-between. The luxury apartments to the south only made the place seem more squalid. I was in no mood to face reality.

"Onward," I said with feeling.

We left Ninety-sixth Street and turned up Lexington Avenue. Things began to improve. No loose debris disfigured the streets. Only a couple of medium-size buildings—including the YMHA, which took up an entire block—and a lot of smaller ones. Darkened storefronts, fresh fruit and vegetable marts, a variety of eateries lined the pavement. Traffic was sparse, pedestrians few and far between. Just what the doctor ordered. I could stand the peace and quiet. It didn't last long. As we neared Eighty-sixth Street what passed for civilization in these parts hit the skids. Tumult rose to greet us. Lights blinked, winked, all but whistled; marquees glared, seemed to reach for the marks. Long lines wound around movie houses like giant snakes. Fast-food joints were doing a booming business and trash cans spilled over onto the roadway. Cars whined, horns jeered, exhaust fumes pelted the air. I leaned my head against the seat, shutting my eyes, and the annoying sights went away. That left the sounds and smells.

"Jim," Harry said.

"Yeah?"

"Something fall on you?"

"Two guys slugged me."

"Hit 'em back?"

"Uh-huh."

"What happened?"

"They weren't impressed."

"Tsk-tsk."

"Yeah, my sentiments exactly."

We rode into the Seventies and the racket fell behind. The engine purred under us. My slick getaway from the sick ward had been my grandstand play. I was ready and eager to rest on my laurels and call it quits for the night. I started to doze off.

Harry's voice jarred me awake. "You want I should chauffeur you around town, maybe show you the high spots, or you got someplace more definite in mind?"

"Home, Jeeves," I said, and went back to sleep.

Harry gently touched my shoulder.

"To hear is to obey," he said.

I pried open my eyelids—no mean trick—and glanced over at the blue awning of my West Seventy-seventh Street domicile, a fifteen-story, yellow brick apartment house.

"Good job," I told him. "I never doubted you for a moment." My mouth tasted like something the cat had dug up in the gutter, and my head was keeping time to a distant drumbeat. My workout on the staircase had left me limp. "Okay pal," I said, "get me outta this damn conveyance."

"How quicky they age," Harry said. Climbing out, he came around to my side of the car. I got the door open and, leaning on his arm, managed to vacate the Ford.

"Pretty spry," Harry said.

"You should see me on my good days," I told him. Harry half carried, half supported me to the vestibule. A locked door blocked further progress. My keys, of course, were back at Ninety-fourth Street.

"We break it down?" Harry asked.

"Uh-uh. We use reason and logic." My finger jabbed the super's bell.

"Yeah?" a voice said through the intercom. I identified myself and was buzzed in.

"The scientific method," I told Harry, "never fails."

The super was a short stocky guy of indeterminate age named Virgil Zacks. He lived on the ground floor next to the service elevator off the lobby. That's where we met him.

Zacks broke into a huge grin when he saw me. "Hey, you're back, Mr. Shaw." His grin faded when he got a closer look at me. "You been sick or somethin'?"

"It's nothing, Virg," I told him, "just a little accident. I'll be fine in a day or so."

Zacks took a second gander at me. My bare legs were sticking out from under the coat; I could feel a draft on them. His mouth opened. "Jeez, what happened to your pants, Mr. Shaw?"

"He gave them to me," Harry said, "along with the shirt off his back. What are friends for?"

"Mr. Zacks, Mr. Canfield," I said. "Can I borrow your keys to my place, Virg?"

"Sure," Zacks said. He went away, returned with the keys. "You back for keeps now, Mr. Shaw?"

"Just a friendly visit," I told him. "If anyone comes looking for a Stuart Gordon, Virg, that's me. Only I moved out four weeks ago."

"Four weeks ago?"

"Uh-huh. Any vacancies around then?"

"Yeah, five C and eight F. Miss Levine got married and took off. Old Mr. Whitler died."

"Both filled now?"

"Sure. Snapped up."

"Make it five C."

"Whatever you say, Mr. Shaw."

"Thanks, Virg." I turned back to the lobby and elevator.

"Come on," Zacks said, "I'll run you up in the service."

That meant less effort, which suited me fine. Zacks unlocked the elevator and we zipped to the fifteenth floor.

I used the keys on my three locks, pushed open the door and stepped in. Harry following. I set out on my own for the sofa, which was some dozen steps away. No mishaps marred my jaunt. I lowered myself carefully, as if my body were made of dried twigs. Harry helped me out of his overcoat, and I put my feet up on the sofa, stretched out my legs, and closed my eyes.

"Go mix us two drinks, why don't you?" I said.

"The usual?"

"What else?"

Harry went off to the liquor cabinet.

I sighed, opening my eyes. Home again. I'd only been gone a bit more than a month. It felt like a couple years. *Jesus.*

During daylight hours from my windows facing west I could see the rooftops of midtown Manhattan. Due to the housing pinch, a swarm of new penthouses had sprung up on them, most no bigger than log cabins. A great buy for wealthy midgets. Down below, Amsterdam Avenue had seen some changes too. Gentrification had turned the street on its ear, sending the mom-and-pop stores packing. The Cottage, where Madame Chiang Kai-Shek's own chef ran the works, had replaced a greasy spoon, The Super Runner's Shop, two doors down, a cleaning store. No one had gone into mourning when the tombstone emporium in mid-block had shoveled off. Beyond that was a piece of Riverside Park, a small gray slice of the Hudson between tall buildings, and the Jersey shoreline off in the distance. All as neat and orderly as my desktop. A mere glimpse usually made me feel that my life was under control. Man lives by illusions, but mine were dumber than most. Right now all I got was a lot of lit windows and twinkling lights. They were cheery enough.

There was a bookcase behind me, running the length of the east wall. My tape deck, on it, was in easy reach. I stuck out a hand, turned a knob, and Schubert's Rosamunde Quartet picked up in the second movement where it had left off four and a half weeks ago. I closed my eyes. This quartet, if it caught you right, could break your heart. Here were snatches of grief, vanished love, promise unfulfilled: a peek at the whole bagful of human woe, but done with a class and elegance that made you glad to be alive. That was the trick. It was light stuff compared to Schubert's later work, which just now would probably have made me cut my throat.

Harry came back with my whiskey sour.

"Cheers." We raised glasses. I drained half of mine in one gulp. Schubert and whiskey would see me through, if not exactly in that order.

Harry pulled up a chair. We looked at each other. "How's your ma doing?" I asked him.

"She's fine."

"Still in Florida?"

"Sure. In Sunrise Manor. Otherwise known to the inmates as Graveyard Gulch."

"She still think you're a social worker?"

"Why not? It keeps her happy."

I took another swig of whiskey. "How's your dad?"

"Still dead. And your folks?"

"Still dead too."

Harry nodded. "Those are the breaks, kid," he said. "So now what?"

"I get out of these hospital duds," I said. "Stay put."

I rose under my own steam, just to show that I could, and

padded into the bedroom. When I came out some ten minutes later I was decked out in civilized garb: dark blue pajamas, red, black, and green flannel robe, and my own slippers. I'd taken two codeine tablets. I had hopes of surviving.

I dropped Harry's slippers onto the floor, stretched out on the sofa again, and took another pull on my drink. I sighed, but it sounded more like a groan. "Anything I oughta know about at the office?"

"Same old bullshit," he said. "It'll keep."

"Thank God."

"Jim," Harry said.

"Yeah?"

"There are times," Harry said, "and now may be one of them, when I wonder about all this."

"What's 'this'?"

"Our work."

"It's not work," I told him.

"It ain't play, either. Or haven't you noticed?"

"Yeah, I noticed. Only you gotta give it a chance. Work," I said, "is going to the office from nine to five and waiting for the coffee break. Every fool knows that. What we do is something entirely different."

"Sure. But is it better?"

I shrugged. "I'll let you know in about five years."

"In five years," Harry said, "we'll be too old and beat-up to care one way or the other."

"Don't say 'beat-up,' it only makes me feel worse."

"I can see why. What's with the stakeout? They on to you?"

"You're not gonna believe this," I said, "but my current condition has nothing to do with the damn job."

"You're right," Harry said, "I'm not going to believe you."

I'd neglected to cue Harry in on most of the Keller doings. Neely's orders. Just one of the small items that was giving me conniptions about this operation. There were lots of others, too, but I'd decided to keep them to myself. I didn't want to seem ungrateful.

"Scout's honor," I said. "Have I ever lied to you?"

"Yes."

"Well, forget that. Some old lady got herself killed in my building. I took on the bad guys and lost."

"For this you worked out and shadowboxed for ten years?"

"That was the problem. I got too involved. I thought I was Joe Louis."

"Joe Louis is dead."

"That's okay. I almost was too. Then, as if that wasn't enough, this cop Danker developed a real interest in the business, and I just about blew the case."

"Surely you jest."

"I was a bit woozy."

"What did you do?"

"Gave 'em this address, for one thing."

"'Woozy' isn't the word."

"Don't worry, I can cover it."

"Good luck. I don't have to remind you, I suppose, that we're eighteen thousand in the red."

"Don't remind me."

Two years ago Harry and I, reaching way down in our pockets, sprang for a swanky new office suite on Madison Avenue. It was a lulu all right, and didn't cost nearly as much as if we'd bought the whole building outright. About half, maybe. Our old office, a firetrap on Eighth Avenue and Forty-fourth Street, had brought in too much riffraff, lowlife, and shyster trade—not to mention bums, cheapskates, and chiselers. Our clients had one foot in the poorhouse, the other in the pokey; there was no future in it. We'd been put on permanent retainer by Gideon Life, and that gave us the push we needed. Only Gideon merged with a larger outfit three months later and we never did get much business out of them, and when time came to renew our contract, they didn't. We let our secretary, Miss Pilgrim, go, and were hunting for the nearest soup kitchen when Neely showed up. He'd seemed a godsend at the time. I wasn't quite so sure now.

"The cops," I said, "aren't going to waste their time on Stuart Gordon. I think."

"Why not? You look suspicious to me. And I know you."

"Suspicious, maybe. But not dumb enough to knock off my fellow tenant for no reason at all, then give myself a concussion."

"So how come they're pestering you?"

"Not they. This nut Danker. He's probably having a slow week. I'll pull some strings and get this mess squared away."

"Sounds simple."

"Nothing's simple. Look, I'm gonna need you tomorrow."

"When?"

"About five thirty."

"In the morning, huh?"

"When else?"

"That's really wonderful."

"Provided I don't have a relapse."

"What is it?"

"More chauffeuring. To the damn stakeout."

"You can't go by cab?"

"It's safer this way."

"Safer? You're afraid of cabbies, now?"

"They keep records."

"You should learn to control this irrational fear."

"I'm doing my best."

"Call me."

"Yeah, I said. "Thanks for tonight, pal. I owe you."

"Don't mention it," Harry said. "But if you gotta repay me, make it in thousand-dollar bills." He picked up his coat and slippers, said, "Try for a relapse, old buddy," waved, and left.

CHAPTER 6

I FINISHED MY DRINK SLOWLY, SAT AWHILE TRYING TO GET IN the right mood. Like a lot of things these last few weeks, the right mood ducked me. There was probably a reason. My hard-and-fast rule never to mix my private and business lives was about to bite the dust again. A man of character would never have stood for it—a good thing no one like that was around. Another shot wouldn't do either. Too much was riding on this dumb call to chance it.

Three rings and the receiver was picked up. I recognized the voice. "Ralph," I said. "Jim Shaw."

"Darn, how've you been, James?"

"Holding my own," I said, "just barely."

"Don't fool an old man, James."

"How old are you, Ralph, about fifty-six now?"

"Fifty-seven."

"Still run five miles a day?"

"Certainly."

"I can hardly make it around the block," I said, truthfully enough.

Clinton laughed. Little did he know.

"How's Jessie doing?" I asked. Jessie was his daughter.

"Fine. Just as happy as can be."

"Expect to be a granddad soon?"

"Have my fingers crossed, James."

"Good luck, pal," I said. "Ralph, I hate to bother you, but I need a small favor."

"It did occur to me," Clinton said, "that you might have a reason for calling."

"Uh-huh. There's a guy may come around asking about me. Either him or one of his boys."

"Yes?"

"I'd like you to tell him I was a salesman at the tool works for six years. Got laid off three months ago; no seniority. I kind of used you as a reference, Ralph."

"Nice to be remembered," Clinton said.

"Can you manage it?"

"Sounds easy enough."

"Guy's name is Danker," I said. "A cop. That make a difference?"

He hesitated. "Is this illegal, James?"

"Hell, no!"

"Positive?"

"Absolutely."

"Forgive me. Are you in trouble, James?"

"Ralph, I'm on a job, undercover; I need a phony background. That's all there is to it, not a thing more."

"I see."

"It's important, Ralph."

"I would imagine."

"My reputation," I said, trying to keep from whining, "is on the line. Make or break."

There was a long, disheartening pause while I sat sweating bullets.

"No risk?" Clinton finally said.

"Guaranteed."

"Very well, James, I will take your word for it."

I let my breath out. "You're a prince, Ralph. Believe me, you have nothing to worry about. I'm using the name Stuart Gordon; that's who Danker will ask about."

"I'll bear it in mind."

40

"Jesus, Ralph, write it down. Don't take any chances. Tell Penny too. They may call or show up when you're out."

Penny was his secretary.

"Consider it done."

"Thanks a million, pal. I really appreciate this."

"My pleasure, James. After all, I was almost your father-in-law."

"So you were," I said, and shuddered.

We exchanged some more small talk, said our good-byes. I replaced the receiver, wiping my forehead with the back of my hand, which seemed to be shaking slightly. If I couldn't handle old man Clinton with dispatch, what would happen when I had to do something really tough, like tie my shoelace?

I got up from the sofa, steered a wobbly course into my makeshift den next to the bedroom, plunked down on my desk chair, and thumbed through the Rolodex. I found the number I wanted and dialed it. A woman's voice answered.

"Sam in?" I asked.

"Who is speaking, please?"

"My name's Jim. We're friends."

"This is Mrs. Klein."

"Sam got married?"

"His mother. Samuel's in California."

"He still with Ajax?"

"Samuel left Ajax two months ago, Jim. He hopes to start fresh."

Don't we all, I thought. I said, "Congratulate him for me."

"You could do it yourself," she said, and gave me his number.

I thanked her earnestly and hung up.

One down, one to go. I could just imagine myself standing in the hall at Metropolitan Hospital, garbed in their finest, cadging quarters from old Boxcar and trying to trace my so-called contacts. My hair would have turned a neat shade of chalk white in the process. Along with me.

I hunted through my Rolodex again, dialed a third time.

"Yes?" A woman's voice.

"Daphne Field?"

"Speaking."

"This is Jim Shaw," I said, "the private eye who lives in your West Seventy-seventh Street building."

"Sam Klein's friend?"

"Yeah."

"This *can't* be about your apartment." She laughed.

"You're right, it isn't."

"Well, I'm intrigued."

I sighed inwardly. Klein I could have handled on the phone, but this lady was too much a stranger. At the very least, I needed eye contact.

"I've got a proposition for you, Miss Field."

"It used to be Daphne."

"Daphne. There's a bit of money involved."

"In my line," Daphne said, "money talks."

"Mine, too. Can I meet you for a drink somewhere?"

"When?"

"Now, if you don't mind. Just for a little while. I know tomorrow's a workday, so I'll try and keep it short. Promise."

"Why not?" she said.

"Great. We're almost neighbors, aren't we?"

"About five blocks apart."

"Know The Shelter?"

"Of course."

"Meet you there in twenty minutes."

We swapped so longs and hung up.

The Shelter was on the northeast corner of Broadway and Seventy-seventh about a block away. With a little luck, I might actually be able to make it.

She was waiting for me by the time I finally hobbled through the café door. Beer odors, chatter, piped rock, and the smell of fancy chow took a swipe at me, making my knees wobble. Solzhenitsyn had called rock misic intolerable, but to my way of thinking he understated the case. I ignored it all, put a grin on my face, raised an arm in greeting. She saw me and shot back a white, sparkling smile. As far as I could tell, it was just a smile. But all on their own, my grin widened, my shoulders grew straighter, my legs stopped shaking. I wondered what my body was up to. Maybe if I were lucky I'd get her to smile again. This time I'd probably sprout wings.

Daphne Field was about five four and somewhere in her late twenties or early thirties. Her hair was sandy blond, long and curly. Large green eyes gleamed behind steel-rimmed granny glasses. High cheekbones, full lips with just a touch of color, and even, white teeth. Looking at her restored my faith in building managers. I used to think them evil, especially when my toilet didn't get fixed, but now I was seeing the light. She had on a short red coat and paisley scarf over a blue and purple blouse and dark navy skirt. Her hand pressed mine. I held on to it. A guy in my condition needs all the help he can get.

Lights in The Shelter were discreetly dim; it took her a moment to size me up. "Have you been ill?" she asked.

"Not until yesterday."

"What happened?"

"I tried to be a hero."

"And?"

"Don't ask."

We followed the hostess, a slender, perky redhead, to a small, candlelit table in the glassed-in sidewalk café. A thick wall mercifully separated us from The Shelter's interior, which was in its usual state of advanced din, most of the hubbub coming from the narrow singles bar that led into the dining section. Here was cozy, reasonably quiet, and if the company got dull there was always a dandy view of the street. Half the West Side boiled and bubbled along that street. You got all kinds out there, depending on the luck of the draw—snazzy dames, fashion-plate guys, tattered bums, professor types on leave from their teaching stints, teens with and without weirdo punk haircuts, and a small army of loonies turned loose from the local funny farms during the budget crunch. This latter bunch was as frisky as bedbugs, but not half as much fun to watch. They came in all shapes, sizes, and ages: screamers, flailers, babblers. But there wasn't enough money in the world to get me to live anywhere else. Right now only a middle-aged couple and some kids were strolling by. I hardly noticed. I was too busy admiring my new friend.

"Seriously," Daphne was saying. "You okay?"

"Sure. A little beat-up is all. I came to the aid of a lady in distress and got the worst of it."

Daphne smiled. "I never know when to believe you."

"Glad I made an impression last time," I said. "Even if it was the wrong one."

"Oh, you made an impression, all right." Her smile widened.

I frisked my mind trying to figure out how I'd overlooked this lady the few times we'd met before. Then I remembered. She'd been with some guy both times. Long gone now, I fervently hoped.

"Daphne," I asked, "what brought you to your job? A love of buildings?"

"When it comes to buidlings," she said, "I can take them or leave them."

"But you took 'em."

"A divorce," she said, "made that necessary."

"Too bad."

"Not really. Marriage à la mode wasn't my style anyway. When our union hit the rocks, I reached for the want ads. The first job that offered a living was in real estate."

"How do you like it?"

"It's fine. Especially on Fridays."

"That's when you get paid."

"Right. It's also when I get off. Not that I mind worrying about boiler breakdowns, leaks, and paint jobs. I consider

44

them a challenge. But frankly, not quite the challenge I had in mind when I was young and innocent."

"When was that?"

"Not so long ago. During college. I went to Queens and majored in English."

"The literary life," I said, "is a noble calling."

"All I had on *my* mind was reading the world's hundred greatest books."

"What happened?"

"I read them, and a few hundred others. After four years I knew I wasn't going to write the hundred and first greatest book."

"So you got married?"

"Not so fast. First I was on the information desk at the Museum of Modern Art. Then I was a waitress at The Village Gate, then an unemployed actress, then a sales rep for Donald and Daisy Duck T-shirts, towels, and bedding."

"I didn't know they had bedding."

"Take my word for it. They even have prophylactics, although that wasn't my specialty."

"Not licensed by Disney, I take it?"

"Strictly illegal."

"Next would've come muggings and bank jobs. It's unavoidable. What saved you?"

"A bit part in an off-off-Broadway show. I lived on my savings. It ran four months. And *then* I got married."

"Congratulations."

"Don't you believe it! At the time, of course, it seemed wonderful. Now you have my *entire* life story, except that next week I get my broker's license, and become an adult."

"Not a moment too soon."

"Precisely. Now it's your turn, Shaw. I bet your story is fascinating."

"Yeah. It begins in the womb and goes on forever. I'd just as soon hire someone to do the recitation. Also, I've been put through the wringer recently and I don't know if I can hold up through all of it. How about I give you a rain check?"

"I can wait. But I'll hate every minute of it. Are you up to telling me about this mysterious lady in distress?"

"Her, eh? My rescue mission was a dud. As in disaster."

"Too bad. And the damsel?"

"No damsel; an elderly woman. She died."

"Oh."

"Yeah. That sort of puts a damper on it." The waitress showed up and we ordered our drinks. "Damn thing wasn't even my case," I said when she was gone.

"Is it your case now?"

"Uh-uh, doesn't work that way."

"How does it work?"

"The cops go hunting while I try to stay out of their way. Fact is, I'm having a tough time holding up my end just now."

"Really?"

"That's where you come into the picture, Daphne."

She smiled. "This I've got to hear."

I told her. Nothing to it. By now I'd had a good deal of practice telling this dumb tale.

"I'm sorry," she said when I was done.

"You aren't the only one. Is Ajax computerized, Daphne?"

She nodded.

"Have access to the computer?"

"It's part of what I do."

"Okay," I said. "There's light at the end of the tunnel." Our drinks arrived, a whiskey sour for me, a brandy Alexander for her. "Cheers," I said. "To nice things."

"Cheers."

We drank. I said, "Tomorrow, a cop called Danker or one of his stooges may get in touch with your office. He'll want to know if a Stuart Gordon lived at one sixty West Seventy-seventh Street until four weeks ago."

"Who's Stuart Gordon?"

"I am. I had to come up with an address, fast. I was flat on my back in a hospital ward when this Danker woke me."

"When did it happen?"

"A few hours ago."

"You get around, don't you?"

"Too damn much. If what I told him holds up, that's it; I'm home free."

"And if not?"

"I'm ruined."

"Ruined?"

"Yes. My career won't be worth a dime. This case is special, Daphne: it's do or die. I don't deserve getting shafted for trying to help someone in a jam."

She took another sip of her drink. "Just what would I have to do?"

"How many buildings does Ajax manage?"

"Hundreds."

"And if someone comes looking for information, how would they go about it?"

"Speak to the office manager."

"Then?"

"One of the clerks would check the computer."

"Okay," I said, "here's what you do. Slip Stuart Gordon's name into your computer. He lived at my address for seven years, vacated the premises a month ago. His apartment was five C."

"That's all?"

"That's it. In a couple days, cancel the entry."

"Is this against the law, Jim?"

"What law? Who's ever going to know it was you? Listen, I've got a pretty good expense account. I'm not asking for a handout. What I said on the phone still goes: consider this a business deal."

"Don't be ridiculous. Why not just take me to dinner sometime. And tell me your life's story."

"That's easy."

"Of course."

"How about I throw in a concert, too?"

She smiled. "I was too modest to ask."

"You like chamber music?"

"You mean classical?"

"What else is there?"

"I like it. But I've got a tin ear."

"Meaning what?"

"I can't make out melodies first time around."

"That's not so bad."

"Second or third time either. Unless I really know a piece well, it sounds like noise."

"Noise?" I said.

"Mozart's Serenade in D—and that's real simple—sounded like tin cans rattling."

"Mozart sounded like *tin cans?*"

"Oh, not just him. Tchaikovsky, Beethoven, Brahms, anyone."

"Jeez. That's a bad case."

"Don't worry. After ten hearings everything starts to sound *beautiful*. Sometimes it only takes eight or nine."

"You've never thought of being a musician, eh?"

"Never."

"Smart move," I said. "Look, there's a strategy even for your problem, unlikely as that may seem. We'll get tickets in advance. Then I buy some records of what we're going to hear, and you play them over till they make sense. Neat, eh?"

"That's a stroke of genius. I usually do it the other way around: first a concert, then the records."

"Very dull, I'd imagine."

"Very."

I grinned at her. "So it's a deal, then?"

She nodded. "A deal."

CHAPTER 7

THE ALARM CLOCK YANKED ME OUT OF A DEEP SLEEP. FIVE
A.M. The thing to do, obviously, was pull the blanket back
over my head and get some more shut-eye. I couldn't do the
thing, much as I wanted to. Instead, I crawled out of bed and
staggered off to the bathroom. I was going to be a hero. In
Russia they pinned a medal on you. Here, maybe, I'd get to
keep my swanky office. I wouldn't mind.

Some forty minutes later, showered, shaved and with two
codeine tablets under my belt, I phoned Harry.

"Jim. Morning, pal."

"Go away," Harry said.

"Up and at 'em," I croaked. I didn't sound any too chipper
myself.

Harry groaned.

"Look," I said, "I'd try it on my own if only I hadn't lost my
crutches. You're my one hope."

"Why are we doing this, Jim?"

"It can't be for fame or glory," I said. "How about dough?"

Harry sighed. "That, at least, I can understand."

The car carried us up Broadway past the all-night bagel
shop, Zabar's, and rows of darkened bars, restaurants, super-
markets, clothing stores, occasional pedestrians, and bums
snoozing away in doorways and on new midlane benches—the

city's gift to the infirm—onto Ninety-sixth Street and then across Central Park. Bare tree branches beyond the roadway waved us on our way. The sky had turned from black to dirty gray. Not much traffic yet. I closed my eyes, put my head against the seat. I'd been doing a lot of that lately.

Harry said, "You almost look worse than yesterday."

With his bloodshot eyes and unshaven face, Harry didn't look so hot either, but I was too much a gentleman to say so. I'm glad one of us was.

"The 'almost' part," I said, "makes it okay."

"It's not okay," Harry said. "Look, Jim, I'm as greedy as the next guy."

"More, probably."

"Sure. But if you keel over on the job, there won't be any dough at all."

"Keel over," I said.

"Or land in the hospital for a couple months."

"Jeez," I said, opening my eyes.

"Take a few days off," Harry said. "Give yourself a break."

"Thanks, pal. I'm gonna. Think I'm up to tailing Keller all over town? Thing is, I gotta be at Ninety-fourth Street in case this Danker shows up."

"Why?"

"You're not supposed to know, remember?"

"Tell me anyway."

"Danker's not the only cop involved. Keller used to be one. There are others. This whole deal is knee deep in cops."

"Cops."

"Right. Danker's gotta think I'm just a hard-luck Joe looking for work. Anything else, even a hint, blows this job to kingdom come."

"You *are* a hard-luck Joe looking for work."

"See? No problem."

We drove around the block once to make sure the coast was clear. Dirty, lopsided tenements leaned against each other like patients in an old-age home, too feeble to stand alone. Battered trash cans crowded the sidewalks. Even the streetlamps were crooked. A lone woman, bent and ragged, shuffled down the street; she turned a corner and was gone.

"You sure can pick 'em," Harry said.

"Not me. This creep Keller."

"The guy who's making us rich?"

"Yeah. If I live through this."

"I thought you were okay."

"I'd forgotten what this place is like."

Harry pulled up and I maneuvered my tired body out of the car.

"I'll be in touch," I told him.

Harry nodded, said, "Take care," and drove away. I stood looking after the car as though I'd lost my one friend. It turned a corner and I was alone again. Here I was, back on the job, the one I wanted and had fought for. So why wasn't I happy? I did a slow about-face, waddled over to the house, mounted the three rickety steps to the front door, and stepped into the dank, smelly alcove. The second door was locked, of course, my keys up in the flat, but I didn't panic. I had an insider's knowledge of this dump. I jiggled the knob awhile and the door popped open. Houdini would have applauded.

I made my way up two flights of stairs, my hand sticking to the bannister as if it had been glued there. I rested a couple of times before I hit 3C. A padlock hung on my door.

I sighed, stuck my hand back on the bannister, and did the whole routine in reverse.

I stood in front of the super's flat on the ground floor, rear, and used my knuckles; his bell had gone the way of the dodo. It took awhile for the door to open.

"Mr. Gordon," he said.

Carlos was a short wiry Hispanic in his mid twenties, with a thin mustache and longish hair. He had on a blue flannel shirt which hung out over faded jeans. He was barefoot.

"Sorry to get you up," I said.

"Is okay."

"Cops padlock my door?"

"No cops. I do this. Door is open, but you no give me key, so I cannot lock. I put padlock on. No one can rob things."

"Thanks, Carlos." I got my wallet out, gave him a ten. He flashed me a white smile and went off to find the key. I trudged up the stairs a few minutes later, clutching my prize.

I unsnapped the padlock and stepped back into my flat. The scraped wooden table, antique bathtub, and facing stove, the peeling walls and tattered linoleum all greeted me like lost kin. A large water bug scurried across the floor.

The light was still on in the bedroom. I went to the closet to inspect my cache. The bugging equipment was untouched under its blanket. I flicked on the radio. A Brahms trio was in progress. Better, but far from perfect. Nothing would be perfect till I earned my dough and left this hole.

I went to the window, gazed out over the back yard. Keller's windows were still dark. He liked to sleep late. I returned to the kitchen, fried some eggs, brewed a pot of coffee. My spirits were sagging, but my appetite, surprisingly, showed signs of life. Here was a sterling example of Schopenhauer's Will to Live. Wasted on me, maybe, but not my stomach.

I carted my breakfast back to the bedroom, sank down in the worn easy chair by the window and, using my lap as tray, fed myself. Being here didn't feel all that unfamiliar, of course; in some ways it was just like home. That was the problem.

My dad had been hooked on the ponies when I was a kid. The guy was a charter member of all the racetracks within fifty miles of Manhattan. In between he gave the chess and card clubs a whirl too. He won plenty—only not half as much as he lost. The guy was a fancy-leather-goods cutter, an okay trade in those days, and would have pulled down more than enough to keep the family in clover if it weren't for his hobbies. Those hobbies were a menace. A gambler needs a money cushion, spare cash to fall back on when luck or talent lays an egg. Dad never had it; his paycheck wouldn't stretch that far, so we ended up camping in one miserable slum after another. It didn't take an Einstein to figure out why this job was getting under my skin. This flea box reminded me of *those* dumps. And it was giving me the willies.

I drained my third cup of coffee. Another glance at Keller's digs told me he was still in slumberland. That didn't seem like such a bad idea. I dumped the dishes in the sink, stretched out on the bed, lowered the radio to a murmur. Steam gently hissed through a radiator. I went to sleep.

In the dream, Dad was seated at a long table, a slender, fiftyish, good-looking guy, dapper in a black three-piece suit and striped tie. He cut a deck of cards, turned the top card face up. My brother Danny and I were suddenly standing next to the table—had been there all along, I realized. I was full grown, but Danny was still a kid. I felt jumpy as hell. "You lose," Dad said, grinning at us. I didn't know whether he meant Danny or me. Then I was all alone, being propelled into the next room, and I knew it was me. The next room was where you died. Only it was Daddy who was dead, I seemed to remember. . . .

I came awake with a sour taste in my mouth and the radio announcer's spiel in my ear. The sun, streaming through both windows, put broken squares of light on the walls. The alarm clock read 10:25. My head still throbbed. I got up, swallowed another pair of codeine pills, washing them down with warm water, and took a third peek at Keller's windows. Nothing had changed. The blinds were raised but no lights shone from inside. The guy could have gotten up while I was snoozing and gone off on his errands.

I hauled the recorder out of the closet and set up shop on the kitchen table. Both phone tap and ceiling mike had been on in my absence. I pressed Rewind, listened.

A phone rang. Keller's voice said, "Yeah."

A male voice said, "It's all set."

"When?" Keller asked.

"Tomorrow."

"Good," Keller said. He hung up. Next, a knock on the door. There was no way of knowing how much time had elapsed. Keller said, "Who's there?"

"Mrs. Rankin."

I heard the door open.

"This package was left for you, Mr. Keller."

"Thanks," Keller said. Mrs. Rankin said good night. I heard the door close.

The next sequence had Keller twisting the dial on his TV set. Apparently, he didn't like what he saw: the set went dead. I heard the toilet flush a couple of times. Keller coughed once.

The rest of the tape was blank.

Keller was no great shakes when it came to spilling the beans, but this was ridiculous. Rankin's "Good night" put their chat at sometime last night. It was now pushing eleven. Was Keller grabbing an extra forty winks? Was he ill? Had he somehow wised up to the mikes and removed them? His package could have contained a bug sweeper.

I left the table, dug my binoculars out of a dresser drawer, and carried them over to the window. If Keller had tumbled to the stakeout, Neely's case was all washed up. Along with my big payday.

I climbed on top of my easy chair and stood far back, so I could see out without being seen.

Ignoring Keller's left window, which showed mostly wall, I sighted on the right one, adjusting the focus. I hit a dresser, a folding chair, part of the bed, the damn TV set. So far, nothing to write home about.

I leaned over a bit, trying another angle. More mattress came into view, unmade, unoccupied. Something caught my attention beyond the bed. I fiddled with the focus again, brought it in sharp.

Lying very still on the floor, palm up, was a hand. Oh, brother! The last thing I needed now was a hand on Keller's floor. I shut my eyes, then opened them very slowly. The damn thing hadn't gone away. They rarely do.

CHAPTER 8

WHATEVER GOOD CHEER I'D MANAGE TO STORE UP DURING MY
short snooze was snuffed out like a candle in a windstorm. My
one hope was that maybe I was hallucinating. I'd have
preferred the bughouse to what I figured was lying on Keller's
floor.

I took a final squint. The hand didn't look like part of a
mannequin or plaster cast. There was no reason to think it
was.

I climbed down off my chair and plopped into it with all the
grace of a boulder bouncing into a ditch. A small, persistent
hammer had started pounding in my skull—again. My legs
felt weak and useless, not unlike their owner.

I had a couple of options to mull over, neither of them
doozies. First, I could do the smart and sensible thing, forget
that I ever saw anything, and let events take their natural
course. Sooner or later someone would find the body, and the
cops would come calling. I'd get an earful through my
bugging devices and have a dandy front-row seat right here by
the window. Sweet and simple. Except for maybe one small
hitch.

If the cops did their job, were the least bit ambitious, and
gave Keller's flat the going-over it deserved, they'd turn up
my bugs in no time. The one I'd stuck in the phone was an
odds-on favorite to come in first; the spike mikes in the ceiling

wouldn't be far behind. I had to count on their going for broke. This Keller wasn't just anyone—he was an ex–rogue cop. He'd rate that extra bit of attention. And finding the bugs would stir up the kind of fuss neither I nor Neely would especially enjoy: even if they couldn't trace the bugs to me, their presence and my proximity to a second body in two days would raise some eyebrows. The cops would start digging in earnest, and my cover was as thin as tissue paper, but not half as firm. I wasn't up to being a suspect just now, or standing off the law about who had hired me. I was hardly up to being a private eye.

No doubt about it, life would be a lot simpler if the cops never found those bugs.

Which led straight to my second option, one I liked even less: I could drop in on Keller for a quick look-see, pay my last respects, and in the process make off with the incriminating devices. A real coup. I might even stumble across something interesting while I was nosing around, proving to me and the world that I wasn't a total washout in this racket. Or at least proving it to me. At the moment, I was willing to settle for small triumphs. But would this really be a triumph?

If someone spied me entering the flat or caught me inside, I was a goner. My license would be up for grabs, and I'd be lucky to stay out of the clink.

I could hear cars out on the street, horns honking, a box radio blaring away somewhere, kids yelling. The clock was pushing eleven and the neighborhood was alive and kicking. I wouldn't be moving in the dead of night this time but in full view of anyone who cared to notice.

I sighed. Both options were lousy. What I needed was a grown-up to make my decisions. What I had was broken-down me, last year's version of the model gunshoe, now, unfortunately, quite obsolete.

I reached for the binoculars, got to my feet, and took another gander at my problem. It hadn't changed. As far as I could tell the hand hadn't moved an inch. No fingers were twitching. No other part of the anatomy had crawled conveniently into view.

But of course if Keller had had a stroke, a seizure, a heart attack he wouldn't necessarily be drumming his fingers on the floor, waiting impatiently for someone to find him. He'd be lying there like a sack of potatoes, out cold, breathing his last. Keller wasn't the suspect I loved to shadow, nor the goon most likely to win your affection. But if the jerk was still alive, I was probably the one guy who could save him. That sort of tipped the scales, didn't it? I waited for a voice to say no, to show me the fatal flaw in my logic. The part of me that hoped to be Bertrand Russell must have been on vacation: no voice spoke up. Just my luck. I was slated to be a Good Samaritan again. As if last time hadn't been bad enough.

I made my way down the stairs and out onto the street without any major mishaps. A couple of attendants and a stretcher would have helped, but that might have drawn attention. In comparison to me, Garbo was a wild-eyed exhibitionist.

A gray sky lowered overhead. Ninety-fourth Street was as empty as a cadaver's future. I tottered around the corner. Cars and buses rattled along on Second Avenue. Blank-faced pedestrians hurried by on their errands. Too much tumult for anyone to notice me or anything, I hoped.

I got past the laundry, candy store, and bar in nothing flat. Sam the Tailor never looked up from his sewing machine. Nobody popped out of the corner grocery to get my autograph as miscreant of the week. Little did they know.

An empty lot was across the street on Ninety-third. Eight lopsided tenements huddled together on my right like vagrants in a blizzard. This block, like mine, was on a steep incline that ended on Third Avenue. I huffed and puffed my way to the sixth house. Nothing to worry about. I was as nondescript as a used matchstick, as invisible as a wino on skid row. Maybe if I told myself often enough, I'd even get to believe it.

I mounted three concrete steps, and pushed open the front door. The inner one swung open at my touch. The odors of rotting fish, kitty litter, and ammonia tied my stomach into small, uncomfortable knots. A TV muttered somewhere overhead.

I reined up on the third floor, the lock-pick in my hand. For an ex-cop, Keller was careless: he'd neglected to buy heavy-duty locks. I'd already had practice with these babies; I got the door open and shut in jig time. I stood leaning against it, breathing like a long-distance runner on his last legs.

For about two minutes I'd all but forgotten about my infirmities: now reality struck back. My breakfast kicked me in the guts, hunting for a way out; the floor undulated under me as it were a giant snake that didn't like being stepped on. The walls began to shimmy. That did it. I half doubled over, closed my eyes, and waited for the end. It couldn't be far off. The sooner, the better, as far as I was concerned.

After a while, things slowly began to simmer down. I managed to straighten up—quite a trick. My knees were buckling; I was soaked with sweat. A sour taste lingered in my mouth, but I seemed to be whole. Not bad. I knew now what they'd put on my tombstone: He Kept His Breakfast Down. My greatest achievement.

I was in Keller's catchall living room–kitchen, replete with bathtub and turn-of-the-century stove. Some chairs, a table, a worn oilcloth on the floor. A print of Hulk Hogan hung near the stove. The walls were a bright, cheerless yellow.

I reached into a pocket for a pair of gloves and locked the door. The bedroom and kitchen were separated by an archway. I could see part of my tenement through one of Keller's back windows. More of my flat came into view as I moved forward: the blackened fire escape, my pair of windows, a slice of wall and ceiling. The only thing missing was me, binoculars in hand, peering at myself.

60

I stepped into the bedroom and stood gazing down. The hand on the floor didn't belong to a plaster cast or mannequin. It was attached to a stocky guy in a brown suit lying face down near the foot of the bed. There was a small puddle of dried blood under him.

I stooped over slowly, took hold of the wrist. Stiff, cold, and pulseless. Far too late for any Good Samaritan. I rolled the body on its back.

The guy was short, thick-nosed and overweight. He was somewhere in his mid-thirties, with thinning brown hair. His gray eyes were open and staring. His thick lips were slightly parted, revealing an even row of yellowish teeth. He still needed a shave.

I hadn't found Keller but one of the two bastards who had killed Mrs. Silbert.

CHAPTER 9

I CROUCHED THERE, STUPEFIED, WAITING FOR THE BODY TO assume the reasonable and expected dimensions of Horace Keller. This stiff just didn't fit the bill, or belong in any scenario I could possibly devise. A bad mistake had been made. If I waited long enough maybe things would right themselves. Then again, maybe they wouldn't.

The floor was showing definite signs of wanting to shimmy again. Bright spots had begun doing stunts before my eyes, almost blotting out the nasty environment. I got to my feet in slow motion, feeling as tough as a cracked eggshell. I was swaying slightly, like a guy standing in a rowboat. It would be a howl it I passed out now and Keller or someone walked through the front door.

Standing tall cleared my head somewhat. I took a deep breath then lowered myself toward the floor a second time and went through the guy's pockets. I could have saved myself the trouble; someone had beaten me to it. Or maybe Shorty liked to travel light. I rose empty-handed, no wiser than before. Wisdom never did come easy.

With a sigh, I stepped over to the phone, unscrewed the mouthpiece and retrieved my bug. At least something was going according to plan. Hoisting myself onto the dresser with some difficulty, I dug a pair of long-nosed pliers out of a back pocket and raised my eyes to the ceiling. I stood there, my neck craned as if I were some dumb statue in Central Park on eternal lookout for pigeons. I could see the hole I'd made, all right, but there didn't seem to be anything in it. I poked around with the pliers. Empty.

I got down from the dresser, and went into the kitchen. Squinting up at where my second mike should have been told me nothing. I shoved the table over a few feet, using a chair to get on top of it. The tiny hole I'd made in the ceiling was as vacant as a store dummy's grin.

I climbed down off the table with all the agility of an octogenarian, moved it and the chair back into place. I understood now why the tape had been blank: Keller had found the spike mikes. No doubt the bug in the phone, too, but for some reason he'd let that stay. Maybe he'd already made his weekly quota of incriminating calls?

I dragged myself back into the bedroom and got down on my knees. It wasn't to pray. Counting eight floorboards from the wall, I used my fingernails to pry a six-inch chunk from the floor. The sending equipment, no bigger than a Marlboro pack, was still there. It went into a pocket, the floorboard back into place.

I stood up and looked around at the peeling walls and beat-up furniture. Shorty matched the decor perfectly. What I wanted most was to leave this place and head for the nearest bar. I needed more than a stiff shot to get over this mess: nothing but a bender would do. With Keller on the prowl, every minute I spent here put me in greater jeopardy. What if he decided to come home? The guy did live here, after all. The only weapon I'd brought along was my pliers. Maybe I'd get to tweak his nose before he shot me. The thought of two bodies in this dump was doubly depressing—especially if one was mine.

But if I beat it before frisking the joint and missed something important, I'd have no one to blame but myself. Enough people were blaming me already without my joining the parade.

I got busy searching the flat. I didn't really think that a guy smart enough to find my bugs would leave behind much of interest. Except for a body. And how smart was that?

There was only one closet. It contained some frayed slacks and jackets and a couple of suits. The pockets held no secrets. Two peaked caps and a gray hat had nothing stuck in them; a pair of scruffy shoes were equally empty. The dresser contained socks, shirts, and underwear. Keller had been shrewd enough not to hide anything under his bed—although making sure of that had cost me a good deal of effort. I decided against pulling up all the floorboards. The water tank in the water closet yielded no hidden treasures.

I waltzed into the other room, light-headed and panting. Thank God there were only two rooms.

The cupboard under the sink held some tools, a carton of trash bags; the cabinet above, dishes, glasses, a few pots and pans. The silverware drawer contained just that; the stove was empty. A broom, mop, and dustpan were in the broom closet. Except for the corpse in the bedroom my suspect had nothing to hide.

I had done my duty, put my neck on the chopping block and come out in one piece—at least, up to this point. If I hadn't found any goodies, those were the breaks. The thing to do now was get out while I still had the chance.

I stood in the kitchen and eyed the joint one last time. No doubt about it, living like this permanently would have made me turn to crime, too. I was beginning to sympathize with my suspect. Now it was *really* time to go, only my feet seemed to have other ideas and had welded themselves to the floor.

I wondered vaguely what was wrong. I knew I wasn't in tip-top shape, but I hadn't expected paralysis to set in so soon.

The print of Hulk Hogan caught my attention.

It was stuck to the wall with four thumbtacks. The paper was warped and crinkled; Keller had hung it too close to the stove, definitely the wrong spot. I pulled off a glove, delicately removed the two bottom tacks—no need to damage a work of art—and peered behind the poster.

The old dumbwaiter was there, just as it was in my flat, in every flat of these tenements. Defunct, useless, painted over countless times these last decades. Tenants brought their garbage down to the trash cans in front of their buildings. No one thought twice about the slight bump in the wall that housed the dumbwaiter.

Except Keller.

He had thoughtfully chipped the paint from around the rim of his. And then hung a poster over it.

I opened the small square metal door. The hinges squeaked but cooperated. I peered inside. Nothing. I stuck my hand down the shaft. Still nothing. I reached up as far as I could, felt around. Something was wedged up there. I gave the something a couple of hard tugs. A small black plastic trash bag dislodged itself from the four walls, fell into my waiting hands.

A trash bag in a dumbwaiter. It figured, didn't it?

CHAPTER 10

I STOOD THERE REGARDING MY PRIZE—A BULKY BUNDLE TIED
with twine—with some wonder, as if I were a magician who
had pulled one rabbit too many out of his hat. I hoped I had
come up with something useful for a change. Even half useful
would do.

I tucked the package under one arm, put on my glove,
closed the dumbwaiter, replaced the tacks in the poster. I was
satisfied. I moved quietly to the door and pressed my ear
against it. Silence. I stepped into the hall. I didn't waste time
fooling with the locks; there was nothing left to steal, anyway.
I scrambled down the stairs. The TV upstairs had gone quiet.
By the time I reached the ground floor, the gloves were back
in my pocket and what I hoped was a sane expression back on
my face.

I went home the long way, via Third Avenue, where no one
knew me. For a physical wreck, I wasn't feeling half bad.

Inside my flat, I used the phone, dialed Lucy Samler, a
mid-thirtyish brunette who could shadow a needle through
the proverbial haystack. A freelancer, she worked out of her
Washington Heights apartment. Luck tipped its hat at me:
Lucy was home and itching for a job.

"A two-month stint would suit me just fine," she said in her
mellow, throaty voice, "but I'll settle for what I can get."

"Bank account hurting?"

"What bank account?"

"Uh-oh."

"Right," Lucy said. "The wolf used to be at the door; he's moved in with me now."

"Good thing I called."

"I was beginning to think crime had dried up in this town."

"Not a chance," I .old her. "Take it from me."

"What's the story, Jim?"

"A guy named Jed Elman needs some watching."

"What did he do?"

"Nothing, as far as I know," I said. "I'm keeping tabs on a pal of his, one Horace Keller. I think he's skipped."

"And you figure," Lucy said, "that they may hook up somewhere along the way?"

"Yeah. There's a chance, at least."

"Anything I should know about this Elman person?"

"Lots, probably. Only I can't tell you."

"Can't, or won't?"

"Can't. Don't know. Elman appears to be Keller's drinking buddy. They meet in some bar and drink."

"That's all?"

"Never did anything else," I said. "Elman showed up in his car once. I took down his license, ran it through Motor Vehicles, and got his address."

"He have a job?"

"Looked well fed," I said. "Probably does something. If he's not at his flat when you get there, ask around. Pick him up at work. I want you on him right away."

"Then what?"

"Stick with him. If he meets up with Keller, drop him. Go after Keller. Got that?"

"Yes."

"Leave word at the office."

"Right."

"And watch yourself. This Keller may be a bad egg."

"What do they look like?"

"Elman's a tall, raw-boned guy, age forty-two. Longish blond hair, nose like a beak, deep-set hazel eyes, long neck. Skinny. Narrow-chested. Swings his arms when he walks. He's worn a brown leather jacket all the times I've seen him. Keller's about five nine, forty-five years old, round-faced. Hair: black, graying, parted on the left; eyes: dark brown verging on black. Nose, long; lips, thin. Weight, about one seventy-five. Looks like a grifter."

"Where does Elman flop?"

"Manhattan. Eighty-third, off First." I gave her the address.

"I know the neighborhood," she said.

"Good luck," I said.

"Thanks, Jim."

I hung up.

I'd done it, hired help. Something I should have done weeks ago. Neely, if he got wind, would pop his cork. Only Neely wasn't going to find out. So why worry? If I thought real hard I would probably come up with a reason.

I'd chatted standing up, my knees locked, the bundle still under my arm. Not bad. All it took were nerves of steel and a will of iron. I had a feeling that if I sat down I might fall apart. Silly thought. I weaved my way into the kitchen, snared a knife from the dish rack, zeroed in on the easy chair, and made a crash landing Chuck Yeager would have envied. I sat, the bundle on my lap, and waited for my breath to catch up with me; it was off somewhere on Third Avenue taking in the sights. There was a slight tremor to my hands, as if I were stirring up an invisible martini or getting set to conduct one of Schönberg's twelve-tone works. Euphoria was fast becoming a distant memory. I seemed to have the tired blood the TV ads warned you against. Worse yet, I'd suddenly acquired the dull wits my brother Danny said came from binging on cola, white bread, and baloney. The snack I had four months ago had finally caught up with me; my keen intellect was kaput. There was no sense to it: any way you cut it, Shorty just didn't belong on that floor. The two theories I had cooked up to fit the circumstances were both disasters.

In the first, my stiff was a common burglar working these houses, who just happened to pick on the wrong guy. In the second, Shorty, Silbert, and Keller had some sinister, devious connection. Objections to part one: any burglar who wasted his time in these dumps was a mental case, not a burglar. Objections to part two: Silbert fit in with those two birds the way I fit in with a punk rock band. Neely's job involved crooked cops, not elderly bakery workers.

Which left me with a third explanation that was no explanation at all: neither of the above, but something entirely different.

So far logic and deduction had led nowhere. I was up a stump, a place where a guy in my condition could least afford to be. It was time to try a more direct approach.

My hands were behaving again, and the rest of me had settled down to a comfortable state of infirmity. My chair was out of line with the window: no prying eyes could see what was on my lap. I took hold of the knife and began slicing the twine. It parted, and I reached inside the package and removed a bulging paper bag, its mouth sealed with tape.

I don't know what I expected to find. If this had been one of the gory comics from my misspent youth, I'd have pulled out a severed head. Right now I was willing to settle for a more mundane object. With Shorty lousing up the works I wasn't apt to get many more cracks at this case. I wanted to bow out with my self-respect intact, and as much of Neely's fee as possible. It seemed a modest enough goal. I could always set the world on fire next time. Provided there was one.

I took a gander inside the bag—then did a double take. I peeked a third time to make sure I hadn't been seeing things the first two times. The guy I heard chuckling sounded a little less sane than the Boston Strangler. The guy was me.

I forgot about my delicate condition. I couldn't have been more surprised if I *had* pulled out a severed head. The last thing I expected from Keller was hidden wealth, but what I was looking at were bundles of fifty- and hundred-dollar bills held together by thick rubber bands. Very carefully, I put the bag down on the floor, rose to pull both window shades.

You had to hand it to Keller. While I was busy going broke, lying to the cops, and getting my brains beat out, this deadbeat was salting away the greenbacks. All *he* had to worry about was a dead guy in his bedroom and my having found his dough.

I could hear the voice of temptation warming up in the wings, getting set to give me the business. I recognized the signs. But could temptation meet my price? What the hell *was* my price? Only one way to find out. I took the bag and emptied it onto my bed. A sheet of paper came floating down onto my blanket—another surprise. I didn't know if I could stand any more. Maybe Keller had written out a confession, a kind of double reward for anyone who unearthed this treasure. Very considerate. I picked up the paper. I had been going to flick on the radio, find some nice Bach, Mozart, or Beethoven to help me celebrate while I tallied up the goodies. Now I needn't bother. I knew exactly how much money I had come into: ten grand. I could even reel off the serial numbers on each and every bill. The great Blackstone himself would have been impressed. But my pal Keller had given me the inside track and had thoughtfully listed the amount and serial numbers on his sheet of paper. Keller or *someone*. Because this was only a carbon, and for all I knew there were dozens of these sheets scattered around town. And even one would be too many.

I stuffed the dough back in its bag, rolled up the shades, reclaimed my easy chair. My narrow brush with sudden wealth had changed nothing—I was still a pauper, and still in the same old pickle. I cast an eye out the window: nothing had changed there either. No cops were swarming through the yard or popping up in Keller's flat; it was still empty. And odds had it that Shorty was still dead. Shorty was going to be a problem. But what wasn't these days?

I reached for the phone.

CHAPTER 11

HARRY CANFIELD LOOKED AROUND THE FLAT. "NICE DECOR," he said. "Skid Row, nineteen thirty, isn't it?"

"Thirty-two," I told him, "You're missing the finer points."

"How stupid of me."

"Can't all be experts," I said. "Takes years of study. See that crack in the west wall? Vintage thirty-two. Costs a mint to duplicate. But worth every cent."

"You're a shoo-in," Harry said, "for Connoisseur of the Year."

"It's my life," I said with simple dignity. "Have a seat."

"In *here*?"

"In there. Here you wanta cut your throat in five minutes; there you get an extra ten minutes of blessed life."

We went into the bedroom. Harry settled on the edge of my bed; I sank into my easy chair. The springs groaned under me. The springs had the right idea.

Harry leered at me. "Got lonely, huh, kid? Needed old Harry to cheer you up."

"Needed old Harry to take over for me, come live here for ten, twenty years while I go to some nice quiet asylum and take the cure."

"Old Harry too old for that," Harry said sadly.

"Old Harry not as dumb as he looks." I tossed him the bag.

He took a peek. "This stuff real?"

"Probably."

"How much?"

"Ten grand."

"Not bad. Eight grand to go and we're out of debt. This a bribe, or you steal it?"

"Actually, I stole it."

"Didn't know you had the sense. Who from?"

"Keller."

"He going to miss this?"

"Not for a while. He's going to be busy. There's a dead guy over in his apartment."

Harry stopped running his fingers through the cash. "Dead—as in killed?"

"Dead, as in shot dead."

"That's dead."

"Can't get any deader," I agreed.

"Our boy do it?"

I shrugged. "He wasn't there to tell me."

"The mikes?"

"Someone thoughtlessly removed 'em. Left the bug in the phone, which didn't pick up a thing. I got the sending gizmo back."

"You implicated in any way, Jim?"

"Only if they use a psychic."

"This money: the killer left it behind?"

"The dough was hidden. I found it."

"Well, that's something."

"Maybe. There was a sheet of paper with it. Had all the serial numbers. The sheet was a carbon."

"Neat."

"Yeah. Someone wanted to keep an eye on that dough once it got into circulation. How, why, or through whom is just one of those little things we don't know yet."

"Yet."

"A mild touch of optimism."

"Or dementia. Look, Jim, this case has been nothing but trouble."

"I noticed."

"We could drop it. And perhaps even manage to hang on to this money."

"You're serious."

"It's only a suggestion. One of many."

"I can hardly wait to hear the others," I said.

"It's mob money, right?"

"That's my guess."

"So hypothetically speaking, it's fair game."

"Probably."

"I mean, we're not swiping the guy's hard-earned retirement fund, for Christ's sake. So what's the problem?" Harry said.

"No problem. Unless I get dragged into this murder."

"Why should you?"

I grinned at him. "I was saving the best for last. You ready for this?"

"I'm not going to like it, am I?"

"You're gonna hate it. The victim's one of the two guys who killed my neighbor and gave me a concussion. Nice, eh?"

"I hate it."

"See?"

"How's that possible, Jim?"

"I'm glad you asked. It shows you have confidence in me. That's more than I do."

"Shit," Harry said.

"Right. Our best bet," I said, "is to sit tight, see what happens. Maybe the cops will miss me. Maybe they'll tag Keller for the shooting. Then we can figure out what to do with all this. Thing is, I've got to stay out of the limelight. If Keller or the guys behind him get wind I've been camping on his doorstep, it might give them ideas about who swiped their dough. I don't want to risk my neck for a lousy ten grand. And Keller may have an alibi. That would change things; the case would still be wide open. We could make a lot more than ten thousand by sticking with it. Keller's covered his tracks so far. Now he knows he's been bugged, there's a dead guy in his bedroom, and it shouldn't take him long to find out his dough's gone, too. Maybe he'll panic and do something dumb."

"And maybe he won't," Harry said.

"We'll help him along. An anonymous tip to the cops ought to get the ball rolling. Meanwhile, you abscond with the loot and listening devices. There's a shopping bag in the next room."

Harry stood up. "Anything else I should do?"

"Yeah. Pray for me."

CHAPTER 12

ANOTHER GLANCE OUT THE WINDOW TOLD ME THAT *NOTHING* was still the operative word out there.

I used my phone, dialed 911.

"There's a guy," I said, "at two thirty-six West Ninety-third Street, apartment three B. He's either dead or dying. Hurry."

"Who's this?"

I hung up.

That did it. Now it was up to the law. *Hurry* meant anywhere from twenty minutes to never. I could always call again if they didn't show up. Good citizens like me never quit.

I stretched out on my bed, turned on the radio, and relaxed. A Schubert impromptu filled my dingy room with light. There was nothing to do now but wait.

Tchaikovsky's First Piano Concerto took over from Schubert and I turned the dial hunting for something a mite fresher, something that wouldn't put me to sleep. I found it in a Vivaldi string concerto. Sirens intruded in the middle.

I lowered the radio and slid off the bed. Getting a small round hand mirror out of a desk drawer, I went and settled down in my easy chair by the window. As long as I leaned back, I couldn't be seen, but by angling the mirror just right—about four inches above my lap—I got a pretty good view of Keller's window. I sat there like an expectant hen waiting for her eggs to hatch. It took a while. Presently two cops popped up in my oval eye, both youngish, one black, the other white. They went in and out of sight. It didn't take lots of imagination to know what they were up to: a glance at the body, a call to the station house, a peek at the rest of the flat while they waited for reinforcements to arrive. More cops turned up, all in uniform. Still the wrong type. They wandered around the flat like sheep hunting for a pasture.

I got up and made myself some lunch: a cheese and tuna sandwich with chicory and sliced tomatoes on rye, a Granny Smith apple, a tall mug of Colombian coffee, and a piece of carrot cake. According to my brother Danny, the coffee alone would do me in sooner or later. The tuna had mercury in it, the cake too much sugar—*any* amount was too much—and the apple, chicory, and tomato had probably been sprayed with deadly pesticides. I had just committed gastronomic suicide. I killed myself three times a day. Better me than a stranger.

I hoped lunch would see me through the next few hours. At least my appetite seemed normal. I decided to lay off the codeine; the stuff made me woozy. If I ran out of luck, I'd need whatever wits I had.

I went back to my chair. The act had changed a bit at Keller's during my absence. A smattering of plainclothes cops were hustling around. I got a lot of shoulders and backs in my mirror. I had trouble getting a fix on any of them, but one party looked especially large. That wasn't so hot.

The knock on my door came some twenty minutes later. By then, the mirror was back in its drawer, a Chopin ballade was tinkling away on the radio, and I was more or less ready. Mostly less.

I opened the door. There stood Detective Danker.

"Your bell's not working, Mr. Gordon."

"That isn't all that's not working," I said. "They catch anyone working on these premises, they chuck 'em out."

I stepped aside and Danker strode in.

"You're still a wit, Mr. Gordon."

"And I still know someone taller than you."

"Who, Wilt Chamberlain?"

"Just a guy."

"He's got my condolences."

"Tough finding clothes, eh?"

"Beds, chairs, you name it. Even dames. There's one consolation: people don't get in your way very much."

"Must help in your work."

"Doesn't hurt. Left the hospital kind of sudden, Mr. Gordon."

"Hospitals give me a pain."

"You okay?"

"I've felt better. Doctors send you after me?"

Danker half smiled and went into the next room. "Cozy," he said.

"Like a closet."

"Nice view."

"If you like back yards."

"Lots of windows out there."

"Life in the raw. Poverty doesn't seem to bring out the best in people. Hear them squabbling day and night. I try to tune it out. Not half as much fun as TV, and I don't watch that."

Danker, hands in pockets, stared out the window. The cops in Keller's flat were still bouncing around for all the world to see, only the world wasn't watching. Just Danker and me. I was starting to sweat.

"There's been a little trouble across the yard," Danker said.

"Yeah?"

"We got a dead guy in one of the apartments. Thought you might want to take a look at him."

"Me?"

"It's not far, Mr. Gordon."

"Across the yard is like another country. I wouldn't know a neighbor from a hole in the wall."

"You'll be interested."

I shrugged. "It's your show."

I killed the radio—my resident mouse had shown scant interest in the classics—put on a jacket, followed Danker into the hallway, locked up, and shuffled down the stairs.

The sky was showing patches of blue between the clouds. No silver linings; this area didn't rate any. I moved slowly as befitted an invalid. Sam the Tailor failed to drop his needle, run out, and ask me what I'd found at Keller's. No one did anything. Danker and I walked in silence, turning up Ninety-third and entering the sixth house.

"How you doing?" Danker asked.

"Awful."

"Only two flights up."

"Only," I groaned.

It seemed a much longer haul this time. But then, two hours had gone by; I was older. The place was noisier now. I could hear voices coming from above. They grew louder as we approached the third floor. Tenants were out on the landing and around the stairwell, about six or seven. Nothing like cops to materialize a crowd.

Keller's door was open. I could see cops inside. We went in.

It was as if I had never left. The lumpy walls, tawdry furnishings, scraped wooden floors seemed to reach out in an embrace. The Hulk Hogan poster leered at me. Any second I expected the cadaver to rise off the floor and stumble over to greet me like a brother. It was all I could do to keep from bolting out the door.

"The bedroom," Danker said.

One of the plainclothes cops trailed after us, the other continued chatting with the pair of cops in uniform.

We went into the next room. I glanced out at my window, then down at the floor. Shorty stared up at me as if he'd seen one live guy too many recently.

"Know him?" Danker asked.

"Yeah," I heard myself say, "that's one of the guys who beat up Silbert."

"You sure?"

"Uh-huh. He live here?"

"No."

"Just visiting, eh?"

"We're looking for the man who does live here. The name Horace Keller mean anything to you?"

I shrugged. "Should it?"

"It's his place."

"I told you, Ninety-third Street could be in Hong Kong for all I know about it."

"Never look across your back yard?"

"What can I tell you?"

"Your window and Keller's are just about level. Take a look."

I did. "Yeah," I said, "I see what you mean. Sure, I probably glanced across lots of times. But I never saw anything. The guy works, he's not going to be home during the day. At night he probably kept his shades lowered. What's to notice? If the guy were a gorgeous lady, maybe I'd've paid more attention. I'm sorry, Danker, I'd like to help, but I just don't know anything."

The other cop drifted away. He hadn't seemed very interested to begin with.

"You've been a help, Mr. Gordon."

I said I was glad.

"I'd like you to come down to the station house, make a statement."

"Now?"

"In a day or two, when you're up to it."

I promised to do that.

Danker told me I could go. I went.

CHAPTER 13

THE CROWD IN THE HALL HADN'T BUDGED. A COUPLE OF KIDS had joined in. They eyed me eagerly as though I might be dispensing free tickets for the show inside.

I got down the staircase by hugging the bannister. Outdoors, I took a deep breath and started off in the direction of my flat. I didn't have to fake decrepitude anymore. I moved slowly, hesitantly, like a guy who'd just been told he was terminally ill. It wasn't me, though, only my career. Sooner or later, Danker would wise up to who I was. Sooner, probably. This second killing would give him an added incentive to hustle. He'd want to know who'd hired me and what the connection between Silbert and Keller was. I couldn't tell him the first and didn't know the second. I was through if my cover was blown; I was through if Keller vanished or landed in the clink for any length of time; I was through if Neely got jumpy over all this—and his nails were already bitten down to the quick. A lot of guys didn't know what they were, but I was lucky, I knew: I was through.

I stopped in front of the pleb bar next to the tailor's shop. An old duffer was seated inside, bent almost double over his drink. The bartender had a face like a pile of raw dough. The joint itself looked as cozy and inviting as the lobby of a welfare hotel. I needed a drink, but not this bad. I could wait till I got back to my own dump. The company would be better, if nothing else. The drink, too, probably.

I turned the corner, went up the rise. The crumbling tenements seemed ready to topple over if anyone glanced their way.

Don't knock it, pal, I told myself, this could be your permanent abode. Better than camping out in Central Park. Just come up with sixty bucks a month, they'll let you stay forever. You'll have your mouse for company and Keller's window right across from yours, a swell reminder of how you screwed up.

I climbed the three lopsided stone steps of my building, a feat that seemed to get tougher each time I did it. In the alcove, I juggled open the front door and went on up the stairs. The outside world was gone. I was back on the staircase, where I seemed to have spent half my life. I began to reconsider. Central Park wasn't so bad after all. It got a bit drafty in winter, but fresh air could be very invigorating.

I let myself into the flat, poured out a stiff jolt of whiskey, took a huge swallow, found Respighi's *The Birds* on QXR, and settled down in my easy chair.

I glanced across the yard—and right away wished I hadn't.

Danker's head and torso were framed in Keller's window. Smoke drifted from the cigar in his mouth. He waved at me. I think he may have even winked. I wagged a hand in his direction, but my heart wasn't in it. I gulped down some booze and almost choked.

I couldn't see myself spending Keller's ten grand. Not with Danker and Lord knew who else poking around.

But that left an interesting dilemma.

Rent was due on both the office and my home; Harry and I owed the bank a small fortune on our loan. Neely's dough had been paying most of our bills, and a king-size bonus, if I pulled off this job, was waiting at the finish line. But did I still have a client?

A lot of nice people had predicted that I'd fall flat on my

face when I took over Uncle Max's agency. I would hate like poison to see them proven right.

I took another mouthful of hooch. A nice mellow streak began to work its way through me. I could feel myself unwinding. Not bad. If a double shot could make me feel this good, what about a whole bottle? Or a case? I used to scoff at rummies, but that was before I'd sampled their wares in earnest. I drank some more. My brain felt as fuzzy as a baby's pink blanket, but underneath I was as sharp as a Gillette twin-blade. I was raring to go, show 'em what I could do. Too bad there wasn't much demand for my brain just now. New York's Finest were on the job, and my all-purpose suspect had taken a powder. Damn inconsiderate. Two bodies in three days. Not a record yet; far too early to call Guinness. Third body bound to turn up, then a fourth and fifth. Gotta have patience. . . .

Trouble was Shorty, of course. He might have been part of Keller's world, all right, but not Silbert's, not without a lot of finessing, which my razor-sharp brain, just now, wasn't quite up to.

Poor old departed Silbert sold yummy little cookies, pies, and cakes across a counter. Maybe Shorty was a *very* stupid burglar who got his kicks knocking over what passed for the local poorhouse. Maybe he was trying to rob Silbert and Keller, after all. That would explain the whole thing. Except, why would Keller shoot him? The guy was an experienced cop. Surely he knew how to say "Freeze." So maybe Shorty didn't freeze and Keller shot him. Why not just call the cops? Because Keller, who was a lowlife and a crook, had some business with Shorty, who was also a lowlife and a crook.

But not upstanding, kindly, innocent Mrs. Silbert, who wouldn't know a crook if he sat on her. Not unless there was something very underhanded and devious about poor old broken-down Silbert, something that didn't meet the eye, and the two guys who were beating the shit out of her had some reason, wanted something from the old dame because, despite everything, there *was* some connection between them.

Very cautiously I put my empty glass down on the floor and got to my feet.

I'd been too busy worrying about my job, about Keller, Shorty, and Danker—all reasonable things to worry about—to give much thought to Mrs. Silbert. That was my error. For Silbert had handed me this vital piece of evidence on a silver platter. And while no doubt I could've ferreted out the whole rotten scheme by sheer analytical power, this made things a hell of a lot simpler. The annals of high-class sleuthing were full of simple stuff, and simple meant easy. And what was wrong with that?

I peeked out the window. Still some activity over at Keller's. No one was giving me the old eagle eye. I chuckled at this obvious oversight.

I made my way to the closet, jerked open the door, bent double, and looked around. At first I saw nothing. Then I grinned. The damn letter had slid under my empty suitcase in a vain effort to escape me. Stupid letter. I scooped it up, tore open the envelope, pulled out a single handwritten sheet.

It was in Yiddish.

CHAPTER 14

I TURNED THE SHEET OVER TO SEE IF SOMEONE HAD THOUGHT-fully provided a translation on the back. I held it sideways and upside down. Enlightenment didn't come. I could understand Yiddish more or less, and even make myself understood in it. Any words a precocious seven-year-old might know, I probably knew too: my parents had spoken the language. When it came to talking like a grown-up, though, I didn't have a prayer. I could decipher a few words in a Yiddish newspaper—I'd had some lessons as a kid—but handwriting always looked like Chinese. Mrs. Silbert's letter meant nothing to me.

It was disheartening.

I stood there by the open closet door, holding the piece of paper. It was a dud, something useless and personal that would get me nowhere. The whole notion of a link between Silbert and Keller now seemed ludicrous, the product of desperation and one shot too many. I could just see the old lady scrawling letters, in Yiddish, about some mug who lived across the yard. The thought was sidesplitting. But the laugh was on me. I hadn't gotten the jump on the cops: I was still at the starting gate.

I put a pot of coffee on to boil. Like a lot of traditional remedies, this one wasn't going to sober me up, either. But it gave me the feeling I was in charge. I liked that.

I was going to check out the letter, of course. I couldn't do less; it was all I had going for me. Long shots had put the Shaw family in hock for years, but I was already in hock, so what did I have to worry about?

I reached for the phone.

I made my way uphill till I hit Third Avenue, turned north, and ambled on toward Ninety-sixth. I walked slowly, like a guy Dr. Frankenstein had just fixed up with a pair of mismatched legs. I kept peering into store windows, trying to catch the reflection of whoever was tailing me. I saw no one.

I gave up the game on Ninety-sixth Street and flagged a cab. Riding west, I twisted around twice to squint out the rear window. The effort made my head hurt. I saw nothing. I settled back in my seat and dozed fitfully for the rest of the trip.

The taxi pulled away, leaving me standing on the corner of Broadway and Eighty-ninth. Coming from my hovel across town, this felt like another country, one whose sanitation department did its job. Any second someone would step up and ask to see my passport.

A block away, Banana Republic peddled safari garb in the heart of the concrete jungle. Where would we be without them? A health food store next door offered cut-rate longevity. The New Yorker movie house across the street, a prime dispenser of illusion, had given way to greater reality, was gone. A giant residential tower had shouldered it into history. Other towers were going up around it. Someday the new residents would all try to get into the local IRT subway at once and make headlines.

I headed east, turned in at The Gotham Arms, got a nod of recognition from the doorman, gave the 10K buzzer three short jabs, and hustled into a waiting elevator at the rear of the lobby.

Ten K was the last apartment down a long, carpeted,

discreetly dim hallway. The door had been left ajar for me. I went in.

I could hear his voice coming from the bedroom on the right. A cramped kitchenette hid behind a wall to my left. I was in a very large high-ceilinged room. Books were everywhere. A bookcase rose from floor to ceiling, running the length of the east wall; plants and smaller bookcases shared the north wall under the windows. There were more bookcases in the bedroom. The books were in six languages. Only a librarian and checkout desk were missing. I made my way around a pile of books lying on the floor and over to a small enclave of comfort: a soft ivory sofa, a lamp, a barber's chair, an end table piled with books and journals. I didn't need a shave or haircut so I sank down into the sofa, sighing, and removed my shoes and stretched out. I was ready to apply for a job here as library mascot, as long as they threw in the sofa.

I closed my eyes, then heard the footsteps and opened them again. This was not going to be a day of rest.

He came out of the bedroom, still gabbing into the phone, the long extension cord trailing behind him.

He was shoeless and had on gray slacks, a white shirt, and yellow and green striped socks, the day's concession to unbridled color. He had a longish head, a straight nose, rather full lips, brown hair over a high forehead. Brown eyes and eyebrows behind horn-rimmed glasses. He was six foot six, which was about three inches taller than Danker, proving that I occasionally spoke the truth, strange as that might seem.

For a bookworm he didn't look half bad. For an athlete he wouldn't have looked half bad either. Nothing to it. All it took was a pass to the Columbia gym, which as a faculty member he got gratis, and lots of sweat—although he probably thought of it as kicks, along with the ton of health food he consumed daily. Here was a genuine hero who single-handedly kept three local health food stores in the black. This was my older brother, Danny.

"Sorry," Danny said, putting down the phone. "That was Linda."

"Linda?" I said.

"I'm seeing her," Danny said.

"What happened to Sue?"

"I'm seeing her too."

"And Mary-Lou?"

"Less than Linda and Susan."

"Ah," I said.

"Linda's a redhead," Danny said, "and a painter. A realist."

"Bet you've wanted another redhead since old what's-her-name, eh?"

"Marsha."

"Yeah. Your second."

"Quite right," Danny said. "This will be my third redhead. They are a rare breed, you know."

"Yeah, I always use a net to catch mine."

"The trouble is Sonya."

"Sonya?"

"She keeps calling up, at the most inconvenient times. It literally takes hours to get her off the line."

"I thought you broke off with Sonya years ago?"

"I did."

"She know about it yet?"

"There are problems."

"When aren't there?"

"Her mother's ill," Danny said.

"Getting worse each day, I bet."

"Bedridden."

"Oughta kick the bucket any minute. Certainly by the turn of the century."

Danny shook his head. "She's in trouble, Jim. Father out of the home, mother chronically ill and dependent on her for financial support. Few friends. And the job at the library far from secure."

"And you figure you're making things better for old Sonya by stringing her along?"

"Can't break her heart now, James."

"How do you do it, Danny? You're seeing three other women."

"It's not easy. She thinks I'm teaching extra courses, doing research for articles. I told her you haven't been well and I'm helping out at the office."

"*Me?*"

"Had to tell her something."

"So you *are* seeing her."

"As little as possible. What I hope is, she'll become disgusted with me."

"Keep hoping, pal."

"And meet some nice prospect somewhere."

"And live happily ever after."

"Why not?"

"Because she's hooked on you," I almost shouted, "and you're encouraging her!"

"What can I do?"

"Tell her it's over."

"She'd die."

"Jesus."

"The burden would be too much for her. How can I let her face all that alone?"

"How alone can she get? You've got three other dames in your life."

"Mary-Lou doesn't really count. I think she's seeing someone."

"You're not sure?"

"She's dropped hints."

"So get rid of her."

"I don't want to hurt her, Jim."

"But she's got another guy."

"I think she's using this fellow."

"Using him?"

"To make me jealous."

"Daniel."

"Yes, James?"

"You are a very sick person."

"Linda's the one, Jimmy."

"That's nice."

"Wait till you meet her."

"A real knockout, eh?"

"She's perfect. Somehow I'll extricate myself from the others; you'll see."

"Let me guess: you've known this Linda less than three weeks."

"Right."

"You always say stuff like that when you know them less than three weeks."

"This is different."

"You always say that, too. What about Sue?"

"I don't know."

"Sue stays, eh?"

"We go way back, Jim. I don't know what I'd do without her."

"Hide her under the bed. Who'd know?"

Danny peered at me. "You don't look good, Jim."

"You just noticed?"

"I noticed before. You know I don't like to pry."

"Yeah, and birds don't like to fly, they prefer hitchhiking. Do me a favor."

"What?"

"Sit down, don't hover over me. It makes me nervous. You slip and fall on me, I go back to the hospital."

Danny shrugged and climbed onto the barber's chair. "Sitting all day, James. Been preparing my lectures."

"Sit some more."

"What's this about a hospital?"

"Jesus, you think I look this way because I've been noshing on hot dogs and white bread?"

"You were actually in a hospital?"

"I was on this stakeout, Danny, in a dump just like the dumps we grew up in—you'd've loved it—minding my own business, when I hear these screams. It's the middle of the night. And like the dummy I am, I jump out of bed and go racing off to grapple with the tough guys."

"There were tough guys?"

"Yes, just my luck. Instead of someone having a simple nightmare, there were real honest-to-God tough guys, a pair of them. They were beating up an old lady on the top floor, don't ask me why. You would've mopped up with 'em. I almost did too, but I got cocky. They banged me on the head when I wasn't looking and I ended up spending the night in the sick ward. I'm okay. The old lady died of her injuries. Not my fault, right? So I should be in line for a good citizen's award at the very least. Instead the law has me pegged for the hot seat. One of these hoods turns up dead in another apartment and the cops drag me over to ID the body. Know whose place it was? The Joe I'm supposed to be shadowing. He's beat it. The cops are suspicious as hell—of *me*. I'm supposed to be invisible, keep a low profile. Only now I've become a star attraction. The job's hanging by a thread. The man I'm working for blew a fuse when I gave him the first part of this mess; he'll go right into orbit when he hears the second. So much for getting rich quick. The trick now is to stay out of debtor's prison."

"You can always borrow from me," Danny said, "you know that."

"Thanks, but you haven't got the bread. This is a big hole I've dug for myself. It'll take mucho moolah to fill it, the kind my client's been dishing out. He's more likely to take an ax to me now than keep the paychecks coming."

"Jimmy, why do you need it?"

"'It'?"

"This so-called business of yours."

"It's no worse than the other dozen so-called businesses I've been in. The only difference is, I like it."

"You don't know if you're coming or going."

"I'm going. I used to be coming, but now that the shit's hit the fan I'm definitely going. There's nothing like knowing where you are in life."

"If you're so happy, James, why do you sound so bitter?"

"Hospital's don't agree with me, chintzy clients give me a pain, I don't like dead guys, I don't enjoy getting tangled up with the law. But most of all I hate the thought of going broke again. I really can't stand that."

Danny sighed. "Uncle Max didn't do you any favors when he handed you the agency."

"All he did was save my life."

"All he did was leave you a hole in the wall on the worst block in town, two months' back rent, an unpaid phone bill . . ."

"We did well enough. We got out of there, or haven't you heard?"

"Certainly. And look where you are, James, you and your novice friend."

"Harry's all right."

"He's not a professional."

"Sure he is."

"He is a *social worker*."

"So what's wrong with that? Best experience in the world. All that snooping into peoples' lives, all that legwork. Perfect for our racket. Kid's a natural."

"You're not much better yourself."

"Come on, Danny."

"Eighteen months in military intelligence does not a detective make, Jimmy."

"Now he's knocking the U.S. Army."

"If only *one* of you had practical experience—"

"Cut it out. I didn't come here to be lectured."

"If our father were alive, James, he'd say—"

"'I got a hot tip at Belmont. Lend me fifty bucks.' Gimme a break, Danny. I'm here on business."

"Business?"

"How's your Yiddish, big brother?"

"What kind of question is that? I teach a course in Yiddish literature."

"In English translation."

"In the original, too. Every three years or so. Small classes. And too many Yiddish professors. That's the problem."

"Four professors?"

"Three now. Gudtkind didn't get tenure; they let him go."

"Cutthroat racket."

"These are *very* small classes, hardly worth the preparation. But I like to keep my hand in, for the good of the cause."

"Some cause. You still teach American, British, French, and German literature?"

"Of course."

"I should have such problems. Your Yiddish okay, or does it get rusty in between your three-year layoffs?"

"It's fine."

"You read handwriting too?"

Danny nodded.

"I've got a letter. The old lady I tried to save gave it to me before we both passed out—she, permanently. It's in Yiddish."

"Let me see it."

I fished the sheet of paper out of my pocket, passed it to him. The big lug sat in his barber's chair and read it. He didn't move his lips over each word or break out in a cold sweat; he just read it. It's bad enough having a brother who looks like Mount Rushmore without him having a brain like Bertrand Russell's, too. At least the older kids never picked on me after school: they were dumb, but not *that* dumb.

Danny raised his eyes.

"So?" I said.

"Fascinating," he said. "If you can tell me what all this means, you really *are* a detective."

CHAPTER 15

"WHO IS THIS WOMAN?" DANNY ASKED.

"Worked in a bakery, I think."

"That's all you know?"

"We weren't exactly chummy."

"This is a funny letter, Jimmy."

"Humorous?"

"Peculiar."

"That's nice. Mind telling me why?"

"It's not a letter."

"What is it, a laundry list?"

"A report. Know someone named Keller?"

I looked at him. "Yes."

"Who is he?"

"The man I've been shadowing."

"You weren't the only one."

"Shit."

"How about Elman?"

I nodded. "Keller's pal."

"Rifeman? Saphire?"

"I don't think so. Any first names?"

"No. Gordon ring a bell?"

"Yes."

"Who is he?"

"Me."

"Congratulations. You're only mentioned once."

"It's nice to be remembered. What does she say about me?"

"That you're still watching this Keller."

"Still?"

"Yes."

"Great. What else?"

"She says Keller hasn't seen Rifeman in over a month. Or Saphire. That he's gone drinking with Elman three times. That Keller has been to McDonald's, to OTB, to a whore-house—"

"A what?"

"*Ah byes zoynes,* a whorehouse."

"I missed that one. She say where it's at?"

"No."

"I have an idea. Maybe in that building with a pool parlor. I waited downstairs."

"It's important?"

I sighed. "Uh-uh. Go on."

"Keller at McGill's."

"A bar."

"That's all for places. She says Keller's behaving strangely."

"Yeah? How?"

"She doesn't say."

"Anything else?"

"That's it."

"Tremendous."

Danny grinned at me. "How did she do?"

"As a sleuth?"

"Yes."

"Dandy. Except for the small matter of getting herself killed."

"Amateurs always run a risk."

"Let's not start that again, Daniel; I'm not up to it." I folded my arms behind my head, shifted my weight on the sofa, put one leg over the other, and tried to assume the posture of a man who knew what he was doing. It wasn't easy. From the corner of Amsterdam Avenue and Eighty-ninth Street, ten floors below and half a block over, the sound of salsa music magnified two-hundred-fold came blaring up at us. "Nice serenade," I said.

"I've spoken to the manager of that store," Danny said, "but he remains recalcitrant."

"Wants all of Manhattan to know he's around. Kind of puts him on the map, doesn't it?"

"Next comes dynamite: I blow up the store."

"They'll hate you in New Jersey. I hear there's a whole community listens to his concerts. Wafts right across the Hudson. Isn't there some law about being a public nuisance?"

"Certainly, if the police enforce it."

"There's always a catch, eh? Listen," I said, "she wasn't tailing him alone."

"The baker?"

"Yes, Silbert. I'd've noticed an old lady like that always hanging around. I all but lived with this Keller for six weeks. She had help, lots of it."

"So?"

"So the cops might've been curious about Keller, or another private eye, maybe. But an old lady with some sort of a staff under her, no less, writing up reports in *Yiddish*! That's too damn weird! I don't believe a word of it."

Danny beamed at me. "It's a mystery."

"Yeah. Along with everything else."

"Right up your alley, I should imagine."

"Don't count on it."

"A man in your line, after all."

"Let's cut the wisecracks, shall we? Any address on that letter? Any indication who it's for?"

"None."

"This gets better every second."

"Want a typed translation?"

"Sure. Thanks."

"I'll make one. Stay for lunch?"

"Love to Daniel."

We had a tall glass of carrot juice apiece; an organic salad consisting of grated raw beets and turnips, sliced radishes, kirby cucumbers, plum tomatos, and chickory, topped with Zabar's extra virgin olive oil and balsamic vinegar; two baked potatos in a dill-tofu cream; cantaloupe; and herb tea.

"I almost feel alive," I told him.

We were seated around a circular table in the main room, where almost everything else was, too, over on the left, between kitchen and front windows.

"Any time," Danny said.

"I can actually feel the herd of vitamins racing through me," I said, "going after the alcohol molecules I had for breakfast."

Danny looked grave. "Can you imagine what Mother would have said to that?"

"Yeah. 'Why did I ever marry that no-good-luck gambler, your father?' and 'Can you spare ten dollars for the phone bill?' "

"The mismatch of the century."

"Another one of those mysteries," I said. "Plan to work on it as soon as I get some free time."

"Are you going to be all right, Jimmy?"

"I hope so. If not, I can always come back here for another meal."

"Seriously."

"I don't know. The bump on the head's nothing. The money outlook's nothing, too—I wasn't kidding about that. And the job's beginning to look a bit tired. But you never know."

"I can still loan you some money."

"And it still wouldn't be enough."

"So what's going to happen?"

"We muddle through. What else?"

Danny shook his head.

"Yeah, I agree with you a hundred percent. Mind if I use your phone?"

"Help yourself."

I went back to the sofa, plucked the phone off an end table, put it on my lap, and dialed Neely's home number. Neely wasn't going to like my bothering his wife. But then he wasn't going to like anything I had to tell him either. I listened to the phone ring a good twelve times before I hung up.

I stared at the wall, hunting for inspiration. It seemed to be in short supply.

Neely's case had taken a decided turn for the worse and was attracting more attention than a nude jaywalker in Times Square. The poor slob didn't know what kind of trouble he had. The cops were likely to start grilling me in earnest soon, probably over a slow flame. Whoever had been getting Silbert's reports could finger me any old time, and maybe would. I was becoming as useful in this business as a Model T Ford in the Indy 500. If I jumped the gun, called it quits and gave Danker what I had, Neely's career was done. Why Wait for Fate to Trip You Up? Go to Shaw and Be Ruined Now. If I opted to stand firm and sat on evidence in a pair of murder cases, I could lose my licence, or worse. Both choices left something to be desired. What I had to do was have a quiet man-to-man chat with my client, and the best way to set that up was to reach him in person. The sound of my voice over his office phone would probably kill him anyway, solving my problem.

I dialed the number.

"Twenty-fourth Precinct, Sergeant Lacovaly," a voice told me.

"I asked to speak with Lieutenant Neely.

"Hold on." I held.

The voice spoke again. "He's not here."

"When's he expected back?"

The voice didn't know.

I thanked the voice and hung up.

"No luck?" Danny asked.

"Plenty," I told him. "All bad."

CHAPTER 16

I CAUGHT A TAXI ON BROADWAY AND WAS HAULED AWAY FROM
the land of plenty. Don't think I went willingly. Only duty
screaming hysterically in my ear could have budged me. That
and the fact that I had no choice. We turned east on Ninety-
sixth, passed the mid-income projects, which valiantly held
upper Harlem at bay, and dived into Central Park. The late
November sky had become a clear, bright blue, but the tree
branches peeking over the roadway were bare and scraggly;
they weren't fooled one bit.

I closed my eyes and mentally played the first movement of
Beethoven's Third Piano Concerto. I played as much as I
could remember and gave myself a standing ovation when I
was done. I wasn't apt to get much applause from anyone else
just now.

When I opened my eyes, we were back on the East Side
among the giant, still-growing construction sites. Three
months from now I'd need a Boy Scout to help me find my
way.

The taxi turned south on Second Avenue. I caught a
glimpse of Metropolitan Hospital behind us before we hit
Ninety-fourth.

"Keep driving," I told the cabby. "Go around Ninety-third
and Ninety-fourth a couple of times, slowly."

"It's your money, bud."

We rolled up the hill on Ninety-third past the row of too familiar tenements, weed-strewn lots, and strolling pedestrians. The latter were a couple of dumpy women and a small kid. Not very menacing. I ignored them.

A third of the north side of Ninety-fourth was taken up by a large laundry where the actual washing got done for some of the storefront chinese laundries scattered around town. The weathered brick rose five stories. The windows were boarded over; the two wide doors were always closed. My hunch was that the joint ran on slave labor, but they could have just been serfs. There didn't seem to be anyplace for someone to hide.

The parking garage and ancient brownstones next to it were more promising. They were also a lot closer to my building. I saw nothing the first time around. We went for a second spin. Seconds came up a winner.

The shoes were first, then part of the legs attached to them. The rest of the guy I couldn't see. He was way over by the east wall, far inside the garage. He could have been sitting down for all I knew.

He still hadn't moved the third time we coasted by. He might have been some working stiff taking a well-earned break. Except that his pants were wrong. Suit pants. Not jeans or overalls. The boss, I figured, would have better places to hang out.

"Let me off on Second and Ninetieth," I said to my driver's back.

"Seen enough, huh?"

"Too much," I told him.

I came hobbling around my corner some fifteen minutes later. Actually, Danny's chow and my short breather from the flophouse had given me a considerable lift. I wasn't ready to take on Marvelous Marvin Hagler yet, but I had vague hopes. Anyone watching, though, would see someone too infirm to worry about, a guy probably on his way home from drawing up a last will and testament.

I didn't even glance across the street at the garage. I just barely managed to crawl up the three steps and into the alcove. I wondered if I was really fooling anyone. I wondered why the cops were bothering me in the first place. I even wondered if I was in the wrong line of work.

Not for long, though. Soon I had more important things to wonder about—like whether I'd make it to the second floor. For the time being, Marvelous Marvin seemed safe enough.

Inside my flat I pitched my raincoat onto the bed and lunged for the easy chair. I sat and eyed Keller's window. The cops hadn't even lowered the shades. Why should they? They were waiting, a pair of them, in the bedroom for their man to stroll through the front door just like any other upstanding citizen, not creep up the rear fire escape. One of the cops was the one who'd been with Danker when I identified Shorty; he still looked bored, only now he had plenty of reason.

Keller's welcoming committee made sense, a lot more than the guy staked out in the garage. I had to figure he was a cop, and that his main interest was me. I'd been bad, all right, but not *that* bad.

More than ever I had to reach Neely. But the phone was suspect now. If Danker had put a man on me, why not go whole hog and bug my phone, too? It stood to reason. Reason was giving me a headache again.

I wasted the rest of the day making periodic trips to Lou's Diner on Second and Ninety-first. It wasn't to sample the food. Lou had a pay phone in back next to the washroom, one that couldn't be seen from the street. I fed the phone quarters and was rewarded with a few words from Sergeant Lacovaly or one of his buddys. No one answered my ring at Neely's house. The guy trailing along behind me during these outings, a heavyset, gray-haired, red-faced party, didn't look much happier than I was.

In between, I lulled in my easy chair waiting for something to happen. I tried reading my dog-eared copy of McNeill's *The Rise of the West*. The general, ongoing mess of humanity usually make my problems seem like kid stuff. Not this time. I closed the paperback and left humanity to fend for itself.

Rachmaninoff's Second Symphony came at me over WNYC. Even on good days the work was a bit mournful; right now it sounded like the end of the world. I was too stupefied to get up and turn the damn thing off.

I eyed my phone balefully, as if it were responsible for getting itself bugged. I kept watch on the cops across the yard. Staring at a brick wall would have been just as useful.

Around six I got up and fixed dinner: sardines with chopped onions, cold canned peas and spinach, a thick slice of rye bread, a pear, and a cup of Zabar's Colombian coffee. Emergency rations, except for the Zabar's. If this wasn't an emergency, what was?

By seven o'clock it was good and dark outside. No light in Keller's windows. The pair of cops—if they were still there—might be whiling away the time by keeping tabs on *my* window. The Jim Shaw show, the dreariest hour in midtown Manhattan. Watch Shaw sit inertly, craftily imitating a cadaver. Humanitarian instincts prevailed. I put any possible spectators out of their misery by dousing my lights. I felt around inside the closet for my wool-lined denim jacket and my jeans and running shoes and pulled them on. I stuck a flashlight in my pocket, closed shop, and paid a visit to the cellar.

Junk cluttered the floor; the smell of mildew filled my nostrils. My flash led me to the back door.

A bolt held it in place. I released the bolt and stepped into the back yard. I climbed over a four-foot wooden fence, made my way to the last building in the row, scaled a six-foot crosshatched wire fence, and came down in a weedy lot.

I looked around hopefully to see if any male nurses had shown up to carry me the rest of the way. Using the fence as a support, I waited awhile; then I tried it on my own. Some of the taller weeds almost got me, but I managed to reach Ninety-third Street.

No one was behind me. No cops loitered in front of Keller's house in an unmarked car; presumably they were all hidden inside. I had the block to myself. I trudged uphill to Third Avenue.

The A&P was dark. Only the gas station across the street and the corner bar showed signs of life. A few cars drove by. No taxis. Tired streetlamps stretched off into the distance. I trekked up another hill to Lexington Avenue.

I stood among people again, lit store windows, moving cars. Presently a yellow cab came along. I got in and rode away.

CHAPTER 17

MY CAR WAS PARKED IN A GARAGE ON WEST SEVENTY-SEVENTH Street, a block away from home. I got it out of hock and drove back across town. I glanced up at my penthouse once in passing. Still there. It hadn't caved in or blown away yet. The way things were going it was probably an oversight. I hit the East River Drive some fifteen minutes later, and turned south. Luxury beckoned on my right. Lit windows in tall, swanky towers twinkled down on me. On my left, the water below was a black streak. A lone tugboat was out there hauling an empty barge. Queens lay on the other side.

I rode across the Queensboro Bridge. Bach's Concerto for Four Harpsichords on NCN rode with me. You can judge a man by the company he keeps. For my money, I'd rather have had Bach running the show than me; the guy never went wrong. The closer I came to Queens, the less I liked it. Danny had a point. This racket could turn sour. Every move of mine was as surefire as a roll of the dice. I was trailing along in Dad's footsteps, a true chip off the old block. The old man had held the great Reshevsky to a draw. Once. In one game. But win or lose he never hit the jackpot. There was no dough in chess. To make dough you played the ponies; any fool knew that. Now it was my turn. I wasn't all that keen on carrying on the tradition.

I rode through the Queens streets. The buildings changed

size and shape every few miles like a deck of cards being reshuffled. I'd neglected to bring salt and pepper, but I figured when you're eating crow, it doesn't matter too much.

It was a quiet block. The two-story frame houses looked like twenty identical twins in the dark, as if their various architects were all buddies who didn't want to outdo one another. Bare trees watched over the pavement. Lawns and hedges in the summer were no doubt perfectly manicured. Only five cars in the street; the rest would be safely tucked away in their garages out back. If this was the good life why was Neely such a jerk?

I had to look twice before I spotted the right number. My client's house was dark in front. That left the back. I pulled to the curb, killed the motor, and stepped out, instantly destroying the block's symmetry.

I went up the walk and tried the bell. Chimes sounded inside. I waited. When nothing happened, I rang again. Still nothing. I went around the back. Dark there, too. I tried the back door. Locked. I went over to the garage. No windows. Both doors locked. *Locked* was the secret word this night, only no prizes were being awarded. I vetoed breaking into the garage just to see if it was empty; my client might not like it. I hoofed back to the front of the house and stood gazing up at it. If it had anything to tell me, it was keeping mum. The trip began to look like a washout.

I hiked over to the house on the left, and rang the bell. A small, beak-nosed, sixtyish lady answered.

"My name is Schwartz," I said. "I had an appointment with the Neelys tonight. No one seems to be home."

"So?"

"You wouldn't know what happened to them?"

"No."

The door closed. A biddy of few words. Or maybe the Neelys had flunked the latest popularity polls around here.

I tried the house on the right. A kid answered this time.

"Your parents home?"

"Nope."

"I'm trying to get hold of the Neelys next door."

"Ring their bell?"

"Yeah."

"Nothing happen?"

"Nothing's the word."

The kid shrugged. "Sorry, mister, can't help you."

The door closed. Some neighborhood.

I headed across the street. Across the street, in urban terms, was as far off as the other side of the canyon. No one would know a thing. But a couple more nos couldn't make matters any worse.

A man answered my ring this time. He was middle-aged, balding and overweight. He had on a plaid shirt.

"I'm looking for the Neelys," I said, jerking a thumb over my shoulder, "I had a—"

"You ain't the only one, son."

"I'm not?" I heard myself say. I was so surprised I forgot the rest of my spiel.

"You're the fourth."

"The fourth? What is this, a convention? They all stopped here?"

"Just you, son; shows intelligence."

"Yeah, I was called the Plato of the First Grade."

"Neely come into money, or what? Hasn't gotten this much attention since his kitchen caught fire. That was some five years ago."

"Beats me," I said. "I used to be on the force with the guy."

"Don't say."

"Yeah. He asked me to drop over tonight."

"Friendly of him."

"Uh-huh. Only he doesn't seem to be home."

"He ain't. Drove away around six. Him and the missus."

"No kidding?"

"Wouldn't kid you, son."

"I guess not. Don't know where he went, I suppose?"

"Ain't a mind reader. Just snoopy."

"Yeah. These other guys—"

"First one, around six twenty; the other two, a half hour later, maybe."

"The two together?"

"Looked that way; drove up in the same car."

"Rang his bell and drove away?"

"Did what you did, son, went all around the house. *Then* they drove away."

"Didn't bother the neighbors?"

"No sir."

"You see a lot," I told him.

"Not so much. Just after work and some weekends. Got my easy chair by the front window. Sony's there too. Along with the evening paper."

"Bachelor, eh?"

"Widower. Children all grown up. Be surprised how dull the TV and paper can get sometimes."

"Not me."

"Well, I look out the window."

"More interesting."

"Pretty dull, too. Just different. Name's Higgens, by the way."

"Schwartz," I said. We shook hands.

"Neely," he said. "What kind of cop was he?"

"When I knew him? Average."

"Just average?"

"Maybe a little below."

"Ain't too neighborly, either."

"Actually," I said, "he stank."

Higgens nodded. "That's what I kind of figured."

CHAPTER 18

I CROSSED OVER TO MY CAR, GOT IN AND DROVE AWAY. NOBODY bounded out of Neely's house to wave good-bye. Nobody did anything. The only mileage I'd gotten out of this visit was on my odometer.

I parked on a side street two blocks away, climbed out and started back. My first breakin had only grossed a measly ten grand, but that had been a whole eight hours ago. Now that I was a seasoned veteran, bigger things could be expected. Like ten years in the jug. But who said a life of crime was a breeze?

Neely's house was near the center of his block. I was on the adjacent block somewhere behind it. I counted houses. Twelve from the corner seemed about right. I went up a driveway. Only one lit window on my left. I went past it. No one started yelling. No dog took a chunk out of my leg in the back yard. A four-foot white picket fence was the only obstacle I encountered. I surmounted it.

Neely's back yard was as I had left it; the back door was still locked, the windows dark. If my client came home suddenly and found me loitering in his living room, he'd hardly call the cops. By the time I was done filling him in, he'd be too miserable even to complain. What I had to watch out for was nosy neighbors. I was lucky. None were in evidence.

The pair of windows facing me were small and screened.

That made them too tough. The side of the house farthest from the driveway was the most secluded. If the old biddy who had given me the cold shoulder spent her spare time staring at her neighbor's wall, I was in trouble. I figured she was probably flying around on her broomstick somewhere.

There were plenty of windows. I chose the first one I came to and stuck my nose close to the pane hunting for an alarm system of some kind. There didn't seem to be any. Very civilized. I tried to raise the window. Locked. Even civilization has its limits. I went back to the rear of the house. A black plastic trash barrel stood next to the drainpipe. I lifted the lid. Empty, rinsed clean. I carted it over to my window, climbed on top of the lid. Digging the flash out of my back pocket, I swung it at the part of the upper pane even with the latch inside. The glass shattered. When no alarms went off and no one screamed "Help," I put my hand carefully through the hole and twisted the latch. I got down from the barrel, raised the window, hoisted myself over the sill. If Neely gave me the gate as shamus, I could still offer my services as security guard. I had just demonstrated his need for one.

I took a deep breath, inhaling stale air and something that smelled like dusty carpet; I was probably standing on it. I waited for my eyes to get used to the dark.

I was in a dining room. Chairs, table, and china cupboard were just dark shapes. I opened a door on the left. Kitchen, the back yard beyond. I went back through the dining room into a living room. Sofas, easy chairs, huge mirror over a fireplace, TV, turntable, speakers. The front room had a closet, which contained outerwear. There was an umbrella stand. I peeked through the front windows. Streetlamps cut solitary figures in the night. Outdoor lights cheerily illuminated housefronts. Lit windows gave off a warm, secure glow. No one was walking around out there. No traffic, either. I felt like curling up on Neely's sofa and taking a peaceful snooze. This place seemed a lot safer than my skid row domicile. The only sour note was the housebreaker. Me.

A staircase in the front room went up to the next floor. I climbed it. Two bedrooms: his and hers. Another room down a short corridor turned out to be a den. His. Small TV, desk, chair, ashtrays—a pair of them, filled to overflowing. If I listened hard I could probably hear the echoes of coughs bouncing off the walls.

I turned on the desk lamp, sat down at the desk, pulled open the top drawer. Pens, pencils, index cards, unopened cigarette packs, postage stamps, a ruler, two bottles of whiteout. This drawer hardly offered the proper incentive to look in the other two. I did anyway. One was full of lined yellow legal pads, packages of typewriter paper, a box of carbons, and envelopes. The other contained documents. I spent twenty minutes going through them. The tax records dating back seven years were cut and dried. My client had no outside income; he lived off his paycheck. The house I was in had a double mortgage against it; the second was only a couple of months old. Maybe that was where my fee was coming from? I did some mental arithmetic. If I stayed on the job another two months and Neely sprang for the bonus, I'd just about clean him out. At least he had the dough; that inspired confidence. No bankbooks. No stocks, bonds, mutual funds. There was an insurance policy with his wife as beneficiary. There was an honorable discharge from the U.S. Army, a B.A. from the John Jay College of Criminal Justice— probably in the use of the billy club. A marriage certificate too. All the milestones. What I had was the guy's life laid out for me on his desktop. The papers forgot to mention he was a shithead, but I knew that already.

What I failed to find was an address book of some kind, a Rolodex, my card, any of my reports, any names associated with the case. Which could mean that Neely had packed them away in his suitcase, or that they were stashed elsewhere.

I put everything neatly back where I'd found it. I'd come a long way to get this unexpected peep at my client's life, and now that I had, I knew as much about him that was useful as a cat knows about American history, even one that's lived in New York all its life.

I frisked both bedrooms and found nothing. I went up to the attic and stumbled over old furniture. I broke open two trunks. Blankets and linens in one, ancient clothing in the other. If the drab fifties ever made a comeback, this family was ready.

I used one of Neely's old shirts to wipe the dust off my hands, took a last look around, and left. I was definitely not enjoying myself. I could feel despondency starting to edge out depression, a bad sign. The only place I had neglected to rummage in so far was the basement. I went down there. No one would be able to accuse me of not exploring every possibility. I stood in the basement and played my flash over the walls, floors, boiler, and pipes. My light fell on a large black plastic trash bag over by the cellar steps, which led out to the back yard, the day's or week's garbage waiting to be put in the nice clean barrel near the drainpipe. Only Neely had left so fast he had forgotten to dispose of it. I could now add to my already vast store of knowledge what the Neelys had eaten recently. I could feel my stomach lurch. As usual, my stomach had the right idea.

I opened the bag and poured its contents onto the floor. Chicken and fish bones mingled with leftover salad and coffee grounds. The odor all but convinced me to give up detective work right then and there. I kicked the refuse, scattering it around for a closer look. The trick was to get my nose in the proximity of the junk without passing out. I took a deep breath and leaned over. The garbage was all garbage. No money mixed in with the lettuce. Two crumpled sheets of yellow lined paper from Neely's legal pad were there too. I dug them out. Doodles on one, a few figures on the other— not the artistic but the numerical kind. I brushed off the bread crumbs, dabs of butter, and pencil shavings, and stuck the second sheet in my pocket. Then I went up the stairs and opened the basement door. I stopped there, my hand still on the knob.

I wasn't alone anymore.

There were footsteps in the living room.

I couldn't have been more surprised if Neely had popped out from behind the boiler and yelled, "You're it!" Good fortune was grinning at me. I was actually going to meet my client. Or was the grin more of a sneer?

Something bothered me about those footsteps. They sounded furtive, too quiet, as if someone were tiptoeing through a nursery.

I peered around the door's edge. The whole place was still dark. I had to listen hard to hear the sounds of someone gliding up the stairs toward the first floor.

I moved from the living room to the staircase. Nothing to see. My mystery guest was off somewhere on the first floor. No lights had gone on.

I went down the basement stairs and found the fuse box on the north wall behind the boiler. I removed the fuses one by one, then moved to the other side of the boiler and waited. Nothing happened. No one came rushing down to see why the lights had gone out. No doubt because they had never been turned on. Ah, yes.

I looked around for something to use as a weapon, but didn't find it. I went back to the ground floor. The kitchen seemed a good bet. I rummaged quietly through drawers and cabinets. The thought of sticking someone with a knife didn't appeal to me. I settled on a rolling pin. Shades of Maggie and Jiggs. At least my weapon was time-tested.

I moved up the stairs, halting on the top step and letting my ears do the work. Faint sounds came from dead ahead: the den. The door was a black patch surrounded by more blackness. I crept toward it. It was closed tight. I put an eye to the keyhole, saw nothing. I laid an ear against the door. The sounds grew stronger. My fingers curled around the knob, turning it gently. One hell of a way to earn a living, I thought, and kicked open the door.

My flash spilled a distorted oval of light across the room. A man, half leaning over Neely's desk, was caught in it. He was medium height, stocky, with a blunt nose, strong chin, black eyebrows, and graying hair. He wore dark pants, an open black jacket, dark blue shirt, and no tie. A large pinky ring glistened on his left hand. A gold watchband glittered around his left wrist. He moved.

His left hand swept down to his hip; a gun sprang up in it, as if the hand had sprouted an extra appendage. This guy had been practicing.

I was going to say freeze, hold it, put 'em up, or something else smart. I didn't bother. I chucked the rolling pin at him and in the same motion hit the deck.

Noise filled the darkness, streaked with a flash of orange-blue light.

By then I was moving fast down the hallway toward the rear of the house, bent double, praying every inch of the way. If I had brought my gun along, this bird would be strumming his harp by now, or more probably stoking some hellish furnace. The guy, definitely, was not wise. I wanted nothing to do with him.

I kept going. I didn't know what I was looking for, a bed to crawl under, or a window to dive out of—right into intensive care.

The guy saved me the trouble.

He wasn't tiptoeing anymore. I heard him come charging out of the den and down the stairs as though he'd bumped into King Kong. I think he slipped once. For my money he could have broken his neck. But he'd have to do it on his own. I wasn't going to help.

I stopped running, did an about-face. I didn't want to catch the guy, merely see where he went next. I figured it might be informative. I got down the stairs all right, but my zip was gone. I felt like an ex-ballplayer at an old timer's game, drafted to play one more inning with the regular team.

I reached the front door in time to see a black Honda speed away. I didn't get the license number.

I used the front door to make my own exit. A parade around Neely's house would have been only a little more conspicuous than what had just happened. Stealth was wasted now. The thing to do was leave. I left. I turned a corner, using another street to reach my car, and drove away.

I called Harry from a Queens pay phone.

"Yes?"

"You home?"

"No. This is a disembodied voice I hire to answer my phone."

"Stand some company?"

"Absolutely not."

"Good, I'll be right over."

"When's that?"

"Soon as I can make it."

"Right-o."

CHAPTER 19

SIXTY-EIGHT JANE STREET USED TO BE ENTENMANN'S PASTRY factory before Entenmann's struck it rich and moved to larger if not greener pastures in New Jersey. The building's a co-op now. Jane Street itself, a quiet residential strip in far west Greenwich Village, is only a half mile away from some of the livelier sections of town. A nice place to live if you're looking for seclusion and carnivals wrapped in the same package.

I found a parking space a block away, walked back, and rang Harry's bell. He buzzed me in after I assured him it was not the Mad Slasher. I cooled my heels in the elevator waiting for him to punch the button on his fourth-floor landing and draw me up. The tenants in this building took no chances; from below the elevator could only be started with a special key. The door to the stairwell was rigged too. If some crook was going to clean out the joint, he'd have to work at it.

The elevator started its upward crawl. I stepped out on the fourth floor, where Harry, in jeans and gray sports shirt, greeted me.

"All suited up in blue," he said.

"The Midnight Stalker," I said, "never sleeps."

"Come in," Harry said. "I've got an iron lung ready if you have a breakdown."

"You think of everything."

"What are friends for?"

Harry had three rooms: a bedroom and storage room off the main one, which was large enough for a skating rink. The place could have used a couple more walls, but my partner had run out of credit somewhere along the line. Probably when he hooked up with me. A kitchen and a table and chairs were over by the north wall. Southeast was a wicker couch, some chairs, and an Australian unbrella tree. I planted myself on the couch.

"Drink?"

"Yeah, thanks."

Harry went off on his errand. I sat gazing out through the oversize windows at brownstone rooftops and taller buildings in the distance. The sight would've driven anyone from Homer's time off his rocker, but I took it in stride.

My host trotted back with the drinks.

"To crime," I said. "Where would we be without it?"

"Better off."

"Yeah, probably."

Harry sank down into the soft pillows of his wicker easy chair and took a pull on his gin and tonic. "Tell me something," he said.

"Yeah?"

"How can you drink that stuff?"

"This?" I held up my whiskey sour.

"It's a lady's drink."

"Big deal."

"It's sweet."

"Uh-huh. And it's got a candied cherry in it, no doubt loaded with deadly Red Dye Number Four; if you won't tell my brother, Danny, I won't either. A guy's gotta have some vices. Gave up sugar in my coffee last year, so I got this coming."

"Aren't you afraid someone's going to call you a sissy?"

"Someone did. About three years ago in a local bar."

"What happened?"

122

"I used reason and logic on him. As soon as his teeth grow back he'll be able to tell me if it worked."

"I don't have to be a straight man," Harry said, "but the union says I get paid double."

"Try and collect. Ever feel this place is haunted?"

"By doughnuts and cupcakes?"

"Yeah."

"Never."

"Me neither."

I downed some more hooch.

"You about ready?" Harry asked.

"Almost."

"I got a feeling I'm going to need some more gin."

"Better fill up the bathtub."

"We can always go back to what we were doing before."

"Who wants to shine shoes in Grand Central?" I asked.

"That was *your* job."

"What's so hot about being lavatory attendant?"

"It was in the ladies room," Harry said.

"Sounds like paradise. You really wanna know what's going on?"

"No."

"Fucking case is unraveling at the seams."

"I'd never have guessed."

"This Neely we're working for is a police lieutenant."

"So it's 'we' now," Harry said.

"Welcome aboard."

"Must be hopeless."

"It's getting there."

"Great."

"Here's the pitch," I said. "Our boy Neely gets wind some of his colleagues are on the take."

"New York's Finest?"

"Must've been Jersey imports. He's all set to blow the whistle, except for one small hitch."

"He wants to go on living."

"Yeah. And he's a bit short on evidence. He isn't quite sure which of his pals are straight and which are crooked. If he spills what he knows to the wrong party, he's a goner. If he hands the case over to Internal Affairs and they develop it, he loses all the glory and in the process earns the reputation of being a grade-A fink."

"Grade A is good in eggs."

"Bad in finks," I said.

"Just what *does* he know?"

"He didn't say."

"You ask him?"

"Sure, more than once. On bended knees."

"And?"

"Tough on the knees."

"Got any ideas, Jim?"

"Dope. Gambling. Prostitution. Loan-sharking. You name it. This was Neely's baby. I was just a well-paid hired hand. The lug almost saved our agency, too."

"Almost."

"Game's not over yet," I said.

"Glad to hear it."

"Our boy wanted to crack this all by himself," I said, "then give Internal Affairs an airtight case and while he was at it pull his career out of the ash heap."

"I take it," Harry said, "he wasn't a comer."

"You should see the creep, Harry. It's a wonder he ever made the force."

"How *did* he make louie?"

"Greased someone; burned the midnight oil; got a lucky break—who knows? How did we get so far out on a limb? Things happen. Anyway, he had a surefire candidate for bagman: an ex-cop. Horace Keller, my Joe. Old Horace was bounced from the force a couple years ago. Shook down some pimps and an undercover cop. The last one squealed."

"They always do."

"Yeah, don't they. Keller never got to court. Departmental

trial. The guy's lucky. He'd opened his mouth on the stand, he'd've gotten the chair. This is the genius Neely had me trailing after for five weeks."

"Come up with anything, Jim?"

I shrugged, finishing the last of my whiskey sour. "Never caught him red-handed slipping dough to the top brass, if that's what you mean. The guy was pretty active the first few weeks, saw a lot of people. After that he became a hermit."

"The wicked often undergo religious conversion," Harry said, "when in the presence of a saint."

"Never got that close to him," I said.

"Think he had you spotted?"

"Could be. The whole thing was dumb. You can't shadow a guy twenty-four hours a day. Not if you go solo. Gotta have some backup, for Christ's sake."

"Neely, the cop, didn't know that, of course."

"He knew it. And how! I told him often enough. The sucker was scared shitless there'd be leaks. He figured his life was on the line."

"And it wasn't?"

"Yeah, maybe it was. But it was still a half-assed way to play this."

"But you," Harry said, "went along."

"Sure. Didn't hear you beefing when the gravy was flooding in."

"Perish the thought," Harry said. "It was a worthy effort. He rich?"

"Uh-uh."

"So how's he been paying us?"

"Mortgaged his house."

"He tell you?"

"Our client wouldn't tell you the time of day. Unless his life depended on it. I'll get to that in a minute."

"Sure. How did this paragon of virtue latch on to us?"

"Andy Grimes."

"Cop who thought his wife was playing around, about two years ago?"

"Right."

"They friends?"

"They say hello. I checked with Grimes. The pair used to work out of the same station house in Brooklyn. Neely got transferred last year. The guy's a loner, so Grimes was kind of surprised to hear from him. Our boy was looking for a gumshoe. Grimes said I'd done okay for him. And that's how we landed the contract."

"Man must have been desperate."

"Probably," I said. "The chump was on the skids. This was his big chance. And he didn't know who to trust."

Harry grinned. "So he came to *us*?"

"We *are* in the business. How would I sell him out? Brace Keller? Run an ad in *The New York Times*? He didn't give me enough dope to know my way around, even. And he paid. Boy did he!"

"Bought himself a friend."

"Some friend. My enemies should have such friends."

Harry drained the last of his gin and tonic and gazed mournfully at the empty glass. "I don't want you to think I'm not getting a big kick out of all this, or that I must resort to artificial stimulants in order to keep my spirits up. But I think the situation calls for another round, don't you?"

"I think what you think."

"Good," Harry said, and went away.

CHAPTER 20

I SPENT SOME MORE TIME SURVEYING THE VIEW. A LOT OF windows were facing me, but nothing much was happening in any of them. No hands lying on floors, no dismembered bodies, no severed heads, no guys chasing each other with guns. A very tame neighborhood. Good thing my sainted mom had gone off to her just rewards. One glimpse of the life I was leading would have killed her. That's all I needed. I never did figure out what Mom wanted me to be when I grew up. Something successful. And respectable, no doubt. Like president. Only she'd have thought the hours too long. Maybe emperor—they set their own hours. James the Merciless. Why not? Tough world out there. Or James the Gross. Might as well have a little fun while I was at it. Fun seemed to be what was missing from this case. Next time, put an ad in the paper: Detective for hire; must be fun case.

Harry returned.

"So where are we now?" he asked, handing me my second whiskey sour.

"Up a tree," I said.

"Sounds safe enough."

"Sure, if they don't toss me in the clink as a material witness."

"Can they?"

"Probably."

"Will they?"

"If they get mad enough." I took a pull on my drink, sighed, shook my head. "It's a pisser, all right. Keller was our ace, the guy who was gonna lead us to the money tree. Now the bum's spooked."

"No sense of fair play."

"Guy's a primitive."

"What does our client say?"

"Here comes the kicker. He doesn't. Our crafty client is unavailable for comment."

"Since when?"

"All day. Couldn't reach him at work, so I went to his home tonight. A neighbor saw him drive away early this evening."

"Obvious criminal behavior."

"Damn right. I wasn't the only visitor he had. Three guys were there before me. We all missed him."

"All four of you?"

"Yep."

"So?"

"So I broke into the house."

"You don't kid around, do you?"

"I couldn't just leave. Things are getting too tight. Found this in the garbage." I handed him the yellow piece of paper.

"What is it?"

"Nothing, probably. Where did you put the sheet of serial numbers?"

"In the office safe. Along with the money."

"Check this out against it."

"Think they match?"

"Figures are figures. Go see."

"They must look familiar, or you wouldn't be pestering me."

"They don't look like anything. If I could remember stuff like this, I'd be Albert Einstein, not a two-bit private eye. I'd be busy digging up the secrets of the universe."

"Three-bit. Don't sell yourself short, kid."

"Thanks. While I was giving the joint the once-over, more

company showed up. Some guy. He started to search the place too. A few more, we could've had a party."

"For a bookworm, you lead an exciting life," Harry said.

"That's my brother. Ex-bookworm, in my case. Hectic, not exciting. Fearful, maybe. I crept up on the guy. Shone my flash at him. He was cornered, outmaneuvered and caught red-handed. He should've surrendered. Instead the moron took a shot at me."

"What did you do?"

"Ran for my life. Guy ran away too. I didn't make him. End of edifying tale." I said. "Now I really gotta talk to Neely."

"You have some scheme, of course."

"Sure. You drop by the guy's office tomorrow and arrange it."

"Me?"

"Not me. At least four cops know me as Stuart Gordon. Danker works out of the same precinct. I'd rather go into the lion's den; it'd be safer."

"What do I tell the desk sergeant?"

"Anything you want. Except your real name. Tell him you're a friend of Andy Grimes. Guy paid us for a month's work—if that isn't friendship what is? And he really does know you. One lie less."

"My conscience feels better already."

"I ever steer you wrong?"

"Yes. Do I have an excuse for this visit?"

"They won't ask."

"They'll ask. Just to be perverse."

"Grimes wants you and Clyde to be buddys. How's that?"

"Clyde?"

"Clyde."

"Andy, Clyde, and Harry. The Happiness Boys."

"The Three Stooges. Look, they buzz Neely, he won't turn you down. He *knows* Grimes."

"So why am I feeling this deep anxiety?"

"You dread Neely's personality."

"Thanks for telling me."

"*I* dread Neely's personality."

"We all do. What do I tell the rat?"

"Tell him the jig's up—but he should still keep paying us," I said.

"He'll love that."

"Better let me tell him."

"Swell. I just set up the meet?" Harry asked.

"Yeah."

"Any place special?"

"Who cares? But he's got to make it snappy. Day after tomorrow's too late. Now's probably too late."

"And yesterday wasn't so good either."

"Yesterday was the pits."

"Why do I have this feeling, Jim, that our case has gone to the dogs?"

"Someone's on to me," I said. "Lots of someones, for all I know. The Silbert woman gave me a letter. In Yiddish. I had Danny translate it."

"How is the Great One?"

"Great. The letter turned out to be a report. No addressee. It was about Keller. And she's got me in it, too. Pegged me shadowing the guy."

"This old lady tailed you?"

"I wouldn't have missed her, Harry. She had help. Plenty of it."

"Who?"

"God knows."

"Why?"

"Ditto."

"That's wonderful news."

"Yeah, isn't it? What it boils down to is, we don't know who we're up against. Or even why. Keller may turn up any second. The cops are breathing down my neck. My cover stinks. One of Silbert's people may have seen me make off with the dough. They could've been hanging around and seen you show up and then leave lugging a shopping bag. Someone's got the serial numbers of every damn bill. This thing blows over, no one fingers us, maybe we've got ourselves a nice bonus. Shit hits the fan, we have something to give back. I see it as a sort of insurance policy. One that could save our skins."

"Our skins."

"Yeah."

Harry sighed, finished his second drink. "Sounds like a worthwhile cause."

"Highly recommended."

"So how come we're not jumping for joy?"

"Old age?"

"Speak for yourself. How about a drink?"

"I'm half pickled already."

"Nothing like a drink to brighten one's future."

"Tell it to the guy I run down," I said.

"Ah, you're driving." Harry waved his arm. "Sofa's all yours, spend the night. Unless business calls, of course."

"Thanks, but tonight I luxuriate at home. Screw business."

"No more stakeout?"

"What's to stake out? Cops're on the job. They nab Keller, we'll read about it in the papers."

"It'll look funny, the cops show up and you're not at your slum."

"Sidesplitting. Now it's *my* slum, eh? Why should I camp in that miserable dump? What for? You think Neely's going to keep forking out dough just for the hell of it? Besides, what am I supposed to tell Danker and company if they turn on the heat? Do I hand them Neely? Do I stonewall?"

Harry leered at me. "Well, do you?"

I shrugged. "You think I know?"

"I had hopes."

"Didn't we all. Neely knows. Only he doesn't know he knows."

"But he'll find out."

"You bet. When I tell him. Look, the guy's still our client. He's got the right to call the shots. There's a lot more to this than he's let on. Silbert's just one of the angles he didn't cover. The two goons may be another. Anyway, I ask him. This time around, I tell him I want the full scoop. No half measures. Then we see if there's some way I can still earn my keep. The guy decides to bounce me summarily, then it's on his head if the cops make me spill my guts. Maybe I will, maybe I won't. Let Neely sweat it."

"That's the plan, Jim?"

"That's it."

"You stoop to blackmail?"

"Man, you spend your life on your knees, you don't need to stoop, you're there already."

"Come on, Jim," Harry said.

"Whaddaya want? We wouldn't be in this mess if the guy had been square with us. Listen, know what really burns me up? The way he talks to me. That drives me up the wall. Look, I don't mind being a high-class servant for a while, if the pay's all right. But I draw the line at being a slave. Guy didn't have a good word for me from day one. It's 'fuck you' this, and 'fuck you' that. He never stops. First time I thought maybe he was having a bad day. Tenth time, I started to see red. I stopped counting after a hundred. What kind of crap *is* that? Figure I hold a little thing like that against a man? Damn right I do. In spades. Now he's gotta do something smart for a change, meet us halfway, at least."

"Think our noble client is up to it?"

"Who the hell knows? Just remember, Harry, blackmail's for *human beings*. Ever hear of blackmailing a jackass?"

"Never."

"Either have I. And that, pal, lets us off the hook."

CHAPTER 21

TENTH AVENUE HAD ALL THE ALLURE OF A GNAWED BONE. Factories, warehouses, grayish tenements, and dingy mom-and-pop storefronts owned the turf. I gave it a wide berth and used the West Side Highway to drive home.

Bizet's Symphony in C came out of my radio. The last time I heard it was at the City Ballet at Lincoln Center. A time of prospects. Harry and I were about to make our big leap to Madison Avenue. Easy street was just around the corner. Too bad the corner was nowhere near Madison Avenue.

Bizet's piece always inspired me to do fancy stunts, but not now. I drove with care through the sparse traffic, like a barefoot man treading over broken glass. Two drinks hadn't quite turned me into Al Unser, but the impulse was there. I put off showing the world what I could do on four wheels and went on living for another day. I hoped the world was grateful.

The Manhattan skyline was on my right, the Empire State Building, its tower ashimmer in white light, the centerpiece. The whole tableau looked as if it belonged in a museum. I was all set to edge closer, continue my appraisal—and plow right into someone's rear fender—when my headlights picked out the Seventy-ninth Street Exit sign. I turned right and was back in the world I knew. It had its points, but a lot of the lights were ads. Knowing how to read spoiled things.

133

I returned my car to its resting place in the garage and walked the half block to my buidling. My gait was almost jaunty. Maybe it was Bizet, or the booze, or swapping lines with Harry, but I was feeling less the invalid and more like my old self. I still wasn't ready for Hagler, or for headstands and cartwheels, either, but the mere thought of them didn't make me want to barf.

I unlocked all my locks, stepped into my apartment, and caught sight of the tiny red light winking at me. My trusty answering machine. Flicking on the lamp, I tossed my jacket onto a chair and went to hear my messages.

There were two of them, the first from Daphne Field, the second, Ralph Clinton. Both asked me to call them. I didn't have to be asked twice.

Daphne picked up on the second ring. I identified myself.

"Someone up there must like you," she said.

"Probably a very minor angel," I said, "specializing in nickels and dimes."

"Don't be too sure."

"Something *nice* happened?"

"Your scheme, Shaw, went off like clockwork."

"No kidding? Cops show up?"

"Simpler than that. They phoned. Mr. Weizer, our office manager, received the call. He had one of the clerks check."

"And the guy came up with a Stuart Gordon?"

"Of course. The whole thing took less than three minutes."

"Tremendous."

"Does this mean I'm ready for the big time, Shaw?"

"Your cloak and dagger is being rushed by pony express. How'd you get wind of all this, Daphne?"

"That's the amazing thing. I was in Mr. Weizer's office when it happened. We were going over a long and very tiresome list of repair expenses when the police called. I almost fell out of my chair."

"But you kept your cool?"

"I feigned a very dainty yawn."

"You're a pro, honey."

"What do you say about your angel now, Mr. Shaw?"

"Must've gotten a promotion. About time, too."

"Are you all right, Jim?"

"Sure."

"Your health?"

"Much improved."

"Your case?"

"Terminal, maybe. But still clinging to life. I'll know more when I see my client."

"When?"

"Tomorrow, I hope.

"I'll keep my fingers crossed," she said. "That concert still on?"

"What a question! Dinner, too. That's for mere starters, of course."

"You get weekends off?"

"I may be off permanently from now on."

"Well, at least I'll get to see something of you."

"Yeah. The bright side of unemployment. I think I could learn to take it in stride. Listen, keep the Stuart Gordon item in the computer a couple more days, in case they check again. Although Lord knows why they should. Then cancel it."

"Roger."

"Your reward will be hundreds of dinners and concerts. I hope you survive all that."

"I'll go into training."

"Darn angel really *was* working overtime."

"Take care of yourself, Jim."

"Count on it."

I put down the receiver, grinning just for the hell of it, and dialed Clinton.

"Yes?"

"Ralph? Jim Shaw."

"James. You got my message."

"Loud and clear, Ralph. Little machine was behaving itself, didn't scramble a word. How are you?"

"Fine. They called, James."

"Ah."

"Spoke to them personally."

"Good. Who's them, Ralph?"

"An Officer Goldsmith."

"Don't know him."

"He sounded quite authoritative."

"Yeah, I'm sure. You gave him our story?"

"Certainly."

"And?"

"No problem, James."

"Run it through for me, Ralph."

"The officer wanted to know if a Stuart Gordon had worked for me. I said yes, told him you'd been one of our ablest salesmen."

"Thanks for the boost, Ralph."

"My pleasure, James. I said you'd been laid off three months ago, through no fault of your own."

"Not a hotshot salesman like me."

"Precisely. I said it was a matter of seniority."

"Right. I can think of at least three guys who should've gotten kicked out before me."

"Well, I wouldn't say that, James."

"Go on, Ralph."

"I assured him that once business improved, I'd be delighted to rehire you."

"I may take you up on that. Anything else?"

"He wanted to know how long you had been with us."

"Six fun-packed years."

"I told him."

"That's it?"

"He thanked me."

"I thank you too, Ralph."

"That's quite all right, James. I trust there will be no repercussions."

"Not a chance, Ralph. You'll probably never hear from them again. They just wanted to make sure I was who I said I was."

"But you're not."

"Yeah, but they couldn't care less. The case I'm on is important to me. For the cops it's strictly routine. This should wind up your end of it, Ralph."

"Well, fine. How is the case progressing, James?"

"Great. It's starting to look like a real winner."

"Glad I had a hand in it."

"A big hand. I can't talk about it now, Ralph, but once I wrap it up, I'll be glad to fill you in."

"I'll look forward to that."

"It's a deal, then. I'll be in touch."

I carried myself into the bedroom, removed my shoes, and lay down on the bed. I didn't turn on the lights.

Leave it to the cops. They'd done it, managed to fool me, after all. I wasn't slated for the third degree. No rubber hoses, truncheons, or thumbscrews for old Jim Shaw. He wasn't even worth checking out in person. Just a couple of indifferent phone calls. At this rate I'd never make Public Enemy Number One. By now the cop on stakeout had probably been pulled, too. Why not? My former boss and landlord had vouched for me. Who could be more honest than a boss and landlord? Just about anyone, I imagined. But if the cops didn't know that, I sure as hell wasn't going to tell them. I was in the clear.

But for how long?

I didn't need a calculator to help me figure the odds. With a couple of unsolved murders on the books, it was only a matter of time before the cops began sifting through their old suspects again—namely me. And if Stuart Gordon upped and vanished, it would take no time at all.

Suddenly, I wasn't feeling so great. I hadn't moved a muscle

137

but I was breaking out in a cold sweat. I couldn't retire Stuart Gordon. I was stuck with the guy for the duration—however long that might be.

I propped myself up on an elbow, staring into the darkness as though the solution to my problem might be hidden somewhere in my bedroom. Maybe behind the bureau.

If Neely acted true to form, chewed me out and gave me the ax, I might be able to make some deal with the cops and still salvage a scrap of professional honor—just barely. Depending on how much I ended up spilling, and how good a lawyer I got. Neither very appetizing prospects. Through it all, of course, I'd be dead broke, the agency floundering, and Harry and I scrambling just to come up with the interest on our bank loans. If worse came to worst, we could always work out of a tent in Central Park and during winter camp with my uncle Max in Florida—provided we could raise the fare. But was there a future in it?

I sank back on the pillow, wiping my forehead with the back of my hand, and considered another possibility, unlikely as it might be. In this scenario, Neely would humbly admit that his unwise reticence regarding the case was more than a little responsible for the mess we'd gotten into and would come clean and keep me on to set things right. Armed with Neely's new data, I'd run rings around the cops, flush Keller out of hiding, nail the bad guys, and earn a whopping big bonus. Only I wouldn't get to spend it, because just then, the Messiah comes riding down Fifth Avenue on a large white horse and abolishes all money. It figures. The millennium would have to be at hand for Neely to step that much out of character.

Leaving a third either/or prospect.

Neely would go on footing the bill, either out of desperation or because I'd blackmailed him into it, but he'd keep me in the dark about the case, either because he didn't know, or did know and wouldn't tell. The cops catch on that Stuart Gordon is really James Shaw, hotshot private eye, and squeeze the living daylights out of me. But rather than squeal on a client, I stay clammed up, lose my license, and land in the hoosegow, where I remain indefinitely.

There was something about this last possibility that was even less appealing then the others.

I sat up slowly, as a convict might who had just learned that the warden had neglected to forward his last appeal. I swung my feet off the bed, put on my shoes, got up, and went into the next room. Retrieving my jacket from the sofa, I flipped on my answering machine, doused the lights, stepped into the hall, locked the door behind me, summoned the elevator, and rode down. What I didn't do was break into tears. Which showed a great deal of character.

I hailed a taxi on my corner. We moved north on Amsterdam Avenue. Huddled against the seat, I watched light spill over the pavement from Sarabeth's Kitchen, a class-act gourmet eatery done up in ochre and green. I bid it and the rest of my neighborhood a silent farewell. No GI ordered back to the trenches ever felt less cheerful. We passed other restaurants, designer boutiques, antique stores and novelty shops, empty storefronts with For Sale signs, waiting to be reborn again, ancient buildings being renovated or razed, high rises going up as the good times rolled toward the nineties. We hit Ninety-sixth Street, turned east. Overhead, clouds hid moon and stars. The sky was a dense black slate. We rode through Central Park

I was let off on Lexington and Ninety-fourth and hoofed the two blocks downhill to my building. No cops, as far as I could tell, were in garages or doorways or peering out of manholes. I didn't exactly feel abandoned.

I wound my way up the stairs and let myself into the flat. I went to my window. Keller's was dark. The cops were probably still there; the guy was legitimate business. Occasionally they might even glance across here, but otherwise I figured I was alone again. Solitude was looking good.

I peeled off my clothes and climbed into bed.

I had an edge on the cops. I knew that Silbert wasn't merely an innocent victim. In some way, she was tied to Horace Keller. If I couldn't find out how and why, I might still survive this mess. And what better place to start than here? A small, still voice said, *Welcome home, sonny.* "Shuddup," I said, and went to sleep.

CHAPTER 22

IN MY DREAM I WAS RUNNING AFTER NEELY. I CHASED HIM UP and down a series of endless stairways in rotting slums. But he always managed to stay a few steps ahead of me. Then I was in Keller's flat. I was searching for something but didn't know what. Harry, I saw, was there too. I knew he was very upset, and I told him, "It's in the bag." Harry ran away and I ran after him, shouting. Then I was in Danny's place. But Danny's was really The Shelter. Daphne was eating a large piece of chocolate cake. I knew it was full of worms and tried to take it away from her. My right arm was very long, but the left one was too short, and she kept slipping from my grip. She didn't look like Daphne any more but like someone I didn't know. The floor was shaking, and I knew something terrible was going to happen. . . .

My eyes opened. I was in bed, the room black. The only light came from a window on the top floor across the yard. I could still hear the shaking. Only it wasn't the floor but the fire escape outside. The damn thing was as old as Methuselah, but in worse shape. It creaked and clattered whenever a strong wind blew. There had been no wind at all earlier tonight, I seemed to recall.

As I lay there digesting this bit of intelligence, a head and shoulders appeared in my window frame. I looked at it. It didn't look back but kept going. It seemed to be a man, though it was too dark to make out any features. The lit window across the yard, momentarily blocked from view, was back in sight, the guy gone. The fire escape jangled a while, then stopped its racket. I heard something which could have been the breaking of glass. A final jolt and the night was peaceful again. I let my breath out, and sounds of traffic took up where they'd left off a moment ago.

I crawled out of bed, still staring at the window, as if I expected an instant replay. The stupid window had me fixated.

I fumbled my clothes on in the dark. It was a toss-up whether I preferred my dream to this new turn of events. I could probably have managed without either.

When my running shoes were firmly laced, I went into the next room, felt around in the cabinet under the sink, and came up with a flashlight and hammer. A gun would have suited me better, but Stuart Gordon, umemployed salesman, had no use for guns.

I stuck the hammer in my belt, the unlit flash in my hand, went to the window, and very gently raised it. Cold air flowed past me. Street noises grew louder, closer, as if someone had turned up their volume. I put one foot over the sill, then, very carefully, the other.

I stood on the fire escape, glancing up. No one above me. I looked around. No lights had snapped on in darkened windows, no outraged voices were raised to denounce me. The night belonged to me and the creeper.

I started up. I moved slowly, cautiously, as if the fire escape were made of fragile gauze and a wrong step would send me plunging through. I climbed past the fourth-floor window. Whole, dark, the curtains drawn. Very normal. I kept on. I could think of a lot better ways to go after an intruder than with a hammer, which by now seemed as formidable as a feather duster. Maybe I'd be lucky. Maybe the guy had reached the roof and had taken off for parts unknown. Except for the sound of breaking glass it was even a possibility. I hit the next landing. The large hole in Silbert's window seemed to grin at me. It wasn't an especially friendly grin. The sight was familiar enough: I'd pulled the same stunt only a few hours ago. Not the master's touch, but it got the job done.

I peered in. El Creepo was barely visible inside, poking around. I couldn't tell at what. His flash kept bobbing up and down like a fish fighting the hook.

Great. Now what?

Raising a holler would get me nothing except a red face. The only one in the house equipped to handle this was me, and I was here already. By the time the law appeared it would all be over. I'd end up tackling the guy anyway as he made his getaway—probably over my body—but without the element of surprise. Nuts to that.

I could go summon the cops in Keller's digs, if they were still there. But unless the guy decided to take a nap on Silbert's bed, he was apt to be gone long before we ever got back.

I could go charging in and get shot.

Or I could wait out here and jump him when he was done rifling the joint. If he used the stairs, I could follow and grab him from behind. Clever.

While I was mulling over this last choice, the flash went dark. A black shape moved toward the window. The guy was making my decision for me.

I ducked, backtracking a half dozen rungs so my head was below the platform. Above me I heard the window rise. A foot slid over the sill, a shoe came down on the iron plank above my head.

My hand reach up, my fingers curled around a skinny ankle. I yanked sideways, hard. The guy came down, toppling over like a sack of grain in a blizzard.

My feet climbed rungs, regaining their former perch.

The guy was up on an elbow. I put a fist in his face. His head snapped back, as if I'd released a hidden spring. His shoulders bounced against the metal landing. The fire escape shook as if it had the chills.

He moved, trying to rise. His chin was still in range, a perfect target. I wound up like a big-league pitcher, whacked him again flush on the jaw. He twitched once, as though shrugging into a tight pair of briefs, then lay still.

The fire escape, meanwhile, was swaying like a rowboat in a hurricane. Any second I'd get seasick. The damn relic screeched like a trapped bird each time it scraped against the brick wall. By now the National Guard should have been called out. But the yard still slumbered. Not another window had lit up during all this hubub. A third world war might rouse my neighbors, but I wouldn't put my last dime on it.

I shoved Sleeping Beauty over the sill, squeezed past him, and pulled him into the flat. The window went down. I dragged him into the kitchen, away from any possible prying eyes, unlikely as that might be.

I had to congratulate myself. I wasn't even breathing hard—much. The Joes who had called me a has-been would have to eat crow now. I was ready for the champ. As long as I could nail him from behind, he didn't stand a chance.

I shone my flash at the guy on the floor—and did a double take. I stopped congratulating myself. I was looking at a skinny kid, not much older than eighteen, maybe a lot younger. I'd risked my neck to nab a diaper-set housebreaker; just what I'd always wanted.

I frisked him. His pockets were empty. No wallet. No weapon. No loot from the apartment, either.

Going to the faucet, I filled a glass with water and poured it over the kid's face. He blinked. His eyes fluttered, opened. He groaned. I knew how he felt.

"Easy does it," I said.

He looked up at me. "What happened?" he asked.

"I hit you."

"Why?"

I grinned at him. "You wanna be a burglar, kid, you gotta learn to take your lumps."

"Huh?"

"You were waiting for a bus here?"

The kid sat up, looked around. He was starting to remember.

"I didn't take nothing," he said.

"Yeah, I noticed," I said. "How come?"

"I got scared."

"Don't blame you. Place is probably haunted. There was a killing here just a few days ago. Need dough?"

"Yeah."

"Do drugs? Crack? Coke? Pop pills?"

"Uh-uh. Not me, mister," he said. "You a cop?"

"Listen, kid, I was a cop, you'd be on your way to the lockup by now. You got a name?"

"Sammy."

"Sammy what?"

"Cohen."

"Manhattan?"

He nodded.

"Must be thousands of Cohens in Manhattan. I look for S. Cohen, in the phone book, I find you?"

"I live with my folks."

"What're their names?"

He was silent.

"Well?"

"I don't want them bothered."

"Sure. You tell me what you want, kid, I'll see you get it."

The kid said nothing.

"Okay, why'd you pick this place?"

He shrugged.

"At random, eh?"

"Yeah."

"Just like that?"

"It was dark."

"How'd you know it was empty?"

"Took a chance."

I laughed at him. "Know something, Sammy, you're full of crap."

"Honest, mister—"

"Listen, kid, you're in deep shit. I'm trying to give you a break. Don't make it tough on yourself. I get mad, you won't like it."

"I don't know what you want, mister."

"Who sent you?"

"No one."

"Uh-huh. Let's try again. Who sent you?"

"I told you—"

"Ever been busted, kid? Ever been in the slam? Know what that's like?"

"Honest—"

"Nice clean kid like you. It's a shame, kid. They'll eat you alive, cut you up into small pieces and feed you to the animals."

"Please, mister—"

"Your own folks won't know you," I said cheerfully. "You got maybe five seconds to make up your mind. Me or the cops." I grabbed his shirt, jerked him to his feet. "*Now,*" I said, "I'm not gonna ask you twice. *Who sent you?*"

The kid squinted into the light. I was holding the flash a few inches from his eyes. He opened and closed his mouth like a guppy in a fish tank. He licked his lips. "A guy," he mumbled.

"What guy?"

"Don't know his name."

I poked him in the ribs with a hard finger. "Not good enough."

Small beads of perspiration were breaking out on his forehead. He shrugged a narrow shoulder. "This guy, Freddie, he's like twenty-two, hangs around the block. He don't work, but he always got money—"

"Freddie sent you?"

"Uh-uh. He said I could make some quick dough, took me to see this guy."

"Where?"

"A street corner."

"His name?"

"He didn't tell me."

"Describe him."

"Short. An old guy, maybe like sixty-five. Kinda stocky. He wore glasses."

"What did he want?"

"I should come here, search the place."

"For what?"

"Letters. Papers. Anything like that."

"Did you?"

"I tried. I got scared."

"How much he pay you?"

"Fifty bucks."

"Big spender."

"I got another fifty coming, when I deliver."

"When's that?"

"Couple hours."

"Where?"

"I tell, you let me go?"

"Sure. After we meet this guy."

"Me and you?"

"Uh-huh."

"What for?"

"Our health."

"You don't need me, mister."

"Sure I do. You're indispensable. This old guy of yours doesn't show, you got to be around so I can beat the shit outta you. Then, I drag you back here, call the cops. It's like we never left. You put up a fight, see? And lost. You follow me, kid?"

He nodded.

"Okay. Tell me again. Some old guy hired you?"

"Yeah."

"You don't know who he is?"

"Uh-uh."

"And all he wanted was letters?"

"Papers. Handwritten stuff."

"What language?"

"English, I guess. He didn't say."

"Where's the meet?"

"York and Eighty-fourth."

"In a couple hours?"

"One hour."

I grinned. "You're learning kid. You may get outta this yet. Anything else I should know?"

He shook his head.

"Okay, kid." I took him by the wrist. "We move. Try anything, I break your arm. That understood?"

"Yeah."

"Behave yourself, you'll be home inside an hour. Get funny, it's the hospital and the slammer. That's all you got to remember."

He nodded.

I pulled him toward the door. If the kid yelled for help outside while a patrol car was breezing by, I'd be in the soup. My word against his wouldn't be worth beans. But the kid was too dumb and scared to know that—I hoped.

I unsnapped both locks, turned the knob. The door didn't budge. The cops had padlocked it from the outside. "We go the way we came," I told him.

We went back into the next room. I raised the window. I had one hand on the kid and one foot over the sill when I caught the movement down below.

A lone tree grew in the back yard. Under it someone had just shielded a flashlight. Either that or we were up against a king-size firefly.

In one movement I was out on the fire escape, dragging my friend with me. "Let's go," I whispered. "The roof."

The roof was only twenty feet away, a reasonable destination. We headed up. A shrill whistle sliced through the stillness. That made it cops.

The kid and I rolled onto the roof. I wiggled around, peered over the edge.

A head was sticking out of Silbert's window, looking up at me. I ducked back.

Keller's cops hadn't been napping after all. They'd spotted either me or the kid. One had covered the yard, the other the hallway. And help wouldn't be far behind. One thing was certain, I didn't want to talk to these people. Not now.

I stood up, sweating plenty. So was the kid. That's when I blew it. The kid pulled, and his wrist came gliding out of my grip as though it were greased. He ran left.

The fire escape began to clatter. The law was on its way. I went right.

All the tenements had one connecting roof with two-foot walls separating the buildings. I hopped over the walls like a track star doing the hurdles. I glanced back. A tall guy had made the roof and was starting after me. Five tenements were between us. Not enough.

Two steps brought me to the roof's edge. A drainpipe went down to the yard below. I didn't think twice. I went flat on my belly, grabbed the pipe in both hands, swung over the edge of the roof, clamped my shoes around the pipe, and slid down to the yard. Douglas Fairbanks lives again.

Unlike Fairbanks, I landed hard. A narrow alley separated my row of buildings from those on Second Avenue. I ran through it and, unlatching a wire gate, out onto Ninety-fourth.

I heard the police sirens then. I sprinted for 242.

The key was in my hand when I reached the front door. I ran up the two flights of stairs on my toes, soundlessly. A neat trick. Nijinsky would have done it better, but no faster. I got my door open and was stripping off my clothes before I was through it.

I chucked jacket, pants, and shirt into the closet, kicked off my shoes, climbed into my pajamas, and dived into bed.

I needn't have rushed. It took the cops a good ten minutes to reach me.

CHAPTER 23

THERE WERE TWO OF THEM, THE TALL GUY IN PLAIN CLOTHES
and a uniformed cop.

I stepped aside and they came into the flat.

"Mr. Gordon?"

"Yeah?" I blinked at the guy, sleepy-eyed.

"You been here all night?"

"Sure."

The uniformed cop was wandering around the joint, trying
to make sergeant. Anything he found I was willing to split
fifty-fifty.

"See anything?"

"Like what?"

"Like two men out on that fire escape?"

I turned my head toward the window, stared at it stupidly.
"I was asleep," I said.

"Hear anything?"

"Yeah."

"Go on."

"Noise in the hallway. Like running. About ten minutes
ago. The racket woke me up."

"That was us."

"Oh. What happened?"

"Attempted robbery. Two floors above you."

"Mrs. Silbert's place?"

151

"Yes."

"Second time in a week," I said. "And there's nothing up there. The first pair killed her, you know. Couldn't've been them. One died. Right across the yard there."

"Uh-huh," he said.

The uniformed cop had joined his pal. They both stood there looking at me.

"Just one thing more, Mr. Gordon," the tall cop said.

"What's that?"

"I'd like to see your palms."

"My what?"

"The palms of your hands. Hold them out, please."

I eyed the guy as if he'd just grown a pair of antlers and I was too startled to tell him about it. I held out my hands, palms up.

The tall cop looked at them, nodded. "Thanks," he said. Both cops left.

I locked the door behind them and flicked off the lights; then I went to the closet, got out of my pajamas and retrieved my street clothes and put them on. The jacket and running shoes came last. The scratch marks were on the jacket sleeves, near the elbows; the shoes were scraped on the rims of the soles. If you're sliding down a drainpipe without gloves, the best way to clutch it is with your feet and elbows. No burns on your palms then. Any self-respecting burglar knows that. Even I do.

The patrol car was still parked in front of the building, its headlights on, its red and yellow spotlights flashing into the night, a sure sign that the search for crime never ended. But the car was empty. I walked past it, turned south on Second, crossed at Ninety-third and headed east. Taxis at this hour, in this neck of the woods, were scarce. After climbing fire escapes, dashing along rooftops, and sliding down drainpipes, what I needed most was more exercise. I was getting it.

No one followed me. As far as I knew it was no crime to go

for a midnight stroll, except that it was three A.M. and I had the cops so jumpy that if I asked for a light they were sure to figure I was trying to send smoke signals.

By now I could smell the East River. I turned a few more corners, took a shortcut through a hulking, deserted low-income project, and emerged unscathed on Ninety-first Street and York with ten minutes to spare. I kept walking.

York Avenue in the mid eighties was a holdover from another era. Only solid middle-class houses here, trim food marts and assorted retail shops. But more like what you'd find on a small-town street in the thirties than today's Columbus Avenue. Already, the nearby concrete canyons were edging toward this mecca. You could almost hear them chortle.

Stray cars sailed by like ghosts on wheels. I saw no pedestrians. I hoped my elderly gentleman wasn't armed. I wanted him docile and infirm, since anything short of a push-over was apt to give me trouble. My hammer was back at the flat, where its presence required no explanations—more than could be said for me.

I was hunting for a convenient doorway in which to hide when off in the distance the figure of a man appeared. He had come out of the shadows to stand under a streetlamp two blocks away. He wore a hat and coat and seemed short enough. Maybe he was even stocky. I couldn't tell his age. But he was on Eighty-third Street—the wrong corner—and ahead of schedule.

I wondered what I'd say to the man if no one else showed up. I wondered what I'd say to anyone. With my guide, the kid, gone, I couldn't be dead sure I'd nabbed the right bird. If my suspect started to holler I'd be the one carried off in a paddy wagon. Molesting old men on street corners wasn't likely to win me new friends at the station house. Maybe the man would simply confess. Maybe they were going to elect me emperor soon. But could I count on it?

I turned into a doorway. The best strategy was to stay put,

153

see what developed. The best strategy, as is often the case, wasn't quite good enough.

Suddenly the kid was at the man's elbow. One second he'd been alone, the next he had company.

They both looked in my direction.

By then I was out on the street running toward them. If he'd walked, the old guy was as good as nailed. Even in my present state, I could outrun an oldster. But I didn't think he had come on foot.

The pair had no interest in seeing how fast I could cover ground. They hightailed it up Eighty-third and clear out of sight.

By the time I reached the lamppost, a car was speeding down the next block. And that was that. I stood there breathing hard, my fingers twitching, itching to close around the kid's throat.

The kid had pulled a fast one, lying about the time and place, though not by much. Just enough to queer my play and tip his pal. The dumb kid wasn't as dumb as he looked.

CHAPTER 24

THE CLOCK NEXT TO MY BEDSIDE RADIO READ 10:30.
I stretched out a shaky hand, fumbling for the radio.
Wagner's "Siegfried Idyll" thundered from the speaker. I
lowered the volume. I wasn't up to thunder. I wasn't up to
much of anything except a quiet burial. Last night's workout
had been too much of a good thing. A guy in my shape ought
to take it easy, hire someone to do his running for him.

I crawled out of bed and headed for the shower, which was
right there across from the stove. Nothing like a brisk shower
in your own living room to start the day off right.

I made myself a full pot of coffee, poured a double shot of
orange juice, ate a large bowl of rolled oats with lots of
sugarless Sorrell Ridge strawberry conserve.

While I waited for the vitamins and caffeine to take effect, I
hung my dime store mirror on its nail over the sink and
shaved. The face I saw could have belonged to Boris Karloff's
Mummy on one of its sprees away from the crypt. I tried not
to cut it. You don't want a face like that mad at you.

I rapped on the door.
"Who's there?"
"Mr. Gordon."
I heard the sound of locks unsnapping. The door opened
and Mrs. Kazmir stood before me. Short, wrinkled, and

stooped in a black polka-dot dress with an open seam down the left side. Her white hair was done up in two long braids. She grinned, nodding me into the flat.

"How are you?" she asked.

"Fine."

"You in hospital?"

"Uh-huh."

"They hit you?"

"We had a tussle."

"I say no go, Mr. Gordon."

"Yeah, I should've listened. It's about Mrs. Silbert that I'm here."

She sighed. "Is very bad, ah?"

"Bad's the word," I agreed. "She worked in a bakery?"

Mrs. Kazmir shrugged. "I no know."

"Ever meet her friends, relatives?"

"Maybe."

"Who?"

"Is young girl. Very nice."

"Know her name?"

"I only see once."

"Remember anything about her?"

She shook her head.

"Silbert close to anyone in the building?"

"I no know, Mr. Gordon. She new here."

"New?"

"She come maybe two months before you."

I looked at the old girl. "Two months?"

"Sure. In summer."

"Say where she's from?"

"I no ask."

"Okay. You hear anything, you let me know, Mrs. Kazmir. I'm trying to find her folks."

I left her, knocked on the door across the hall. A Hispanic lady answered. Three young kids peered out at me from behind her. She spoke no English, so I gave her a nod and smile and went away.

A fat bald-headed guy lived in the flat opposite Silbert. I'd seen him around. He wore a hearing aid, and at night you could hear his TV all through the building. He wasn't home. He probably worked for a living.

The Irish lady on the floor below was a part-time maid on Park Avenue. She had tried chatting with Silbert a couple of times, but the conversation had never gotten beyond the weather. "She was a bit standoffish, rest her soul," she told me, "but she never did no one any harm."

"Never," I agreed.

I spent another ten minutes knocking on doors. A Hispanic guy who needed a shave shrugged. An elderly party in white shirt and thick glasses was sorry he couldn't help. So was I. Nobody else was home. My last stop was Carlos, the super, on the ground floor. By then I wasn't feeling all that optimistic. Which just goes to show.

"Mr. Gordon," Carlos said. He grinned at me from under his thin mustache, ran a slender hand through his longish black hair. "Is something you need? Something I fix?"

"Just information. You knew Mrs. Silbert, Carlos?"

"Sí."

"I'm trying to track down her friends, relatives, find out where she worked."

Carlos flashed white teeth. "Wait," he said.

I waited.

He returned with a folded piece of paper. "This, maybe."

I unfolded it. The word *Sheila* and a phone number were on it.

"What is it?"

"Mrs. Silbert, she give me this."

"When?"

"Back when she move here."

"In August?"

"*Sí*. She say call this number if she sick or there is problem."

"What problem?"

"She did not say."

"The police know about this?"

"They did not ask."

"You call her?"

"I think police, they handle everything."

I reached for my wallet, pulled out a ten-spot. He waved it away.

"You've earned it, pal." I said. I folded it lengthwise, slipped it into his shirt pocket, got a grin of thanks in return.

Back in my flat, I dialed the number. No answer. I hung up. Nothing doing across the yard. I called Harry; he wasn't in either. I got QXR, caught the last two movements of Mozart's Sinfonia Concertante. Stern and Zuckerman played it as though a cantor were singing his heart out in synagogue during the High Holy Days. Vaughan Williams, Scarlatti, and Liszt followed. I tried Sheila again. Still nothing. She could be anywhere, of course; at work, shopping, on vacation. Maybe she'd moved out by now and no Sheilas were in a hundred miles of here. If I put my mind to it, I might just come up with a better way to spend my time than sitting around and sweating over this lady. Tapes, notes, and copies of my reports to Neely were back at the office. A long, hard, maybe lifesaving look seemed in order.

I decided to wait until the conclusion of Haydn's Oxford Symphony. The maestro deserved no less.

The cops came for me during the third movement.

CHAPTER 25

THE PRECINCT HAD THAT SPECIAL ODOR YOU FIND IN PUBLIC schools, courthouses, and welfare centers. It's sprayed on every night before closing. One whiff is guaranteed to demoralize you. The stuff was wasted on me; I was already demoralized.

The cops put me in a small airless room and went away. The walls were a brownish, off yellow. Three chairs and a table—my sole companions—had enough nicks and scratches to have seen combat in at least one war. A closed window covered by a wire mesh grating looked out on a concrete wall. Twenty minutes of my life dragged by, plenty of time to reflect on my crimes. I was ready to confess to them all just to get out of that room.

The door opened and Danker came in. I was glad to see him. I'd've been glad to see *anyone*.

"Sorry to keep you waiting, Mr. Gordon."

"No problem," I said.

He still looked like he needed a shave. His suit was blue now but just as wrinkled. He hadn't shrunk any either; he made the room seem a lot smaller merely by being in it. He stood leaning against the door.

"How are you feeling?"

"Better."

"That's what I heard. Miller said you looked okay."

"The tall cop?"

He nodded.

"No one looks okay at two in the morning. What's this about?"

"Nothing special, Mr. Gordon. Just your statement."

"Thought I had a couple days."

"Might as well get it over with, since you're up and about."

"You sent two cops for *that?*"

"Sure. Why not?"

"A phone call would've done the trick."

"Free transportation, Mr. Gordon. At the city's expense. Don't knock it."

"Few more rides like that, I'll be back in the hospital."

He grinned. "Figured it for a pinch?"

"It crossed my mind."

"They handcuff you?"

"Uh-uh."

"Then it wasn't a pinch."

"I'll try and remember that."

Danker pulled up a chair. "Any luck job hunting?"

"I haven't looked lately."

"Expect to?"

"Pretty soon."

I gave them their statement when the guy with the tape recorder showed up. Except for the fact that I left out who I was and what I was up to, it was fairly straight. But they weren't going to like the omissions, if and when they got the whole picture. I wasn't too crazy about them myself.

It took fifteen minutes. The recorder was clicked off and carried away.

I rose. "That it?"

Danker stood up. "Not quite," he said. "My boss would like a word with you, Mr. Gordon."

Captain Paul Rogers wore a neat gray jacket and a yellow and green striped tie. He appeared to be in his mid fifties.

His thick dark hair was graying at the temples. Thin lips, straight nose, a tapered chin. His gray eyes were slightly bloodshot; there were bags under them. He looked tired. Everyone in the precinct looked tired. Being a cop was apparently even more exhausting than my job. Rogers was probably around five ten, but I couldn't tell for sure. He was seated behind a wide cluttered desk when Danker and I entered his office, and he remained that way for the duration of our chat.

Danker sat a little behind me and to my right, one leg crossed over the other, his face impassive. Rogers found a pipe under some papers, stuck it unlit between his lips. Danker removed a cigar from his jacket pocket, stripped away the cellophane, bit down on one end. He didn't light the cigar, either. Being a nonsmoker put me at a disadvantage. I had nothing to fidget with. Rogers gazed at me. I could hear the faint sound of voices coming from somewhere in the station house. There were footsteps in the corridor, the click of a typewriter, a door banging shut.

"Things happen around you, Gordon," Rogers said. He had removed the pipe. His voice, an even tenor, didn't sound tired at all.

"Yeah," I said, "I suppose so."

"You intervene in what appears to be a burglary. The victim dies; one of the robbers turns up dead in an apartment across from yours."

"I don't like it either," I said.

"No one likes it, Mr. Gordon," Danker said.

"There's another burglary attempt at the victim's apartment. Two officers who happened to be on stakeout went after the perpetrators."

"They got away," Danker said.

"Over the rooftops," Rogers said.

"I slept through that one," I said.

"Sergeant Miller," Rogers said, "was under the impression that *you* might have been one of the perpetrators."

"Me?"

"Someone who looked like you," Danker said. "It was dark, of course."

"Our men," Rogers said, "caught sight of someone climbing the fire escape."

"The fire escape," I said. "Look, in the first place, only a mental defective would rob that dump. Secondly, if I'd taken leave of my senses and wanted to clean out Silbert's junky flat, what would've prevented me from using the stairs like anyone else who lives in the building? Takes a hell of a lot more than someone breaking a lock to bother my neighbors. And why do it at night? House is just about empty in the afternoon; I'd've had it all to myself. Come on guys, let's be reasonable."

"The perp our boys saw on the fire escape," Danker said, "looked like a kid."

"That lets me out," I said. "I used to be a kid, but I outgrew it."

"There were two of them," Rogers said.

"Our boys saw only the kid climbing," Danker said. "They called in and took after him. Imagine their surprise when two guys crawled out of Silbert's window."

"The second man," Rogers said, "must have waited down below until the other was at the window before he started up. By then Miller and Neighborg were on the staircase of their building heading down. So they missed him. Either that, or you could have been the second man, Gordon."

"Me again. Think I'd need a kid's help in cracking Silbert's flat?"

"Maybe," Danker said, "or maybe you spotted him on the fire escape and decided to grab him yourself."

"Gimme a break, pal." I said. "I'm in no condition to be a hero. You know that. And why would I beat it with the culprit just when the cops arrive?"

"We thought you might enlighten us on that point," Rogers said.

"This is screwy," I said. "I'd've had to be hit on the head a lot harder, brain-damaged probably, to pull a dumb stunt like that. Your guy Miller checked me out at the scene. I came up clean."

"We know that, Mr. Gordon," Danker said. "You're not being accused of anything."

"You could've fooled me," I said.

"An ex-member of the force is involved in this," Rogers said.

"Yeah?" I said.

"A guy named Keller," Danker said. "The stiff was in his apartment."

"That makes it special," Rogers said.

"We kind of figure," Danker said, "that maybe there's a tie-in between the two killings."

"We expect to know more when we locate Keller," Rogers said. "One thing should be quite clear to you, Gordon: this case won't go away. If you know anything, now is the time to get it off your chest."

"If I knew," I said, "I'd tell you."

"Maybe, Mr. Gordon," Danker said, "it'll come to you."

"Think it over," Rogers said.

"You've got a couple of days to refresh your memory," Danker said.

"But no more," Rogers said. "We find out you've been holding out on us, Gordon, it's your ass."

Rogers found a box of wooden matches under some papers, lit his pipe. Danker stood up. "Thanks for your time, Mr. Gordon," he said.

I rose.

"Find your way out okay?"

"Sure."

"Take care of yourself," Danker said.

Rogers sat back in his chair, puffed on his pipe. He didn't say anything.

I left.

* * *

I had covered less than a block when I spied the guy, a storefront window giving me a dandy eyeful. Heavyset, gray-haired, red-faced, wearing a brown suit and an open tan raincoat. The cop who'd been staked out across from my slum and had dogged my footsteps for half a day. Great. I couldn't tell if he was out for a stroll or back on the job. I turned into a Chinese restaurant, went into the kitchen—surprising chefs and waiters—and out the rear door, then followed an alley to a side street and was alone again.

CHAPTER 26

A HANDY PAY PHONE ON A WINDSWEPT CORNER, A REAL BOON to humanity, let me check in at the office. Harry was out but the answering service had a message from Lucy Samler. She wanted a powwow, asked when I'd be reachable.

"She calling back?" I said.

"Every hour," I was told, "if she can."

"Okay. Anytime after two."

A bus carried me to within six blocks of the office. I walked the rest of the way, tallying up all the nickels and dimes I'd saved by not taking a taxi. Fifty more years of taxi abstinence and frugal living, I'd be able to afford a two-week paid vacation in Long Beach. It didn't seem worth it.

The office was stuffy, devoid of life, as if my prolonged absense had somehow broken its spirit.

A note on my desk told me that Harry expected to spend the afternoon reporting to our client on the Hoffman case. I used my palm to dust off the desk. I sat down in my swivel chair and found that it still fit. I was reaching for the desk lamp to turn it on when the phone rang. I picked up.

"Shaw," I said.

"Lucy Samler. Boy, am I glad to find you in."

"You're early. Elman acting up?"

"He's peaceable enough," Lucy said, "but he's moved."

"When?"

"This morning. Eight trunks. He rented a U-Haul and two guys."

"Where is he now?"

"Lower East Side. Orchard Street, between Rivington and Stanton. Apartment one A."

"Some neighborhood."

"It's the middle of the month, Jim. He just upped and left. Thought it might have something to do with your case."

"It might. Anything on Keller?"

"Not yet."

"Elman home now?"

"Probably unpacking."

"Where are you?"

"At a pay phone on Houston."

"I'll join you."

"Okay. You know my car?"

"Green Pontiac?"

"Right. I'll be in it. If I'm gone, our boy's on the town."

Orchard Street was boiling over. Merchandise clogged the pavements. Cheap shoes, dresses, shirts, slacks, briefs, and stockings filled the bargain bins in front of small cluttered shops. Cardboard boxes overflowed with damaged goods: skirts, pants, jackets. A sleeve missing from one garment, a leg from another. Some were stained, ripped, or buttonless. The stitching was uneven on a lot of the stuff, as if the people hired to run the sewing machines were crippled or feeble-minded.

Other shops sold TVs, VCRs, radios, phonographs, Walkmans. Some of the items even came with a warranty, one in Japanese, good anywhere on the Ginza. Shoelaces, toothpaste, and shaving cream were a going concern in adjacent stores. If happiness came cut-rate, this was the place to find it.

I looked around for Lucy. Shoppers filled both sides of the street, a milling throng. They came in all ages, shapes, sizes.

Years ago, when I was a tot, Mom had been one of them, with me in tow. I wondered if her spirit still hovered over the area, hunting bargains.

I caught sight of Lucy's green Pontiac and headed for it. Bucking the crowd, I felt as though I'd landed in the middle of a tag-team wrestling match. I waved at her through the windshield and she let me in.

We exchanged greetings. "How'd you manage to park?" I asked.

"Street's empty in the morning," she said. Lucy was a short perky lady with inquisitive brown eyes, bangs, and an upturned nose. She looked as much like a detective as I did a bathing beauty. That made her perfect for shadowing.

"Any action?" I asked.

"Still as a placid lake," she said, "on a sun-drenched day."

"You've got the wrong neighborhood. Mind if I keep you company?"

"Does a cat mind cat food?"

It took Jed Elman another hour before he decided to leave his new lodgings and mosey out onto the street. With his long-legged walk and worn leather jacket, the tall, blond guy was hard to miss. Lucy and I watched him amble toward Houston. She went after him on foot. I went up to an ancient six-story tenement, past a storefront sign that said BEST FABRICS, rang a couple of bells, and was buzzed in. No questions through the intercom; the tenants here liked to be surprised.

I hid in back of the staircase for a while just to be on the safe side, then went up one flight of rickety stairs. I smelled garlic, hamburgers, and onions, mixed with the musty odor of terminal wood rot. The noise from outside climbed with me. I used my lock-pick, again wondering if I was in the right racket, and entered apartment 1A in nothing flat.

Two rooms and a kitchenette. The place needed a paint job and smelled of ammonia. The trunks were still on the floor,

167

most of them unpacked. No sheets or blankets were on the bed in the next room, just a naked, lumpy mattress; I was almost embarrassed to look at it. I wondered what Elman had been up to these last few hours. It sure wasn't getting things in order.

Elman's inactivity put a crimp in my plans. I had been hoping to search the joint, give it a good going-over. But everything was still buried in the trunks. That killed one bright idea. The other was to bug the flat. I had all the equipment in a small Zabar's shopping bag dangling from my right hand. Even that seemed chancy now; the place was too bare. While my eyes hunted for a decent spot to stash my gear, the door swung open.

I looked over my shoulder.

The guy in the doorway wasn't Elman. He wore a gray sports shirt with the sleeves rolled up. His hair was black with plenty of gray in it and parted on the left. His eyes were dark, round like two marbles. A long nose and razor-thin lips were set in a pudgy circle of a face, the visage of a card shark. The gun in his right hand belonged to a mugger. But he was neither, just a crooked ex-cop who had probably killed a guy in his living room a few days ago. I knew now why Elman hadn't been busy attending to household chores. He'd been visiting with his neighbor, Horace Keller.

"What the hell you doin' here?" he demanded.

This was the first time I had heard Keller's voice live. It sounded deeper than on my tapes, but no prettier.

I turned slowly to face him.

Keller looked at me, his eyes narrowing. "Hey, I know you, don't I?"

I said nothing.

Keller stared at me. "Sure," he said. "I seen you lotsa times."

"That's news to me," I managed to say.

"Whaddaya want here?"

"Heard the apartment was vacant," I said, "and came to take a look."

"Bullshit."

I shrugged. "Who're you? The super?"

Keller ignored my question. "Know where I seen you?"

"Where?"

"In bars. In lotsa bars. You a drinkin' man?"

"Every now and then."

"Sure. And at OTB. You bet, right?"

"Sometimes."

"Know what else? I seen you in McDonald's. Lotsa times. You ever go to McDonald's?"

"You got the wrong guy," I said.

"Everywhere I go I seen you."

"You're nuts."

"Where do you live?"

"Near Eighth Street."

"That so? I got this feelin', Mac, we usta be neighbors. Funny, ha?"

"You got the wrong guy," I said.

"Uh-huh." Keller leveled his gun at me. A small, mirthless grin twitched at his lips. "You been snoopin' all over the place, breathin' down my neck for weeks now. Why? I gotta ask myself, why? Could it be, Mac, because I usta be a cop?"

"How should I know that?" I said.

"Yeah, how? Maybe someone told you? Maybe some little birdy whispered in your ear that I got in dutch with the big boys on the force. Lotsa hanky-panky goin' on. Maybe they needed a patsy to take the fall. Maybe I got the job."

"You really *are* making a mistake," I said. The back of my shirt felt wet and sticky, as if it had begun to weep on my behalf. Stupid shirt.

"Sure I am," Keller said. "I make lotsa mistakes. Maybe, Mac, you're makin' one too. Maybe someone's given you a bum steer. Ever thinka that? Maybe someone needs a fall guy again, and figures I fit the bill."

The door had been half open through all this, as though Keller hoped an audience might gather to take in his performance. Now, without turning, he kicked it closed. The noise of the street crowd was instantly shut out, became a distant murmur, like waves breaking on a beach. Crowds give me a pain, but I missed that noise. It had become a friend. I didn't know if I could make do without it.

"The cops found a dead guy in your flat," I heard myself say. Keller knew too much. Another tack couldn't make matters any worse.

Keller scowled. "What the fuck you talkin' about?"

"A short, stocky guy," I said. "He'd been shot. Thick-nosed. Needed a shave. Someone you know?"

He nodded slowly, as if his thoughts were elsewhere, far away, on a sunlit desert island maybe, where no cops, bodies, or private eyes would bother him. I could've used a place like that myself.

"Yeah, I know a guy like that."

"The cops are looking for you," I said.

"The cops are always lookin' for me," Keller said. "What's your angle, Mac?"

"My name's Duffy," I said. "Mike Duffy. Up until six months ago I used to tend bar, down in the Village. A place called Max's. Ask anyone in the neighborhood, they'll tell you that's so. Then the bar folded and I went on unemployment. This guy Freddie used to come in to Max's sometimes. I met him on the street. He said he knew how I could make a few bucks. He took me to this old guy. Short, heavyset, in his mid sixties. Wore glasses. Never told me his name. We always met in a bar. This old guy paid me to keep an eye on you. That's the God's truth. Listen, every Friday, eleven sharp, I meet him at The Lion's Head, give him what I got. This was gonna be my last week. My sister found me work in L.A. I'm all packed and ready to go. I don't know what this is about, but as of now, I'm off the job, finished. Look, I never did you any harm, just kinda tagged along when you went out—"

The door opened. Jed Elman came through it carrying hot dogs, coffee, and doughnuts in an open cardboard box.

I tensed my knees, ready to jump. Keller's gun remained steady. He never took his eyes off me. Cop training. It was going to do me in.

"What's this?" Elman said.

"I found him here," Keller said.

"What was he doing?"

"Getting set to clean you out."

"What's to take?"

"He didn't know that," Keller said.

"I'll call the cops."

"Uh-huh," Keller said. "We can handle this ourselves."

"I dunno . . ."

"We don't need no cops."

"What do we do?" Elman asked. He seemed genuinely perplexed. He wasn't the only one.

Neither of us ever heard an answer. Lucy Samler crept up behind Keller, through the open door, and yelled, "Freeze!" Her hands were empty. Too bad.

Keller threw himself sideways, turning his gun toward the door as he fell. I leapt, threw himself on him, grabbing his gun arm. We sprawled on the floor.

Elman didn't hesitate. He dropped his snack-filled box and landed on my back. It felt as if part of the roof had come down on me. Lucy piled on top of us all.

The gun went off three times. Plaster chips flew from walls and ceiling, sprayed over us like confetti. Hands poked, tore, chopped, and pounded. Bodies squirmed, tried to tie each other into knots. Legs kicked, knees jabbed and hammered.

The gun let loose another blast.

Elman wrapped his arm around my throat, trying to pull me off his buddy. I put an elbow in his face. He let go. Keller swung his gun my way. Both my hands fastened on it; I held on as though trying to strangle a wiggling snake. Keller

171

clipped me on the jaw with a left. I sank my knee into his stomach.

Suddenly, Elman was off my back, dragged away by Lucy. Keller heaved and I was off him. Keller rolled sideways, went up on one knee, and dived through the door. Houdini never vanished quicker.

I managed to get to my feet. Lucy and Elman were banging away at each other, my Zabar's bag with its tape recorder serving as a bludgeon in Lucy's hands. Another hundred bucks bites the dust. I yanked them apart, bawled, "We're cops!" in Elman's face, and took off after Keller.

He was out of the building by the time I hit the stairs. I went down them two at a time. A sea of people greeted me on the street: bodies heaved and twisted, heads bobbed. I saw no sign of Keller.

A kid sat near the doorway of Best Fabrics, guarding the junk in the stalls.

"The guy who ran out of here," I shouted, "which way did he go?"

"That way, around the corner."

That way was Rivington. I pushed through the crush, reached the corner. No one who vaguely resembled Keller was in evidence. I made my way down the block, peering behind parked cars, in doorways, through plate glass windows. He was gone, lost in a swarm of bargain hunters.

"You're private cops," Elman said.

We were seated on his trunks.

"A phone call brings the real thing," I said.

"No."

"Okay," I said, "tell us about you and Keller."

According to Elman, there wasn't much to tell. He and Keller had been friends for close to twenty years. Sometimes they went to the races or the fights, but usually they just got together for serious drinking a couple times a month. Elman was a shoe salesman between jobs. He didn't know what

Keller did for a living these days, but figured it was probably shady; they never talked about it.

"What are you doing here?" I asked.

Elman shrugged. "Place is rent controlled, dirt cheap. Ace has had a room here for about a year."

"That's Horace?"

"Yes."

"The guy keeps two apartments?"

Elman nodded.

"Why?"

"Search me," Elman said. "The lady who lived here died. Ace called and I moved in. I get to save nearly a hundred a month."

Keller's room was down the hall. Aside from a bed, table, pair of chairs, and small dresser, the place was bare. Some clothing hung in the closet: I found nothing in the pockets. A racing form lay in the wastebasket. I fished it out. There was handwriting in the margins. It took me a moment to decipher the scrawl. Lucy and Elman helped.

"Horses," I said.

"He's big on horses," Elman said.

"Saphire a horse?"

"I guess."

"It's down here twice."

"Must be a winner."

I shook my head. "I thought you were going to level with me."

"What do you mean?"

"Saphire's the name of a person," I said, "one known to your pal Keller. And me."

Elman and I looked at each other. Saphire had been mentioned in Silbert's letter. I didn't think old Ace had been referring to either the gem or a pony.

Elman shrugged. "Gloria Saphire."

"Why the clam?"

"Look," Elman said. "The guy's a friend of mine. I figure the best thing I can do is forget about this Saphire woman."

"Yeah?"

Elman nodded. "It's like he's obsessed. He's talked about her three, four times today."

"What did he say?"

"That's he's going to kill her."

CHAPTER 27

KELLER HAD TOLD HIS FRIEND THAT GLORIA SAPHIRE LIVED near Scarsdale, but no more. Elman told me nothing else that seemed important.

"There's going to be trouble?" he asked.

"No."

"Thanks."

Lucy and I left him.

Outside she got a big hug for her neat rescue job. Only a few people in the crowd turned to gawk.

"Sorry I didn't have a gun," she said.

"Or at least a baseball bat."

"I go home now?"

"Uh-uh. Stick around here for a couple of days, see if Keller comes back."

"Think he will?"

"No. But I can't take the chance. Got someone to work night shift?"

"Yes."

"Okay. If our boy shows, stay with him. I don't think he got a good look at you. And call Harry first thing."

"What do I do with Elman?"

"Nothing. Unless he does something funny."

"You believe him?"

"Who knows? I don't see him leading us to Keller just now,

and that's my main concern. Elman's too poor to find a new home anyway. He'll keep for a while."

I left Lucy seated in her green car and went to find a phone booth. Information had one G. Saphire listed in Scarsdale. I took down the address. A taxi carried me to my garage. I got my car out and headed for Scarsdale.

Turning off the main road, I followed a narrower one leading through a thickly wooded area. The Saphire mansion, a white four-decker job, was at the end of it.

I had time to take a number of deep breaths of country air and admire the darkness, which had slid over the countryside, before my ring was answered.

A tall elderly man of seventy or so clad in formal black attire opened the door. He had a high forehead, long face, and plenty of white hair. Thick eyelids half hid a pair of dark probing eyes.

"Yes?"

"I'd like to speak with Miss Saphire."

"Missus," he said. "Are you expected, sir?"

"No, but it's important."

"Who shall I say is calling?"

"Martin Sanger," I said. I got the Sanger card out of my wallet, handed it to him. He glanced at it as though I'd given him a dead fish.

"Mrs. Saphire knows you, sir?"

"No."

"You wish to see her about what?"

"A mutual friend."

"Kindly wait here."

The door closed. I waited. Presently it opened again. The guy, who looked like the chairman of the board, was back. "This way, sir."

We went down a long hall. Paintings in ornate frames filled the walls. An oriental rug stretched underfoot. Soft lights lit our way. I felt as though I ought to be paying admission to be here.

The butler opened a door and I went into a large room. Plush chesterfields and lounging chairs in wine-colored leather took up a lot of space. Logs in a fireplace were all set for roasting. Thick wine red drapes framed huge windows that looked out at the night.

"Mrs. Saphire will be with you shortly," he said, and went away.

The room was done in walnut hues. Everything shone. The half naked long-haired lady in the painting over the fireplace seemed to chide me for treading on the rug. For a dame who was maybe a hundred years old, she didn't look half bad. There were a couple of framed photos on the mantelpiece. I went over for a better view. One showed a black-haired woman in full equestrian regalia mounted on a horse. The other had the same woman in the company of a man. She was smiling, a big grin that showed even, white teeth and dimples. The guy was staring deadpan at the camera. He was much older than the woman. The skin on his lined, bony face was stretched tight. Strands of black hair were combed over a bald head. Big ears and a large Adam's apple should have given him a comical appearance but somehow didn't.

I had made three circuits of the room, with a stop at the windows, when the lady from the photos showed up.

She came striding through the doorway dressed in an ivory silk blouse and skirt, her black hair bouncing against her shoulders. She wore a red kerchief around her neck.

"Mr. Sanger," she said, in a low musical voice.

"Mrs. Saphire."

She gave me a firm hand, nodded me to a lounging chair, and took one opposite me. "What can I do for you, Mr. Sanger?"

She was somewhere in her thirties. Her eyes were large, deep, and the color of amber. A high-bosomed figure was curved just right. Her full lips, strong chin, even nose, and smooth complexion were a dime a dozen on Hollywood stars after they'd been worked over by the makeup man, but Saphire seemed to have come by her endowments naturally.

"I'm a private detective," I told her. "The case I'm working on just now has nothing to do with you, Mrs. Saphire."

"That's reassuring," she said, smiling.

"It gets less reassuring," I said, "as it goes along."

"Oh dear." Her amber eyes twinkled at me as though we shared some secret joke. Here was a lady immune to troubles. If something bad came up, she could always swat it with a checkbook.

I said, "I think some guy's out to get you."

"Get me?"

"Bump you off."

"You mean, kill me?"

"Yeah. That's what I was told."

"Told? By whom?"

"That's not important."

"What is, then?"

"The name of your would-be assassin."

"You know who it is?"

"Horace Keller," I told her.

She stared at me woodenly, nodded once. Her smile was gone.

"Someone you know?" I asked.

"He had business with my husband."

"Maybe I'd better speak to him, too."

"I'm a widow, Mr. Sanger. My husband died last year."

"Sorry."

"Thank you. . . . This Keller person, he used to be a policeman?"

"That's right."

"He tried to blackmail my husband," she said. "Mr. Saphire was a financier. He was on the board of a number of corporations. One of these, Wendflex, got into trouble. The president and treasurer were both indicted for trying to bribe some city councilmen."

"In upper Manhattan."

"You remember the case?"

"Vaguely," I said. "It made the papers."

"Yes. They tried to change some zoning laws so they could build a huge housing complex."

"Councilmen wore wires."

She nodded.

"The Wendflex crew was convicted," I said, "and sent off to prison."

"Yes, but my husband had nothing to do with it. He had only attended a few board meetings. This Keller person was one of the detectives assigned to the case. And he hounded my husband until the day that he died."

"But he had nothing on him?"

"Nothing," she said. "He threatened to reveal my husband's connection with Wendflex, but that was already public knowledge. He claimed to have evidence that my husband had engaged in wrongdoing while on the Wendflex board, but he never produced it. The man was simply crazed. He was here twice last month at the house. But I was out. And now you say he's made threats against me?"

"Yeah."

"It's insane," she said.

"Maybe so. But you still might want police protection."

"And have some officer seated here in my home for days on end?"

I shrugged. "Suit yourself, Mrs. Saphire, but Keller's no one to fool around with."

"I am quite capable of taking care of myself."

"Okay," I said. "You've got my card. If you hear from Keller, or if something happens, call me."

She nodded.

"I'm on the move a lot. You'll probably get my answering service. Just leave word for Martin Sanger. I'll get back to you."

She said she would.

The butler showed me to the door.

"Who's the old guy in the photo?" I asked.

"On the mantelpiece, sir?"

"Yeah."

"Mr. Saphire."

"Looks like a tough cookie," I said.

"Quite indigestable," the butler said.

My headlights cut long slices through the darkness. My rearview mirror showed no cars gaining on me, ready to send slugs through my windows or force me off the road. A nice night.

Back in Manhattan, I left my car in its garage and took a taxi to my slum. Neither Harry nor Sheila answered their phones. I went to sleep.

CHAPTER 28

THE NEXT DAY I HAD A COURT APPEARANCE ON AN OLD embezzlement case. I got up bright and early with a solid eight hours of sleep under my belt, fixed myself the usual breakfast: rolled oats, jam, orange juice, and coffee. I added an egg this time, one of the three I allowed myself weekly since Danny had put the fear of God and cholesterol in me.

I put on an olive green cotton shirt, brown tweed Stanley Blacker sports coat, and dark brown wool slacks. I got into my Bogie trench coat, left some chow for my house mouse, and caught the Lex to City Hall. The Civic Center was only a few blocks away.

I spent most of the morning reading the *Times*, waiting to take the stand. My turn came around 11:30. I recited the facts as I knew them, keeping one eye on the courtoom door. I expected Danker or one of his helpers to come strolling in any second and cart me off to the lockup for impersonating a private detective. I wasn't sure myself anymore whether I was Stuart Gordon, Martin Sanger, James Shaw, or a guy called Duffy. Some racket.

The attorneys raked me over the coals only a little bit and by twelve noon my testimony was completed. I went outside, stood on the stone steps, and gazed up at the blue, sunny sky. I took a deep breath. Still a free man. The court has that effect on me.

*   *   *

"Hello." A woman's voice.

"I'd like to speak with Sheila, please."

"This is she."

"My name's Stuart Gordon."

"Yes?"

"I'm a friend of Mrs. Silbert," I said.

"Ah."

"You knew her?"

"She was my aunt."

"You've got my condolences. Your aunt was a fine woman,"
I said. "I live in her building."

"Ninety-fourth Street?"

"That's right."

"Her home was really in Brooklyn," the voice told me.

"I'd heard that."

"We never understood what she was doing in the other
place, never."

"You ask her?"

"If you knew my aunt Mr. . . . ?"

"Gordon."

"Yes, Mr. Gordon. If you knew her then you must know
how futile that could be. She wouldn't say a word unless it
suited her. Could talk a blue streak, of course, when the mood
hit her. Were you at the funeral?"

"I couldn't make it," I said. "I was in the hospital at the
time."

"I'm sorry."

"You don't know about me, do you?"

"I beg your pardon?"

"I'm the man who tried to help your aunt."

"What?"

"The police didn't tell you how she died?"

"She was robbed and beaten."

"Beaten. I don't think they took anything. I heard your aunt

182

screaming and tried to help. There were two men there. We fought. They got away and I went to the hospital."

"I didn't know that," Sheila said.

"There may be other things you don't know, Miss . . . ?"

"Goldberg."

"Right. I'd like to talk with you. In person, if I may."

"Other things? I don't think I really understand."

"Miss Goldberg, your aunt gave me your number, asked that I call you if there was trouble. I think she believed that something like this might happen."

"But *why?*"

"That's what I'd like to discuss with you."

"Goodness. I can't imagine what I could possibly know."

"May I see you Miss Goldberg?"

"I suppose so. Certainly. When did you have in mind?"

"As soon as possible," I said. "This afternoon, if you can manage it."

"I'm free around six."

She gave me her address, on West Twenty-eighth Street, and we said good-bye.

Next I dialed the office.

"Canfield speaking."

"It's me. Free for lunch?"

"Sure."

"Get something, Harry?"

"Yep."

"Me, too. The Jap place?"

"Sounds good."

CHAPTER 29

THE EATERY WAS MODISHLY DIM. SMALL TABLES LINED THE walls. A U-shaped counter with high-backed stools took up the middle. Some of the customers looked as if they'd just stepped out of a swanky display window—Bloomingdale's, perhaps—and expected to be recalled as soon as they were fed; the rest appeared to be run-of-the-mill citizens. A white-aproned Asian chef, presumably Japanese, had cooked our beef and chicken teriyaki in a wok right at our table. Impressive as hell, if you're easily impressed. I was. We were into our sixth little cup of sake and I was feeling properly mellow. The current case no longer seemed like the hot potato it was. With a little luck, I'd wrap it up in a couple of days and then take Daphne and go off on a three-week concert spree. A few more drinks, I'd have settled the Israeli-Arab fracas, too. Harry and I chatted between bites.

Harry said, "Busy couple of days, I bet."

"Had its moments," I said.

"Name one."

"Think I can't? Silbert's niece."

"What about her?"

"Tracked her down."

"No kidding?" Harry said. "How?"

"Privileged information. But since you seem like a nice chap, I'll let you in on the secret. Might do you some good when you grow up and become a gumshoe like me. The super gave me her phone number."

"Got to hand it to you," Harry said. "That's what I call sleuthing. Lots of legwork, keen deductive reasoning, and the judicious use of force. Right out of the book. Should win the Detective of the Year Award hands down."

"Didn't I say so? Got an appointment with her later today."

"Not bad. Want to hear what I did yesterday?"

"No."

"Dropped around to the Twenty-fourth."

"Fat guy at the reception desk. Got a double chin and gray mustache. Lone begonia on the second windowsill over on the right as you come in. Needs watering. How'm I doing?"

Harry put down his sake cup. "You were there?"

"Cops pulled me in."

"What time?"

"Around noon."

"Close. Eleven thirty for me."

"We almost rubbed elbows."

"We could have all gone to lunch," Harry said. "You, me, and the officers handling your case."

"My case hasn't quite hatched yet," I said.

"Give it time. What did they want?"

"My rank and serial number. I made 'em sweat for it."

"Anything else?"

"Yeah. Wanted me to spill my guts. Danker and a Captain Rogers put me through the ringer. Great team. Would've made Laurel and Hardy green with envy. I've got a couple more days to come clean, or it's the firing squad."

"They on to something?" Harry asked.

"Just guessing. Or I wouldn't've gotten off so easy. How about you?"

"Thought you'd never ask."

"I'm asking."

"Great success. In a small way," Harry said.

"Sounds familiar."

186

"First, the figures on that piece of paper have nothing to do with the serial numbers on that ten thousand. You'll find it in the safe."

"That's success?"

"Hold on. I chatted up Peters the desk sergeant."

"Small world. Give him the Andy Grimes spiel?"

"Yep."

"What happened?"

"Peters never heard of him."

"Didn't faze him though."

"Nope."

"And Neely?"

"Neely was out," Harry said.

"Out."

"As in away somewhere."

"Where, away?"

"That's the question, all right," Harry agreed.

"Any answers?"

"Now, that took some doing. Explained about my job difficulties: how I can't find one, how my buddy Grimes had the advice I needed."

"Suicide?" I suggested.

"Neely."

"I was close."

"Neely has a job waiting for me."

"Private eye?"

"Doesn't pay enough. Security guard."

"One opening, eh?"

"Sorry, kid," Harry said. "Find your own job. By now I had old Peters crying down his mustache."

"And double chin."

"Yep. So he called his buddy in personnel."

"Gonna make you a cop?"

"Get the dope on Neely."

"And?"

"Got it."

"Coungratulations."

"I'll drink to that," Harry said.

"Me, too."

We drank.

"Neely," Harry said, "had some health problems."

"Don't say?"

"Yep. Sounds like a nervous breakdown to me, but who knows. Leave that to the MD."

"Think I drove him crazy, Harry?"

"Who else?"

"Jeez."

"Only he isn't taking the cure, that much I know."

"Not dead, I trust?"

"Your trust is well founded. I think. Can't be sure. You'll see why. Old Peters naturally didn't want me pestering poor Neely in his moment of need."

"Guy's got a heart," I said.

"Right. Didn't want me to miss out on my job, either. Not with a wife and six kids."

"You told him that?"

"Well, almost," Harry admitted. "Held it in reserve. I didn't need it, though. Peters came through with flying colors. I promised not to bother the patient if the doctors nixed it, and Peters told me where he was."

"Where?"

"Kingston Hospital."

"That's where he is?"

"Yep. Only he's not."

"Not?"

"You've got it, kid," Harry said. "I called up. This isn't some private hole in the sticks. They got ten charities supporting the place. They don't lie. Neely never checked in. I made a big fuss. Neighbor saw him yesterday, you said. So he had to have checked in last night. Three ladies checked in last night. And a guy in his eighties. Neely in his eighties?"

"Uh-uh."

"Then that's it, kid. That's all there is."

"Not quite," I said.

"There's more?"

"The best for dessert," I said, and gave him the rundown on Keller and Saphire.

"That's the best?" Harry asked.

"Uh-huh."

"So what's the worst?"

"That Saphire goes and calls Sanger and the dumb answering service forgets the drill and gives her my real name."

"That's not the worst."

"Guess not. How about Neely calling it quits now that I've had a run-in with Keller?"

"We are," Harry said, "way beyond that stage. Besides, for Neely to call it quits, we've got to find him first."

"Maybe there isn't any worst," I said.

"You've had too much sake," Harry said. "What do you make of the tale Keller gave you?"

"Won't win the Pulitzer this year."

"Or any other," Harry said.

CHAPTER 30

HARRY AND I WALKED BACK TO THE OFFICE.

From our windows, which face west on Madison Avenue, a bank could be seen. That's where the money was, as Willy Sutton had so wisely pointed out before he got nabbed and tossed in the clink for twenty years. The bank left me cold. Other people's dough, unless they were spreading it my way, hardly rated a second thought. The view also included a card shop, a designer boutique, an overpriced hi-fi outlet, and lots of towering office buildings. There was probably a good reason why we'd moved here, but I couldn't seem to remember what it was. Possibly to build character as we battled against insolvency, and lost. At least on Eighth Avenue the bums had vaguely resembled real life.

I waited until the alcoholic haze parted a bit and got busy. I went to the wall safe, worked the combination, opened it, pulled out the Neely file, and hauled it back to my desk. Settling comfortably into my swivel chair, I started wading through the Xerox copies of my reports. Six weeks worth. Not as much fun as *Catch-22,* but it seemed just as long.

Next I went over the tape transcripts. I didn't expect much from them and wasn't disappointed. Keller had had no visitors during the time I'd spied on him, unless you counted the delivery boy from the corner liquor store. His phone calls couldn't be termed frequent by any stretch of the imagination, but he'd had some. No one had used first or last names, or referred to anything that made the least sense to me. Very suspicious. In less enlightened times something like that would have been enough to land him in the clutches of whatever passed for the local inquisition. Me, him, and everyone else I knew would have been sharing the same cell. No trouble keeping tabs on him then, eh?

There was nothing in the transcripts worth jotting down. I skimmed my handwritten field notes. All of their wisdom was already distilled in my reports. The rest looked like junk.

I now had a full page of names and locations. I carried it into Harry's office.

My partner was on the phone. I took the client's chair, waited till he was done.

"Customer?" I asked.

"Competition. The Fleischman agency."

"Getting advice?"

"Farming out business."

"Good," I said. "I was afraid we might make some dough and it would go to our heads. This way we stay pure."

"This way," Harry said, "we've got a fighting chance. Six cases will keep for a while, no one'll notice. We've closed the books on four since your departure, including the Hoffman job. Money's in the bank."

"Thank God."

"And I've just unloaded three. We get a pittance when and if Fleischman delivers. The best I could do, Jim. No way to handle them and Neely at the same time. And you're going to need all the help you can get."

"True."

"So what have we got?"

"Plenty. Too much, maybe." I handed him the list. "Keller's contacts, the ones I was able to ID. The rest are places he visited while I lurked outside. Couldn't get close without tipping him. Most of this is from the first couple weeks, before he slowed down. This guy Jed Elman needs looking into. Also

192

Gloria Saphire. And this Wendflex outfit. Elrex Imports is on Twenty-fourth and Broadway. Keller went there twice. He was the only one using the elevator. It stopped on eight. I used it next, loitered on the staircase for about half an hour, saw our boy leave the suite. So that's definite. Who he saw and what his business was is anyone's guess. This guy Ranky is one step removed from a street bum. Dottie Sampel's a waitress at Lenny's Diner at York and Eighty-ninth. Keller's spent time chatting with both. I haven't got much of a handle on the rest of this crowd. We'll have to do some work on them."

"Any photos?"

"Uh-uh. Neely said no. Figured our boy might notice."

"He's never heard of telescopic lenses?"

"Didn't think it necessary. Said descriptions would do, that he knew what to look for. I wasn't about to argue with him. All I really did, when you get down to it, was supply him with raw data. He processed it."

"So what we know," Harry said, "is next to nothing."

"That's what we know."

"Sure gives us lots of room to maneuver," Harry said, "doesn't it?"

"Sure does," I said.

CHAPTER 31

SHEILA GOLDBERG WAS A TALL ANGULAR WOMAN IN HER MID thirties. She had short black hair, brown eyes, a long neck, and lots of rings on her fingers. She wore a pleated green skirt, white frilly blouse, and low-heeled shoes. She ushered me into the living room.

"Can I offer you something, Mr. Gordon?"

"Thanks, I'm fine."

I sat on a yellow sofa, she in a wide chair with blue stuffed pillows. A small green jungle sprouted under windows affording a dandy view of a parking lot.

The ILGU projects are between Eighth and Ninth avenues and run for six blocks. David Dubinsky had intended them for his garment workers, but the project was funded under the Mitchell-Lama Law, which meant anyone under a certain income could get in. Sheila Goldberg was one of the results.

"Mind if I smoke?" she asked.

"Not at all," I said, "pretend you're at home."

Sheila Goldberg lit a Parliament. I hated to see anyone commit suicide right before my eyes. I hoped she'd last through the interview, at least.

"Quite frankly," she said, "I expected an older man."

"An older man," I said, "would still be in the hospital. Or worse."

"I'm thankful for what you tried to do, Mr. Gordon."

"We were friends."

"Over the phone you said something about . . . about my aunt *foreseeing* her death?"

"Not quite. It wasn't a premonition. She had good reason to fear a beating."

Sheila took a drag on her cigarette. "I'm truly mystified."

"I'm sure you are," I said. "It's like this, Miss Goldberg. Your aunt confided in me, perhaps because I was the only other Jewish tenant in the building. Or maybe because I was young and she figured she might need help. I was to call you if anything went wrong, fill you in as best I could."

"Yes."

"There was a proviso, though."

"I see." She didn't.

"You must agree," I said, "to tell no one."

Sheila Goldberg looked at me. Her cigarette smoldered untended in an ashtray.

"That means," I said, "literally no one. Not even the police."

Silence for a moment. I shifted my gaze to the parking lot below. A red Toyota drifted through the gate, pulled up next to a dark blue Chevy. A plump woman in a red suit got out, went away. Not the stuff of dreams.

Sheila said, "Surely the police—"

"It was your aunt's wish, Miss Goldberg. I gave my word."

"I can't say I understand the need for all this secrecy."

"You will."

"It's only temporary, you said?"

"Yes."

"Well I suppose there's a good reason."

I nodded.

"Oh all right, Mr. Gordon. You have my word. Now what is this deep dark mystery?"

I sat back on the sofa, crossing my arms over my chest. "Did your aunt ever mention a Horace Keller?"

"I don't believe so."

"He lived across the yard from her."

"No, she never mentioned him."

"Mrs. Silbert was keeping him under surveillance."

"My aunt?"

"Uh-huh."

"What on earth are you talking about?"

"Keller was a member of an organized crime ring, Miss Goldberg, a man involved in a number of illicit operations. Your aunt was trying to get the goods on him."

"Why, that's utterly absurd."

"One of the two men who killed her was found dead in Keller's flat a few days ago."

"Mr. Gordon—"

I held up a hand. "Please, let me finish. Before she died, your aunt gave me a letter. It was in Yiddish. It turned out to be a detailed report on Keller's movements. I believe that Keller or the people around him became aware of your aunt's activities, tried to find out how much she knew, and killed her in the process."

"This is all so fantastic," Sheila said. "Where's this Keller person now?"

"He's disappeared."

Sheila Goldberg rose. "I think I'll treat myself to a drink," she said. "I can use one." She went into her kitchenette. "One for you?" she called.

"Thanks, no."

She returned carrying a large glass of pale liquid and sank back into her chair. "I'm still in shock." she said.

"Understandable."

"Who *are* you, Mr. Gordon?"

"A tenant."

"You don't *sound* like a tenant." She took a long pull on her drink. "You're involved in this somehow, aren't you?"

"I want to find the people behind your aunt's death, Miss Goldberg."

"There's more than that. Tell me."

I shook my head. "If there is, you don't want to know it."

"I do."

"Not now."

"Why not, in heaven's name?"

"Because it could get us both in big trouble. Your aunt put her trust in me, Miss Goldberg, or I wouldn't be here. Why can't you trust me too?"

She reached for her cigarettes again, managed to get one out of the pack, and lit up. Between the booze and the tobacco the pleasure centers in her noodle ought to have been tickled pink. But Sheila Goldberg didn't look pleased.

"What is it exactly you want me to do, Mr. Gordon?"

"There was an attempted robbery at your aunt's place yesterday."

"I didn't know."

"The police take their time. You'll hear from them. What were you planning to do with Mrs. Silbert's things?"

"At Ninety-fourth Street?"

"Yes."

"Frankly, nothing."

"Just leave them there?"

"Why not? They're worthless."

"The burglar was almost definitely sent by Keller or some of his people. My guess is, they were after the letter your aunt gave me. There may be other items, too. The letter was hidden in a book."

"Books and clothing were all she took from home. The furniture was bought secondhand in Yorkville."

"We need the books. Clothes, too."

"You want me to claim them?"

"Yes."

"I hardly have room here for all those things."

"Don't worry," I said, "I'll take them off your hands. Just notify the police that you're getting the stuff. A friend of mine, Harry Canfield, will go to the apartment with you. The furniture needs to be gone over too. Then he'll haul away what we need. What do you say, Miss Goldberg?"

"It's frightening."

"But you'll do it?"

She hesitated. "I suppose so."

I smiled.

"I must be insane."

"Your aunt wouldn't think so."

"Is that all?"

"Almost. I need a list of Mrs. Silbert's friends, relatives, coworkers; anyone she might have known."

"By when?"

"Now."

"I couldn't possibly. Our relatives, yes; there aren't many. But I never really knew her friends and wouldn't have the faintest idea how to reach them. There's an elderly cousin who might help. I could ask him. As for her coworkers, I met them only once, at a benefit."

"I can handle that," I said, "just give me the name of the bakery."

"Bakery?"

"Where your aunt worked."

"Is this a joke?"

"I hope not."

"Aunt Liuba held an advanced degree from Warsaw University."

"That wouldn't be in baking, would it?"

"History, Mr. Gordon."

"History," I said.

"She retired last year. For twenty-two years my aunt was a senior research associate at the Jewish Archives Institute."

"That's something like a professor," I said.

"That *is* a professor."

"Yes," I said.

"Whatever possessed you to think my aunt was a *baker*, Mr. Gordon?"

"Sheer stupidity, Miss Goldberg. It gets us all from time to time."

CHAPTER 32

I STOPPED OFF AT A JOINT ON NINTH AND TWENTY-THIRD, took a booth by the window, and had a workingman's special: split pea soup, a couple of pastrami sandwiches on rye, french fries, a half sour pickle, a dish of coleslaw, a slice of peach pie, and a mug of decaf coffee. The place smelled of fried onions and perking coffee. It catered to a crowd that didn't know a vitamin from a mineral. A pleasant change. The meal set me back a big fifteen bucks. I took it in stride. It was cheaper than a week in Acapulco, but for some reason, maybe because it went against the family grain, it seemed almost as restful.

I went out into the night and turned north on Ninth Avenue, away from the antique and nostalgia shops, boutiques, and renovated brownstones that stretched off toward the Hudson. Soon Dubinsky's projects were behind me too. I could see some factories over on Tenth, across a parking lot and vacant field. Bleak office buildings alternated with seedy tenements on my right. A bag lady snoozed peacefully in a doorway. No one bothered her. Presently even dourer tenements, probably from the turn of the century, took over. Lit windows showed bleached curtains, soiled window shades, an occasional flowerpot. I tried hard not to imagine what the insides were like. A slew of cut-rate stores held sway at street level—butcher shops, coffee and tea importers, fruit and vegetable stands, junk stores, old-world eateries. A few

201

hookers, spillovers from the more crowded and lucrative Eighth Avenue trade, worked the territory around Port Authority. Stray drunks and hopheads used the sidewalks for mattress and pillow, a sight which would have kept anyone with an IQ above 79 on the straight and narrow.

I crossed Forty-second Street. One block east, the blazing neon of porno flicks, nudie shows, fast-food dives, and video-audio outlets bloomed like toadstools.

Again the area changed. A classy high-rise block gave way to more mundane fare: bakeries, shoe stores, thrift shops, drugstores and candy stores, mom-and-pop groceries going head to head with Korean food marts. The tenements above all this were only a touch more refined than their thirties counterparts.

Fifty-ninth Street was the great divide, the gateway to the Upper West Side. I crossed the line and was back on home ground.

The old Art-Deco Sofia warehouse, a red brick tower that was yesterday's gift to a future that never arrived, had been turned into a condo. I crossed over at Fordham U., then hit Lincoln Center. Dad had lost his shirt at a number of racetracks. When I was flush I left some of my money here. Hardly a big-league vice, but there were a lot dumber ways of going broke. The place was all lights and glitter now. I walked on. I felt swell.

At Ninety-sixth Street I got on a crosstown bus and went back to the East Side. The ride took ten minutes. I only fell asleep in my seat twice.

I got off at Third Avenue, hiked over two blocks, and strolled downhill to my house. The block was empty. I turned toward the front door with my usual reluctance, as though I were going back to my cage at the zoo.

A voice said, "Mr. Gordon."

I glanced around. Still no one on the block. I saw the car then. It was parked right by the curb.

No gun barrels stuck out of it. No one had done anything bad yet.

I went over to the car. "Yeah?"

The front window was down. The bird next to it held up a hand. A leather card case was in it. The streetlamp was just bright enough for me to see the card's inscription: IMMIGRA-TION AND NATURALIZATION SERVICE. The name underneath was in smaller letters: NED BRADY.

"What can I do for you, Mr. Brady?"

"Keep off my toes."

Brady had a pasty face and black hair slicked down with stickum. Definitely not the natural look. His voice and face held as much expression as a block of concrete. The two guys with him, one behind the wheel, the other in back, were bulky, shadowy shapes. They hardly moved at all.

"I don't think I even know you," I said.

"Right. But I know you Gordon—or whatever your name is."

"Come again?"

"Don't be a wise guy," the man behind the wheel said. I took a closer look. He was a pudgy guy with grayish hair and a red face. My former shadow, the guy I'd figured for a cop.

"Mr. Gordon," Brady said, "we know about you."

"What's to know?" I asked.

"I don't want to lose my patience, Mr. Gordon," Brady said. "We've been waiting here for an hour."

"I'm sorry."

"It's been a long night," Brady said.

"Tell me what you want."

"Lay off Keller," Brady said.

"The missing guy," I said.

"Cut the bullshit," the driver said.

"I told you, Mr. Gordon," Brady said. "We know. You've been shadowing Keller for more than a month."

"And you're still nosing around," the driver said. He sounded disgusted. Brady didn't sound like anything.

"You're in the middle of something you don't understand," Brady said.

I looked at him with admiration. He'd told the truth, at least once. "This is all a mistake," I said.

"Yes," Brady said, "and you're making it. You're interfering with a federal investigation."

"I'm not doing anything."

"Hey, Gordon," the driver said, "don't be a shithead. We're not playin' games here."

"We've had you under surveillance for some time," Brady said.

"Waste of taxpayers' money."

"We can have you held as a material witness," Brady said. "Go away somewhere, Mr. Gordon."

"Where?"

"Anywhere," Brady said. "Take a vacation."

"You guys paying?"

"Just get lost," the driver said.

"You've been told," Brady said. "You get told only once." The driver started the motor.

I pointed at the man in back. "He doesn't talk?"

The back window slowly rolled down. A large head with a bulldog jaw became visible. It couldn't have been old J. Edgar, he was dead. "Fuck you, asshole," the head said.

The car pulled away.

CHAPTER 33

I AWOKE AT SEVEN THIRTY. OUTSIDE WAS A CRISP AUTUMN DAY. Blue sky peered through both windows. Snippets of Mozart, Dvořák, and Strauss bubbled out of my radio while I shaved and showered. An extra teaspoon of grape jelly went into my rolled oats. I took my coffee mug to the old easy chair by the window. A cheerful voice recited the usual calamities during the five-minute newsbreak. Keller's shades were lowered. A couple of birds pecked at the ground in the back yard. Long johns, panties, sheets, and shirts dangled from a clothesline two houses down. A few windows showed parts of bodies drifting by. Vivaldi came through my speakers. I got up and went to the closet to put on a dark blue shirt, gray slacks, and sports jacket. No tie. I only wore ties to impress the nobility. I hadn't met any lately. I went to the phone and dialed Harry.

"Morning," I said.

"The partner."

"This, pal," I said, "has gotta be a good day."

"You up yet or still dreaming?"

"Listen. Three guys claiming to be feds tried to scare me off the case last night."

"That makes it a good day?"

"They weren't feds."

"No, huh?"

"Uh-uh. They didn't know who I was."

"The existential dilemma. They were probably philosophers. Anything else?"

"You hear of three feds camping in a car till all hours just to tell some turkey to lay off? They said they were on to me from the word go."

"Smart cookies."

"Sure. The Leonardo da Vincis of the Immigration and Naturalization Service, no less. Maybe Keller's an alien, eh? Jeez. They look like pickpockets. They wait six weeks before reading me the riot act. And meanwhile I'm stepping all over their so-called case. Whatever that is."

"Has possibilities," Harry admitted. "Got their license, I presume."

"I'm old and feeble," I said, "but not quite senile." I read the number off to him. "Let's run it through Motor Vehicles."

"Let's."

"Got another errand for you." I told him about my visit with Sheila Goldberg. "Rent a U-Haul. Pick up the niece and get up here. I'll talk to the super, give him some money. He'll round up a few guys to help out. Load the books, clothing, anything that might contain a slip of paper. Frisk the joint before leaving."

"Where do I dump these treasures?"

"Your place."

"You jest, of course."

"Goldberg says her place is out. Mine is the kiss of death. And it'll take time to go through this junk." I gave him Sheila's number.

"Why doesn't this sound like fun?" Harry asked.

"Because it isn't. Make sure you're not followed."

"I'll plant mines behind me."

"That's the spirit."

CHAPTER 34

THE SIX-STORY TOWN HOUSE ON SEVENTY-EIGHTH STREET AND Madison had once belonged to the Morgans. It now housed the Jewish Archives Institute. I went into the vestibule. Two heavy glass doors faced me. A sign said PLEASE RING BELL FOR ADMITTANCE. The sign didn't lie: I rang and was admitted.

The floors were marble. A winding staircase led up to the second floor. Glass exhibition cases contained old Yiddish books, manuscripts, newspapers, letters, photographs. A typewriter sounded from an office on the left. The receptionist was a small elderly woman seated by a switchboard. I asked for the executive director.

"Dr. Benish?" she said.

"Yes."

She pointed to a large room on her right. The doors were open. "In there. Ask him if he's busy."

I thanked her and walked in.

Yiddish books lined one wall. Across from them, oversize windows looked out on Madison Avenue. I could see the movement of cars, a bus, pedestrians; their racket intruded into the stillness here as if trying to reclaim the premises for modern times. Fat chance.

A long conference table surrounded by empty chairs filled the center of the room. A small man with a full head of gray hair and a graying Vandyke beard was working at a desk by the far wall. I went over to him.

"Dr. Benish?"

He looked up. "Yes?"

"You busy?"

"Of course."

"Spare a few minutes?"

"Why not?"

I pulled up a chair. Benish had a large head and a full nose and mouth. His eyes were brown. He wore a dark gray jacket and blue tie. His glasses were pushed down low on his nose.

I said, "I'm here about a former colleague of yours, Liuba Silbert."

Benish folded his hands, nodded. "Yes, a fine woman, may she rest in peace. What is it precisely that you wish to know, Mr. . . . ?

"Shaw. James Shaw. Daniel Shaw's brother. I think you may know him."

Benish smiled. "Of course. I am pleased to meet you, Mr. Shaw." He extended a hand. I shook it. "Dr. Shaw has been a friend of the archives for many years. He participated only last year in our Mendele Moykher-Sforim symposium. You speak Yiddish?"

"Not like my brother," I said. "Mine is more the broken kind."

"Aha," Benish said. "Mendele was the grandfather of Yiddish literature."

I nodded. "If you speak slowly and use a seven-year-old's vocabulary I'll probably understand you."

"But the seven-year-old will want it back." Benish beamed at me. "Fortunately, we can converse in English."

"Yeah. Thank God. What did Mrs. Silbert do here?"

"What did she not do here? At the Archives, Mr. Shaw, no one is completely a specialist. We all assist each other. Mrs. Silbert's field was modern Jewish history. Mostly Polish, but some Russian, too. She gave also a seminar on Yiddish schools

208

in Poland between the two world wars. This is the sort of information you are looking for?"

"I don't know. I'm a private detective, Dr. Benish."

"Daniel's brother?"

I nodded. "Runs in the family. Our uncle was one, too."

"Aha," Benish said. "And you are investigating Mrs. Silbert?"

"Her death."

Benish sat back in his chair and removed his glasses, polishing them absently against a sleeve. "She was killed accidently during a robbery. Yes?"

"Maybe."

Benish replaced his glasses, fixing his gaze on me, "Why maybe?" he asked.

"Her niece, Dr. Benish, thinks she may have been killed because she knew something. About someone."

"Who? What?"

"We don't know. That's what I'm here for."

"The police share these suspicions?"

"Not yet."

"Surely you do not believe that someone here at the archives, God forbid, may be involved in this tragedy?"

"No. What I think is that Mrs. Silbert was engaged in some kind of investigation of her own. And that she had help."

"Aha," Benish said.

"Help from here, maybe."

"And what is it you wish me to do?"

"Speak to her colleagues," I said, "privately. See what you can learn. Even if she got her help elsewhere, she might have confided in someone."

"That is certainly a possibility," Benish said. "I will gladly ask."

"Good. Another thing, I could use a list of her friends; who they were, their addresses, what they do. As many as you can dig up. That goes for aquaintances, collegues from other institutions she might have worked with from time to time—stuff like that."

Benish smiled. "And that is all?"

I nodded.

"You do not want much, do you?" he said.

"Tall order, eh?"

"Mr. Shaw, how many people do you imagine would appear on such a list? Would you care to guess?"

"A good many," I said.

"Hundreds. To adequately compile it would require some weeks, and no doubt entail a staff of researchers. Who, if I may ask, would fund such an undertaking?"

"How about just *very* close friends?"

"Easier, by far."

"I'll settle for that," I said. "It's got to be less than a few thousand, right?

Benish smiled. "Considerably."

"Okay. I don't want to sound like a slave driver, but the faster, the better."

"I understand," Benish said. "I will do my best. It is, after all, in a good cause."

"Thanks. I think so. What happened to her husband, Dr. Benish?"

"He perished during the Second World War. One of the six million."

"She never remarried?"

"No."

I stood up, gave him my card. "Call this number if you come across something important. You'll get my partner, Harry Canfield, or our answering services. I'll get back to you fast. Otherwise, you'll hear from me in a couple days."

"Very well," Benish said. He rose. We shook hands across his desk.

"I'd be grateful," I said, "if you could keep me and the niece out of it for a while."

"My dear young man," Benish said, "under ordinary

circumstances, I must tell you, I should think twice before doing any of this. However, your pedigree is outstanding."

"Daniel, eh?"

"Yes."

"Always knew there was a reason for keeping him around," I said.

CHAPTER 35

I PUT A QUARTER INTO THE PAY PHONE, DIALED MY ANSWERING service, and was told that a Gloria Saphire had tried to reach Martin Sanger. I dug more quarters out of my pocket, dialed Saphire's number. The butler asked me to wait. I was on the corner of Madison and Seventy-ninth. A wind was blowing. I buttoned my Bogie trench coat and watched the traffic put gas fumes into the air.

"Mr. Sanger?" Saphire's voice.

"Yeah."

"He's called again."

"Keller?"

"Yes. He sounded wild."

"What did he want?"

"Money."

"Just like that?"

"He said my husband had helped bribe the councilmen."

"Kind of old hat, isn't it?"

"Yes. Only this time he told me what his evidence was. Tapes, Mr. Sanger. He says he has tapes of my husband planning the operation with the two men who went to prison."

"Think it's possible?" I asked.

"Utter nonsense. The man's a mental case."

"The cops are looking for him," I said.

"Why?"

"Found a dead guy in his flat."

"Do you think they'll catch him?"

"Sooner or later."

"Well, I can tell you what I plan to do, Mr. Sanger."

"What's that?"

"I have a home in Florida. I shall be leaving for it tonight."

"Good idea."

"Perhaps by the time I return, this lunatic will be safely put away."

"He will be," I told her, "if I have anything to do with it."

"Thank you, Mr. Sanger."

"Thank *you*, Mrs. Saphire."

CHAPTER 36

THE BUILDING ON EAST NINETY-FIRST STREET WAS MIDWAY between Second and First avenues. Strictly working-class, the houses only a mite better kept than my own current tenement.

I rang the bell marked BASEMENT. There was no response. My finger pressed SUPER. I was buzzed in and walked down a short hallway to the last door in the corridor. A dog was barking behind it. The door opened.

A short stocky Hispanic with a pockmarked face stood before me sporting army fatigues. Rin-Tin-Tin didn't quite come up to his waist. The dog growled at me. I hoped it wasn't hungry.

"I'm looking for a guy called Ranky," I said.

"He don' live here no more," the super said.

"Moved?"

"Yeah. Last week."

"Where to?" I asked.

"He don' say, mister."

I eyed the guy. I might be able to bribe him. Then again, I might not. And for all I knew he was actually telling the truth. Every once in a while someone did.

I said, "Keller sent me."

The super nodded. "Why don' you say so?"

"I just did."

"Yeah. Don' go away."

He left me. The dog and I looked at each other. He came over and stuck out his head. I patted it. The super came back with a notebook.

"He stayin' with a guy called Vinnie over on 101st and Park." He gave me the address.

"Why'd he leave?" I asked.

"He don' have the rent."

"Kick him out?"

"I do what t' landlord say. Ranky, he waitin' for some cash from your frien' Keller, but nothin' comes."

"Yeah," I said. "I'll take care of that."

The super thought that was a good idea and said so. We said good-bye. I went back onto the street, walked over to First, and caught a bus.

I walked the few blocks to Madison Avenue and took the elevator up to my office. Aside from the new coat of dust on my desk, the place looked the same. I had been away so often I almost felt like an interloper. The real James Shaw was bound to show up and kick me out. I hoped he was in better shape than I was. The guy had a lot of problems to solve. I got a .38 automatic out of the safe, along with my ID card. They went into my pocket. I gave Neely's yellow sheet of paper some attention but made no breakthroughs. I toyed with Keller's bag of dough. It didn't make me feel rich, just guilty. When I called Harry a half hour later he was home. I told him I'd be right over. Harry thought he could hold out that long, but no longer.

"Jesus," I said.

Harry nodded. "Disheartening, isn't it?"

Books and clothing were strewn pell-mell on the floor. The place looked like a low-grade junk shop.

"You could've been neater," I pointed out.

216

"Why? This is permanent? What was she doing with all this, opening a bookstore?"

"Made her feel at home, probably. The old girl was a scholar, lived in Brooklyn. Gave it all up to join our profession. We shouldn't begrudge her a little thing like books."

"I can begrudge her anything I want," Harry said. "Coffee?"

I peeled off my jacket, hung it on the back of a chair. "Uh-uh. What happened with Motor Vehicles?"

"The guy who owns the car isn't Ned Brady. It's a Joe Blakey. Resides in lower Manhattan. A neighbor, almost. Know him?"

"Not by name. What'd you get?"

Harry pulled a piece of paper out of his pocket. "Age, forty-six. Height, five foot nine. Weight, one seventy-two. Eyes, brown. Has a half dozen tickets for speeding. Never confined to a mental institution. Never did time."

I shrugged. "Could've been any of the three creeps in the car."

"Let's get this stuff off my floor, Jim."

"Yeah, let's."

The next hour was spent leafing through books, hunting under dust jackets and in the lining of ladies' dresses. Only some of the volumes were in English. Mostly history, social sciences, anthropology. A few dozen were memoirs. The rest were in Yiddish, German, or Russian. I had some coffee around four. Schubert lieder came over the radio, followed by a Haydn symphony and a Borodin quartet. That made the work pleasanter, if not quite a treat. By five, we had gone through the whole pile and come up with a few items: a yellowing clipping from some Yiddish newspaper, a page torn from a Yiddish magazine, two scraps of paper, and a sheet with writing on it. In Yiddish. All of it had been stuck in books.

"Well?" Harry asked.

"Darned if I know. Gotta call our resident expert. Sheila change her mind, want any of this back?"

"Nope."

"Smart lady."

"It's an eyesore."

"We could donate it to a library. They'd be grateful."

"We could do lots of things," Harry said, "most of them easier than that. Like chucking this crap out."

"Maybe they're classics, unattainable elsewhere."

"You are demented."

"How about we let Danny take a look?"

"He'll eat me out of house and home."

"Not the stuff in your fridge, he won't. Guy's got principles, which is more than can be said for some of us."

"Three days, that's all he gets. If he doesn't show in three days, out they go."

"You are a benefactor of culture," I said.

"I'm a sucker," Harry said.

The books went into Harry's storage room, the clothing, into black trash bags and down to the basement next to the garbage cans. Harry and I grabbed a bite, a couple of corned beef sandwiches on rye, a mug of beer.

"What next?" he said.

"We take a ride."

"Now?"

"Soon. After dark."

CHAPTER 37

HALF THE BUILDINGS ON THE BLOCK WERE RAZED, THE REST looked like war casualties. The sidewalk was cracked, the street pitted. Garbage overflowed from battered trash cans. Some urban critics had smashed all but two of the streetlamps, but the ruins were still too visible. A couple of kids walked by lugging box radios almost as big as themselves. Grating noise blared over the dead street. If these kids didn't get a hernia first, they'd probably go deaf. Punishment to fit the crime. They vanished into the night.

I entered the building.

Here the blackout was total, but that failed to improve matters. The hallway stank of sweat, urine, mold and decay, as if some rotting carcass were buried in the walls. I took a pencil flash out of my pocket and started up the stairs. I heard a TV behind a couple of doors: civilization, such as it was, even here. Voices came through the wall on the third landing. Nothing else indicated this hole was inhabited by anything but roaches and rats.

I rested a second when I hit the top landing, then used my knuckles on 6C. I waited. I was getting set to try again, without much hope of a response, when the door opened suddenly.

He was about five nine, but round shoulders and a stoop made him look shorter. His brown shirt was stained. He hadn't shaved for a few days and smelled of whiskey. The guy could have been forty or sixty. He stood blinking at me as though I might be a mere side effect of his last drink. In my racket you get to meet all the right people.

"Ranky," I said.

"Yeah?"

I put my palm against his chest, shoved. He staggered back into the flat. I followed, kicking the door shut behind me.

"Hey—"

"Shuddup," I told him.

I was in a large, almost bare room. The walls had once been off white; they were grayish now, and peeling. The ceiling had so many cracks it looked like a road map. The floor was bare weathered wood. A sagging couch was propped up against one wall, a long chipped mirror against another. There were no shades on the windows. Pale light on my left came from a naked bulb in a floor lamp. This dump made my place on Ninety-fourth Street seem like Versailles.

"Whazzis?" Ranky demanded.

"You're through," I growled, "finished."

Ranky opened his mouth. No words came out.

"They're gonna toss you in the can," I yelled, "and throw away the key."

"Why?"

I said one word: "Keller!" I made it sound like bubonic plague, something contagious that Ranky had already caught.

"Na. Listen—"

"You listen." I stretched out an arm, pointed a finger at him, the finger of guilt. "You were teamed up with Keller. The pair of you worked together."

Ranky's jaw dropped; it was news to him. He started to shake his head.

"Keller's on the lam," I shouted. "He knocked off a guy in his flat and ducked out. He left you holding the bag, Ranky. I'll get a medal for turning you in."

"You got me wrong," Ranky howled. "I dunno nothin' about no killin'. Who said I ever—"

A door on the left came open. I didn't hear it open—Ranky was making too much racket—but a flash of movement in the long mirror caught my eye.

A man stood in the doorway, tall, thin, with a long nose and jaw. He was in pants, undershirt, and bare feet. He looked as if he'd been napping.

He wasn't anymore.

I knew this guy. He and his pal had knocked off Silbert and managed to give me a king-size headache into the bargain.

It was a toss-up which of us was more surprised. For an instant, the whole room seemed frozen in time, as if some cosmic clock had malfunctioned. Then the guy moved.

A sweep of his arm sent the lamp flying. The bulb shattered as it hit the floor.

I spun left, doubled over—my chin almost scraping the floor—pulled at the gun in my pocket, and made for the doorway, all in one motion.

Two shots came from the door.

I dived down, rolling sideways and managing to put two slugs somewhere in the vicinity of my target; then I gathered myself up on hands and knees and charged again.

I sailed through the door like a cannonball and would probably have gone right through the wall and into orbit if I hadn't collided with the guy's back. He seemed to be bound for a window across the room. We went down together in a tangle of arms and legs.

I used my head, driving the top of it against his chin. That got us unglued. I heard him scramble to his feet, saw him outlined against the window. The window was closed. That didn't stop Tall-and-Skinny. He went through it, glass and all.

I went after him.

He was only a few rungs down when I vaulted over the sill and landed on the fire escape. Errol Flynn to a T.

The guy didn't hesitate. His gun swung up at me. His face

looked wild and distorted in the half light. Reason would be wasted here.

My leg was already raised. I brought my foot down in his face.

He tottered, groped for the railing, and missed. He went tumbling over the side. The arm I stretched out was three feet too short. He screamed all the way down.

I stood on the swaying platform, dumbfounded, peering into the darkness below, unable to see a thing. I got back through the window without noticing how I did so.

The place was empty.

I managed to get down the stairs. Harry's car was on the street where we had left it. Harry wasn't in it. I found the key in the glove compartment. I got in and drove away.

CHAPTER 38

I WENT HOME TO MY PENTHOUSE. WILD HORSES COULDN'T HAVE dragged me back to Ninety-fourth Street. I ran a hot bath, put the phone next to the bathtub, and climbed in. Beethoven's String Quartet in A minor was on the turntable. The piece is full of abrupt changes and hidden meanings that still give the experts a run for their money. It's murder to play, too. But every once in a while some group catches fire and little windows pop open, giving you the barest glimpse of eternity. Right now, the big picture was what I needed.

I augmented Beethoven and the steaming water by thinking of Daphne, what her voice was like, how her hair curled, the curve of her neck, and how her eyes, which were green, sparkled when she laughed. Prospective lady-friend therapy.

After a while I stopped seeing the skinny long-nosed guy taking his plunge off the fire escape. It made a difference. I found I could breathe freely again without feeling that a chain was wound around my chest. And even, more or less, get my mind to focus.

Of course, I'd never have seen the guy at all if I'd sensibly hung on to any of my dozen ill-chosen jobs during the last decade. Except then *I* might have been the one taking the dive. Out of boredom. And Silbert would still be dead.

Some ten minutes later the phone rang. I stuck a hand out of the tub, picked up the receiver.

"You're alive," Harry's voice said.

"I think so."

"You okay, Jim?"

"Taking a bath and giving old Beethoven the ear. I must be."

"Don't go away. I'm coming over."

"When's that?"

"About half an hour."

"Good. By then maybe my hands will have stopped shaking."

The bell chimed.

I opened the door and Harry breezed in. I hung his jacket in the closet, threw an arm around his shoulders, and we went into the living room, where I handed him a drink. It wasn't carrot juice. I was halfway through my second whiskey sour.

"This'll make things seem better," I said, "even if they're not."

"A likely story," Harry said.

Bach was on the tape deck by now. I lowered the volume and stretched out on the sofa. I had on a dark blue robe over lightweight slacks and a black T-shirt. I'd gotten into my slippers. If I relaxed much more they'd have to scrape me off the floor with a razor blade. Could euphoria be far off? You bet.

Harry was in the easy chair. "You had me worried, Jim."

"I had *me* worried."

"What," Harry asked, "were those shots?"

"That was Tall-and-Skinny, the creep I tangled with in Silbert's flat. He came back for a second try."

"Incredible," Harry said. "I didn't even see him go into the building."

"Yeah, that's because he was already there," I said. "Guy's name is Vinnie. He's Ranky's new roommate. Or was. You hear the window break and the nice scream?"

"What scream?"

"Vinnie's. When he flew off the back fire escape."

Harry looked at me. I told him about it.

"How do you feel?" Harry asked when I was done.

"Lousy," I said. "This Vinnie wasn't even gunning for me, just trying to get away. He doesn't do us any good dead, either."

"You in the clear?"

"Think so. No one saw the fracas," I said. "Ranky can place me at the scene, provided he was sober enough to know what I look like, which is highly doubtful. Somehow I don't see him getting too chummy with the cops, in any case."

"I didn't hear a thing after the shots," Harry said.

"The living room faces an alley, and Vinnie's bedroom faces a vacant lot out back."

"Just as well," Harry said. "It would only have distracted me from the task at hand. I might have turned back to save you and blown the game."

"How did you do?"

"Aside from agonizing about your wellbeing, which aged me ten years?"

"Yeah."

"Not bad. I was camped where you had left me, in the safety and comfort of the car, awaiting developments."

"Nice cushy spot."

"Not for long. What I expected was that you would scare the bejesus out of Ranky and rejoin me. Then said subject appeared on the street going lickety-split. Dead drunk, it seemed, but still making good time. You were nowhere in sight. Perhaps if Ranky had been waving a gun around I would have gone hunting for you."

"Thanks."

"But he wasn't. And I couldn't believe you would let him get the drop on you. So I went after him, on foot. Riding behind him in those empty streets at five miles an hour might have proven too conspicuous even for our befuddled friend. As it was, he kept looking over his shoulder."

"Guilty conscience."

"I was on the other side of the street, a block away and in the shadows. My one fear was that a taxi might materialize, but there weren't any."

"The gods were feeling generous," I said.

"From what you had told me, Ranky probably couldn't afford the fare."

"Didn't have a pot to piss in."

"We went south out of the Hundreds and into the Nineties. For a wild moment I thought he was about to visit someone in your row of tenements, but he kept going. By now the streets had more people in them, so I was able to get closer. When we reached the Eighties I was almost at his elbow. He headed east on Eighty-ninth Street. I dropped back a bit. He turned on York Avenue. I ran for it and rounded the corner just in time to see him go right into Lenny's Diner."

"Place must have a magnetic attraction," I said. "Keller liked to eat there too. Used to chat with one of the waitresses."

"It was a man this time," Harry said. "The counter guy went into the kitchen and got him. Stocky, medium height, mid thirties or early forties, had a short black beard and mustache. No apron. White open-necked shirt. The manager, possibly."

"Or even Lenny himself."

"Sign's old and weathered. Could be Lenny's son, of course, but doubtful. The two huddled, went into the kitchen or office or whatever. That gave me a bad moment. Ranky walks out the back door, I wouldn't even know it. A couple minutes, the pair comes out again, leaves the diner. They do not go far, just one door over. Same building, tenants' quarters. Turn key, climb stairs, light snaps on in second-floor apartment, front. The bearded chap lowers the shades himself. A moment later he's down again and back at work. That's it, the whole story. And what a story it was. I hope it has a happy ending."

"You and me both. Anyone minding the diner?"

"Carl Springer. I caught him at home."

"How are we paying for this?"

"The Hoffman fee."

"Good old Hoffman," I said. "We clear two grand?"

"Twenty-two hundred."

"Thank God," I said. "We'll need more than Springer out on the street."

"Bob Perry? Dick Hanks?"

The pair were part-timers; they hired out cheap. "Sounds good," I said.

"Ready to call it a night?" Harry asked, "or do you have some grand surprise up your sleeve?"

"Not me. I've had it. Everything's tidied up. All we need now is for Ranky to deliver the goods before we go broke."

"And if he doesn't?"

"We sue the creep," I said. "What else?"

CHAPTER 39

I WAS PARKED DOWN THE BLOCK FROM LENNY'S DINER. I wore a gray tweed jacket, cream shirt, and dark gray trousers under my tan trench coat. I had been warming my car seat for a solid five hours. Each hour I put in meant less money for the hired help. I could hear the meter clicking in my mind.

I didn't spot Harry's stocky party with the beard. A night shift guy. The shades were down on Ranky's windows. He hadn't shown either.

I had a thermos of coffee with me. Whiskey sours would have been more like it. Pedestrian traffic ebbed and flowed outside, depending on the hour. I had seen the sky turn from black to gray to misty blue. Diners in Lenny's had changed from working stiffs to the golden-age set as the morning wore on. When my nerves began to jangle from the coffee overdose, I switched to herb tea. I had a tuna sandwich around ten thirty. Bob Perry showed up to relieve me around eleven.

"Harry brief you?" I asked.

Perry said yes. He was a big dark-haired man with a lined face. He wore a plaid shirt, work pants, and a lumber jacket. In a neighborhood like this, he really *was* invisible.

"Parked nearby?" I asked.

"Double-parked, around the corner."

"Okay, get your heap and I'll pull out."

I left him perched in my old spot. He had my condolences. By week's end he'd have some of my money, too. Things balance out.

"Dr. Benish?" I said.

"How are you, my friend?"

"Fine," I said. "Just passing, Doc. Dropped in to say hello."

"I was going to call you this afternoon, Mr. Shaw."

"Any luck?"

"I have your list."

"Fast work," I said.

"It is, of course, incomplete."

"Of course."

"But a start, ah?"

"Every bit helps."

He pushed a manilla envelope across his desk toward me. I picked it up, pulled out nine pages.

"An embarrassment of riches," he said, beaming at me. "It was difficult to know where to draw the line. So many colleagues."

"You're the expert, Doc."

I scanned the pages, which were crammed with names, addresses, phone numbers. None of them meant anything to me. "These should keep me busy for a few years. Any of these special friends?"

"They are *all* special."

"How about extra special, Doc," I said. "Think you can check those?"

Benish stretched out a hand and I returned the nine pages to him.

I sat and stared at the hundreds of Yiddish books on the shelves. I wondered how many of them Dad had read. He and Benish shared the same accent, almost. I wondered if they had anything else in common. I wondered what I shared with Dr. Benish. Danny, probably. Did that make us coconspirators?

"It is done," he said.

I thanked him, put the sheets back into their envelope, folded it over a couple of times and slipped it into a coat pocket.

"Anyone here," I said, "able to shed some light on our little mystery?"

"No."

"Too bad."

"Let me assure you, Mr. Shaw, it was not for lack of effort. I can recite half a dozen projects which Mrs. Silbert held dear to her heart. They ranged from literary to historical studies. One provided money for young scholars in Yiddish literature."

"Doesn't sound promising."

"I thought not. Everyone I questioned here recited these same projects. Aside from this, they were of no help whatsoever. They were, I might say, as puzzled as I."

"And me, and Danny."

"Daniel is helping you in this affair?"

"Yeah, I've appointed him my chief assistant. Only he doesn't know it yet. The pay's nothing, but he gets to work with his kid brother. He finds that thrilling. Look, maybe you should jot down these projects for me. I mean the names of the projects. You can never tell."

Benish shrugged, said, "Gladly," and I got another piece of paper to add to my collection.

"If any of this pans out," I said, "it'll prove the higher powers speak Yiddish."

Benish smiled. "They do."

We said our so longs and I went away from there.

CHAPTER 40

DANNY WAS PARKED IN HIS BARBER'S CHAIR LOOKING DOWN AT me. I was sunk in his sofa, a better deal by far. I took another chocolate chip cookie from a large plate on the coffee table. No sugar. No milk products. No chocolate. No taste, either. You can't expect everything. It was, however, free. That made it irresistible.

"I've got something to show you," I said, reaching into a pocket and pulling out my goodies. "The envelope's from Dr. Benish."

"You saw him?"

"Yeah. Twice. The last time a couple of hours ago. He says hello. Guy thinks the world of you."

"The feeling is mutual."

"Uh-huh. I had him draw up a list of Silbert's buddies and projects. The other stuff, in Yiddish, we found in the old girl's books."

He stretched out a long arm and I passed him the material.

I sat and surveyed Danny's domain. I wasn't especially intimidated by the number of books. I was a fast reader myself, and if I put my mind to it I could probably get through a third of them in a lifetime. In the last years I'd need a Seeing Eye dog to finish for me, but I'd get the job done. It was the sitting I couldn't stand. If I had to sit long enough to read most of this stuff, I'd become mummified, as immobile as a plaster dummy. And that left the books in the other room.

It took Danny about eight minutes to scan the whole works. He looked up.

"The two scraps of paper, James," he said, "are recipes."

"Recipes?"

"Are you interested in baking a peach pie, or a chocolate fudge cake with whipped cream?"

"Not at the moment."

"The clipping from the paper is about Nazi war criminals."

"Keller's too young. Although the criminal part fits. What does it say?"

"The writer favors catching them."

"That's nice."

"He cites a number of Nazis still on the loose. However, some have since been caught. Klaus Barbie is in a Paris prison. Ivan the Terrible, an especially sadistic Treblinka guard, is on trial in Israel. Mengele is dead. The Yiddish press always prints articles of this sort, Jimmy. The readers expect it. This one appeared sometime after 1967."

"Yeah?"

"The piece says Franz Stangl's in jail. He was caught in sixty-seven."

"Smart."

"It was published in the *Forvertz*, Dad's favorite Yiddish daily, now a weekly. I know this, James, because of the byline, Shmuel Hersh. He has been a *Forvertz* writer for thirty years."

"Impressive."

"The magazine piece, also by Hersh, is from *Di Goldene Keyt*, a very prestigious quarterly journal. It concerns *Die Yunge*, the Young Ones, a group of Yiddish writers formed in 1907; they helped refine poetry and prose. All dead now of old age."

"You're only young once. What about the handwritten sheet?"

"That may be interesting."

"Thank God."

"These appear to be notes."

"As in Beethoven?"

"As in field notes. I think this is the raw material that went into the report you showed me."

"What makes it interesting?"

"Hersh. He's mentioned."

"The same Hersh?"

"I think so."

"What does she say?"

"'Ask Hersh about the son.'"

"Very enlightening."

"This, Jimmy, is obviously a note to herself."

"Yeah. Hersh a common name?"

"Not as common as Cohen, Levine, or Schwartz, but common enough. It can be a first name, too."

"Great. So why's this the same guy?"

"Because Shmuel Hersh is on Dr. Benish's list. The *Forvertz* is given as address."

"That," I said, "is more like it. Know anything else about him?"

"Only what I've told you."

"I thought you knew this stuff hands down."

"The average age of the *Forvertz* reader, Jimmy, is in the mid seventies."

"Hang in there," I said. "You'll make it yet."

"I expect to, easily. But the *Forvertz* won't. Mostly I read Isaac Bashevis Singer and skim the rest. I'm not what you would call a devoted fan."

"We need a fan."

"We have one," Danny said. "Right in the family."

"Uncle Max?"

"Who else?"

"We're going to pester Uncle Max in his retirement?"

"He'll be delighted, James. Max reads the *Forvertz* from

end to end. He grew up with some of these writers. His first office was a block away from the old *Forvertz* building on East Broadway. He's not just a walking encyclopedia of Yiddish culture, he's a piece of living history."

"That's our Uncle Max you're talking about?"

"Of course, he has other interests, too."

"Yeah, a couple at least."

"He doesn't flaunt his knowledge, Jimmy. He just has it. It's part of his heritage."

"If you say so, Danny."

"I do. He is the *ideal* man for this job."

"Call him, okay?"

"Definitely."

I asked, "What about the other names on that list?"

"I know some of them personally, the academics. A few others are familiar, too, the ones from the Jewish organizations. The rest are strangers."

"Let's put them on hold," I said.

"Hersh first?"

"Hersh first. Anything I should know about Silbert's projects?"

Danny glanced down at the piece of paper. "All worthwhile, Jimmy, either from an academic or humanitarian standpoint. But I can't even begin to imagine how scholarships for budding scholars or 'Trends in Yiddish Literature Between the Two World Wars' can have anything to do with this sordid case of yours."

"Neither can I." I stood up. "Call Harry at the office. He's got some Yiddish books for you."

"Silbert's?"

"Yeah. And thanks, Danny."

"Any time. Going to see Hersh?"

"Later. First I go see a dead body."

"Is that meant to be a joke, Jimmy?"

"Some joke," I said. "Give my love to Max." I took another cookie and left.

CHAPTER 41

THE SUN WAS OUT, BUT NINETY-FOURTH STREET LOOKED NO better for wear. Worse, if anything. You could see all the cracks in the brick walls. It didn't inspire confidence. I went into my building. Carlos was busy mopping the floor.

"The police, Mr. Gordon. They were here earlier."

"Looking for me?"

"They say you should call."

"Thanks."

My mouse popped out and squeaked at me accusingly when I opened my door. "Hi, pal," I said, "still holding down the fort, eh?"

I got some cheese and bread out of the fridge, filled a small dish with water, and set it all under the sink, out of harm's way. The mouse didn't stand on ceremony, he just plowed right in. What I needed in life was another responsibility. A mouse, yet.

I took off my jacket and dialed the Twenty-fourth Precinct. Sergeant Lacovaly identified himself. I asked for Detective Danker.

"Hang on," Locovaly said.

I hung.

"Danker," a voice said.

"Stuart Gordon," I said.

"How you doing, Mr. Gordon?"

"Holding my own, I think."

"Up to taking a ride?"

"Sure," I said. "What is it this time, a free tour of Riker's Island?"

"Nothing's free in this world, Mr. Gordon. Haven't you heard?"

"Yeah, I guess I have."

"Got a body for you," Danker said.

"For me? Another one?"

"Uh-huh."

"What've I done to deserve all this?"

"Been in the wrong place at the wrong time, Mr. Gordon. I'll send a car. Stick around."

"I'll be here," I said.

He used the sirens. The patrol car whisked through traffic as if responding to a major disaster. If the cop at the wheel didn't watch it, the disaster would be us. I was the lone passenger, the reason for all this tumult. It didn't quite make me feel like royalty.

We raced downtown on Second Avenue, turned west on Canal, then south again past the criminal justice complex. The pokey and City Hall were there too. Sometimes they even housed the same suspects.

The cop and I followed the morgue attendant through a grayish corridor. A large elevator carried us down to the basement—"the icehouse"—where they kept the stiffs. Chill air touched us when we stepped out, a foretaste of winter. For the cadavers, laid out on pale green stretchers, six to a tier, the winter would be permanent. We went single file down a narrow aisle. The odors of death and decay tinged with formaldehyde reached out as if welcoming another candidate for the autopsy table. We halted in front of a stretcher. The attendant pulled back the sheet. I looked down at the remains of the tall skinny guy, my victim.

238

"Recognize him?" the cop asked.

"Uh-huh."

"This the man you caught in apartment five C of two forty-two East Ninety-fourth Street?"

I said it was.

The cop nodded. The attendant pulled the sheet back over the body's face. We went back the way we'd come.

"Anything else?" I asked the cop.

"Yeah."

"What?"

"The station house. Detective Danker wants you back there."

The Twenty-fourth Precinct was its usual hectic swirl of activity, as if crime were going out of fashion next Thursday and the blueboys wanted to get their last licks in now. Voices babbled, cops hustled, perps were ushered in and out of offices like some endless dance that led nowhere.

This time I waited for Danker on a bench near the sergeant's desk. I was half tempted to take a stroll and see if I could dig up Neely's office. I wasn't bonkers yet, so I didn't do it. I wondered where Sergeant Lacovaly and his telephone were stashed; I didn't worry about it. Danker appeared in the corridor, waving a hand at me. I rose and joined him.

"Thanks, Mr. Gordon."

"For what?"

"The ID."

"A pleasure."

"Any doubt in your mind?"

"Nope. That's the guy all right."

"Well," Danker said, "I'm glad to hear that. We couldn't be sure. You're our only eyewitness."

"Yeah. Mark it closed. I'd make that bird even in the dark. How'd you get him?"

"On a silver platter. He jumped or was pushed out of a window."

"Avenging angel on the job, eh? This wrap up my end in it?"

"Maybe."

"Why just maybe?"

"Loose ends. Mind visiting with Captain Rogers awhile?" Danker asked.

"Yeah."

"Come on, Mr. Gordon, it wasn't that bad, was it?"

"Bad enough," I said.

"This will be almost painless."

"You and my dentist have the same writers."

I trailed after him into the captain's office and sat down. The place smelled of pipe tobacco. Danker stood leaning against the door.

Rogers was on the phone. He wore a black pin-striped suit. With his graying temples, straight nose, thin lips, and neatly tapered chin he seemed a model of rectitude. A tired one. No simple chore keeping this part of the city in line. Look at all the trouble he was having just with me.

Rogers hung up the phone and turned his gray eyes my way, seeming to gaze right into me. His face assumed an expression of distaste, as though he either saw something there he didn't like or was thinking of sucking a sour lemon.

"Detective Danker tells me you've IDed the other assailant."

"Yeah. They keep turning up dead, and Danker has me check them out. This last one just about exhausts my usefulness, I'd imagine."

"You're quite certain of your identification?"

"I'm positive."

"It was dark when you fought these two."

I nodded.

"See in the dark, Gordon?"

"You punch a man in the face, Captain Rogers, you get a pretty good view. Those guys were all over me; we were jowl

240

to jowl. There was light coming from the window, too. No way I could mistake them. You've got your killers," I said.

"Possibly. We have only your word for that."

"Why would I lie?"

"Why would you visit Sheila Goldberg? How would you even know about her?"

"The super had her number," I said. "My going to see her is no big deal. I wanted to know as much as I could about her aunt. I was trying to find out what if anything she had in common with her killers."

"What did you learn?"

"Nothing."

"Why even bother, Mr. Gordon?" Danker asked.

"Because you two guys think I'm involved in this. And I'm not. As long as you've got me in your sights, you're looking in the wrong direction. If I could come up with something about Silbert, I might be able to get you off my back."

"It ever cross your mind, Gordon, that you were meddling in police business?" Rogers asked.

"What am I supposed to do, sit tight while you guys run roughshod over me?"

"Hardly that, Mr. Gordon," Danker said.

"You got another name for it?" I said. "Anyway, it doesn't matter anymore, does it? It's over."

Rogers said, "Not really, Gordon. Assuming we have the right pair, we still don't know who killed them. Or what part Keller or Silbert played in all this."

"Or what part *I* played. Is that your point?"

"Thought did make the rounds," Danker said, "but you say you're clean?"

"I'm clean."

"Then you have nothing to worry about," Rogers said. "Just leave the police work to us and go about your own affairs. Think you can do that?"

"Sure."

"But will you, Mr. Gordon?" Danker asked.

"Yeah, I will," I said earnestly.

"Very well, Gordon," Rogers said. "I believe we understand each other."

"I can go?"

"No one's stopping you," Danker said.

I rose.

"Don't disappoint us," Rogers said.

"I won't," I promised.

I went.

I'd disappointed my mom, who had wanted me to grow up to be a millionnaire, or at least respectable. I had disappointed more than a dozen bosses. I had run out on a number of ladies who had wanted me to settle down, raise a family, and become an adult. I felt for my two cop pals, but the odds were pretty good that I'd manage to disappoint them, too. Why should they get a break when no one else had?

A taxi took me back to my slum. I grabbed a bite of cold cuts and coffee and called the *Forvertz*. Shmuel Hersh worked out of his home, I was told, and delivered his pieces twice a week to the office. When I said I was with *The New York Times* and hoped to do an article on him, they gave me his home number.

I took a sip of coffee and dialed Hersh. A woman answered.

"Mr. Hersh in?"

"Who is this?"

"Jim Shaw. I'm a friend of Dr. Benish at the Jewish Archives Institute."

"What do you want with my husband?"

"It's about Liuba Silbert. I was told—"

"No! He is very busy. I am sorry."

"This won't take long. I just—"

The phone went *click*. I was left listening to dead air. Jesus.

I dialed Danny at home. No answer. I tried his office at Columbia.

"Dr. Shaw."

"Mr. Shaw, here. How come you got the better title?"

"This will have to be quick, Jimmy, I'm teaching in five minutes."

"Glad I caught you. I just called Hersh. His wife wouldn't let me talk to him."

"Did she have a reason?"

"Said he was busy and hung up."

"Strange."

"She sounded edgy."

"Jimmy, I spoke to Uncle Max."

"How's he doing?"

"Sharp as ever. I told him the whole story," Danny said. "He was quite interested."

"Any insights?"

"Only that Hersh is a fine fellow. He knows him."

"So all I've got to do is get past the wife."

"Want me to try?"

"That's what I had in mind. Speak Yiddish. A taste of the old mother tongue ought to loosen her up. Worse comes to worst, we can have Max call from Florida. They really friends?"

"He said he knew him, personally. That's all. Look," Danny said, "I've got to run."

"I'll call."

"Right."

CHAPTER 42

HARRY WAS ON STAKEOUT DOWN THE BLOCK FROM LENNY'S Diner. Same spot I had sat in that very morning. The place was beginning to seem like a bargain basement extension of the office. I slid into the car.

"Our boy still up there?"

"As of ten minutes ago. He keeps coming to the window. Stick around, you'll get a thrill."

"I've already had the pleasure," I said. "What I'm trying to do now is drive it from my mind. Anything new on your end?"

Harry nodded.

"Something nice?"

"Uh-huh. I had our Wall Street whiz, Sol Bloom, call his friend at Dun and Bradstreet."

"Didn't know Sol had a friend."

"At least one. He rushed through the corporate report on Elrex. I picked it up this morning. Left one copy on your desk, and brought the other."

"Not bad," I said. "If this starts a trend, we may actually get somewhere."

There were only three pages. I read them with care. Elrex imported a number of items, including figs from Turkey and dried fruits from some five other countries. Cheap tools and textiles were listed, along with coffee from Columbia. They pulled down about two million in sales before taxes.

"A going concern," I said.

"Elrex means 'the king.'"

"Wishful thinking," I said.

The firm employed eighteen people. Sixteen names meant nothing to me. Two did. "I think we just struck oil," I said. "Rifeman, the president of Elrex."

"His first name is George. All you had on your list was Rifeman."

"That's all Silbert had in her letter."

"Couldn't be two Rifemans."

"With our luck, sure. But let's ignore the possibility. Notice anyone else?"

"Gloria Saphire."

"Yeah. On the Elrex board. That yarn she told about Keller trying to blackmail her husband was a crock of shit."

"Why'd she bother?"

"Bought her time and gave her a reason for pulling up stakes. She's supposed to be in Florida now. Wanna bet?"

"Look, Jim. No crime in being with Elrex, is there?"

"Not yet."

"Got a plan, huh?"

I nodded.

CHAPTER 43

"THIS IS RIDICULOUS," RALPH SAID.

"This is your big chance," I said, "to do something good for humanity."

"James, for all your considerable virtues—"

"Thank you, Ralph."

"I hardly think of you as a champion of humanity."

"Ralph, I haven't killed anyone in almost twenty-four hours," I said with absolute truth. "Doesn't that prove I'm on the side of the angels?"

"This is no time for levity, James."

"Sorry, Ralph. Look, did anything bad happen when you told the cops Stuart Gordon used to work here? Did you get into trouble? Do you have any regrets?"

"No."

"Okay. This is even easier. All it will take is a couple of phone calls to get the right reference, a quick trip uptown, and a short chat with a businessman. Nothing to it."

"It is not easier."

"Maybe. But it's not hard either."

Ralph Clinton looked at me from across his desk. We were in his Canal Street establishment on the first-floor balcony. Down below on ground level, where the blue-collar boys put in their time, was large, dark and gloomy. The place reminded me of prison. Up on the balcony under bright neon lights were five desks. One for the boss, Clinton, and the rest for his sales staff. The warden's office.

Ralph reached into his desk drawer and took out two pony glasses and a bottle of Dewar's. He filled the glasses, pushed one across to me. We drank.

Clinton was a ruddy-faced, gray-haired guy with narrow lips and brown eyes. His eyebrows were jet black. He was about five ten and still pretty trim. He wore a sleeveless red pullover, white shirt, red and blue striped tie, and gray slacks.

He said, "What I sell is drilling tools, James."

"I know that, Ralph."

"Monkey wrenches, screwdrivers, and hammers are not in my line."

"That's your in. You want to expand."

"I do not want to expand."

"Ah, but you can explore the idea, can't you?"

"There are times, James," Clinton said, "when I am quite gratified that you are not my son-in-law."

"A joint effort?" George Rifeman said.

"Why not?" I said.

"Roy Hartman thought it was worth looking into," Clinton said.

"Yes," Rifeman said, "we are one of Roy's suppliers. But couldn't this wait?"

I said, "Why put off for tomorrow what you can do today? We have a fine sales staff just raring to go." I wondered what I was talking about. Maybe someone smart could tell me.

Rifeman looked smart. But he didn't seem to know either. That made three of us.

Elrex's president was a tall slender man with a dark, even suntan that made him seem more playboy or sportsman than importer. He wore a well-tailored navy blue three-piece suit and blue tie. His hair was a mixture of blond and brown with touches of gray. It was combed back over a high, narrow, slightly lined forehead. He had high cheekbones, a longish nose with a bump on it, and a cleft chin. He looked to be in his late forties but could have been older. Here was the kind of guy you often see in vermouth ads, decked out in a white dinner jacket, with a Matisse hanging on the wall and a knockout dame on his arm. It was probably an honor to meet him.

His office was something else again. The walls were a grayish off white. A desk, green filing cabinet, and two windows that looked out over rooftops and chimneys were all the amenities in evidence. Not very classy. Except for Rifeman himself.

"This must be a mistake," Rifeman said.

"Hardly," Clinton said.

"We are a wholesale outfit," Rifeman said.

"I understand that," Clinton said.

"And you," Rifeman said, "if I am given to understand correctly, are *also* a wholesale outfit."

"Yes," Clinton admitted.

"Well . . . ?" Rifeman seemed genuinely puzzled, as if he had been asked to play ring-around-the-rosy with us or to jump rope.

"We're thinking of going retail," I said brightly.

"I see," Rifeman said.

"Open a few storefronts," I said, "see what happens."

"That is still on the drawing board, of course," Clinton said.

I glanced sideways at Ralph. A thin coat of perspiration covered his brow.

"Well," Rifeman said, "you might also call us competitors."

"Colleagues," I said.

"There is no reason," Clinton said, "why we cannot do business together."

"Certainly," Rifeman said. "Once you become operational."

"I was hoping," Clinton said, "that we might get some figures from you now."

"Now?"

"Only a few," Clinton said, "to give us an idea of what our costs might be. . . ."

I got out of my chair, stretched, put my hands in my pockets, and ambled over to the window. I stood there looking out, as though chimneys and rooftops when seen from Elrex were a splendid sight. Ralph and Rifeman were reflected in the glass. They were still yakking away. By humming a bit of Schubert under my breath I was able to drown them out. Rifeman glanced over at me once, then lost interest. His eyes seemed a bit glazed. Ralph can have that effect.

I took my right hand out of my pocket. The spike mike was in my palm. I put my hand on the sill, slipped the mike in the crack between window and sill. A couple of card tricks would have made a nice follow-up, but I wasn't sure my audience would appreciate it.

I turned, went back to the desk.

"Mr. Rifeman," I said.

Rifeman barely looked up. By now he knew whatever I had to say was worthless. I didn't disappoint him.

"You got a men's room here?" I asked.

"Out. Make a right, then a left. Second door."

"Thanks. Back in a jiffy, Ralph."

I got out of there before Clinton could denounce me for the traitor I was. Walking by a number of partitioned cubbyholes, I found the men's room. It was empty. The sending equipment for my mike was about the size of a deck of cards. The question was where to hide it. Behind the radiator was too hot. The air vent up near the ceiling would have been perfect if I'd remembered to bring my ladder with me. I settled on a more reasonable, if not more secure, hideaway and taped the device to the underside of one of the sinks. No-frills bugging. Someone creeping around on hands and knees might notice—a drunk or washerwoman, maybe. Judging by the way the place smelled, I was at least safe from the latter.

I strolled back slowly, giving the joint as much scrutiny as I could without peering into people's desks. I also looked at faces. If this crew were part of a crime syndicate, they were doing a good job of not advertising it.

I went up a short corridor. More desks and faces. I saw Clinton waiting on the far side of the room; he seemed fit to be tied. I saw someone else too, and slowed down to a crawl. I was so surprised I almost dropped my teeth. I had only glimpsed the back of the guy's head on my trip to the john. The view now was better.

He was stocky. He had black eyebrows and a full head of graying hair. His nose was blunt, his chin firm. He was talking on the phone, the receiver in his right hand; his left was on the desk, a large pinky ring prominently displayed. I could have been wrong about the face, but the ring made it more certain. This was the guy who had broken into Neely's home. Jesus!

I stretched my neck, caught his extension number—15— and kept going. My legs felt weak, as if I'd just climbed out of a sickbed and was taking my first steps.

"James!" Clinton said. His face was red. If the top of his skull had had an opening, steam would be pouring through it.

"Watch the blood pressure, Ralph."

"I have never been—"

"Shh." I steered him by the elbow toward the door.

We took the elevator down in silence. Clinton spoke when we were out on the street. "I do believe that was the most humiliating experience of my life."

"Don't exaggerate, Ralph."

We headed for Clinton's car, two blocks around the corner.

"We made fools of ourselves, James."

"Come on, Ralph, we did great."

"Great?"

"Don't yell, Ralph. That was a very distinguished performance."

"How can you say that?"

"Because we weren't trying to make a good impression."

"We made a terrible one!"

"Sure. But who cares?"

"This will give me nightmares, James, for weeks to come."

"No it won't. Look, were we trying to start a new business back there?"

"Of course not."

"We were trying to get information, right?"

"Yes."

"Well, I got it. In spades, Ralph. You don't know how much you've helped."

"I find that hard to believe."

"Listen, there's a guy sitting at one of those desks who may be the key to all this. And he just fell into my lap. Because of you, Ralph. I could never have gotten in there without you."

"You actually accomplished something?"

"Brother, did I! Ralph, you're an angel. Gimme a week or so to wrap this up and we'll get together for dinner. I'll tell you the whole story; you'll love it."

"Well, James, I am gratified if I did help. It was, however, a dreadful experience."

"That's the detective game, all right," I said cheerfully.

"James."

"Yes, Ralph."

"You would have been better served by marrying Jessie and entering the business with me."

"That's what Jessie wanted," I said, "a husband with a steady job."

"What could be more steady than working for your father-in-law?"

"A stint on a chain gang?"

"You always were too cynical for your own good, James."

We had reached Clinton's car. I retrieved my bag, we shook hands, and he drove away.

I found a pay phone, dialed.

"Elrex," a voice said.

"Extension fifteen, please."

"Hello." A man's voice.

"George?"

"You've got the wrong extension."

"Who is this?"

"Lynch."

"Sorry. I'll try again."

I hung up. Lynch. I fished the Dun & Bradstreet report out of a pocket. Tony Lynch was listed as a vice president. Good old Tony!

I hurried back to the building. The last thing I wanted was to run into Rifeman on the street or in the lobby. I didn't have to use a lock-pick on the door leading to the basement: it was unlocked. I got the tape recorder out of its bag, tested it, heard nothing, left it hidden in the back of a broom closet, and beat it for home.

I put Mendelssohn's Third String Quartet on the turntable, made myself a whiskey sour, and got out of my respectable duds and into a better outfit: midnight blue corduroy slacks, a heavy blue chamois shirt, a narrow black leather belt, thick white socks, and my running shoes. When you feel the enemy gaining on you, it's nice to have your running shoes handy. I put a .38 automatic into the pocket of my lined denim jacket, taking a quick look-see out my window at the warm light gushing from hundreds of other windows. My pals.

I dialed Harry at home. He picked up on the second ring.

"It's me."

"Hi, kid."

"Things are buzzing," I said.

"Here, too."

"Any dinner left in your fridge?" I asked.

"I'm having it sent up. Probably bean curd and yogurt delight."

"A Danny special."
"Yep. And he's bringing it."
"Jeez. Save some for me."
"Have no fear. You can eat mine."
"Coward," I said.

CHAPTER 44

"Not bad," Harry said.

"Vegetarian meat loaf," Danny told him.

"What's in it?" Harry asked.

"You don't want to know," I said.

"It can't be something disgusting," Harry said, "like lizard's guts or reptile snout. So what's to worry?"

"The general public," Danny said, "has quite a few prejudices about healthful eating. More salad, Jimmy?"

"Yeah, thanks."

"If you mean me," Harry said, "I'm just a bundle of prejudices. If I enumerated them all, you would probably never speak to me again."

"I may never speak to you again, anyway," I said. "On general principles."

"Didn't know you had any," Harry said.

"I don't. Danny loaned me some."

"Only monumental ignorance," Danny said, "can account for the public's dietary habits. That, or an unconscious urge to self-destruction."

"Monumental ignorance is my middle name," Harry said.

"I thought it was general public," I said.

"First and last name," Harry said.

"What's for dessert?" I asked.

"In that bowl," Danny said.

I removed the cover. "Fruit cocktail, eh?"

"Homemade," Danny said. "Organically grown."

"But will I like it?" Harry asked.

"I think so," Danny said, "if your taste buds haven't been corrupted beyond repair."

"Put some bug spray on it," I told Harry, "it'll taste more natural to you."

"A veritable eruption of mirth," Danny said. "When you two gentlemen are confined to nursing homes in a few decades—"

"Few weeks, most likely," I said.

"—I will certainly visit you both, provided I can take time off from my teaching duties. I called Mrs. Hersh this afternoon."

"Speak Yiddish?"

"Of course."

"She roll over and wag her tail?"

"She hung up."

"So much for child psychology," Harry said, clearing the dishes.

"You sure that was Yiddish, and not Greek or Latin?" I said. "Sometimes you scholars mix things up."

"She sounded extremely upset," Danny said.

"Didn't say why, I suppose?"

"No. I called Uncle Max."

"What did *he* say?"

"That he would call her."

"At least he didn't hang up on you," Harry said, pouring water into our cups. "Two folks do that, it must be your personality."

We broke out the banana cake and dunked our herbal tea bags. Danny said, "I looked through the books here."

"Any classics?"

"Not really."

"Dump 'em out?"

"I'll take them to the Archives," Danny said. "You never know."

"Make it soon," Harry said. "I'm not used to so much culture under my roof."

"A day or two. Some books had underlined passages, Jimmy."

"About what?"

"Nazis."

"Like Hersh's piece in the *Forvertz*?" I said.

"More or less."

"What's this about?" Harry asked.

"Nazi war criminals. Silbert had an interest in them," I said. "She lost a husband in the death camps."

"Mean anything?"

"Probably not."

"Okay," Harry said. "I've got some news too. Want to know about Ned Brady?"

"It's one of my life's ambitions," I said.

"He's not with the Immigration and Naturalization Service. But he used to be. I called their Washington office," Harry said, "and asked for him. The direct approach. They told me he wasn't there anymore; he'd quit."

"Find out when?"

"About two months ago. I asked if he'd left a forwarding address. They said sure and gave it to me. Guess what? It's the same as Joe Blakey's on White Street. About a mile and a half from here."

"Blakey," I told Danny, "was maybe one of the guys with Brady. It was his car."

"What I did," Harry said, "was call Tom Parker and put him on it."

"Jeez," I said.

"Have a better idea?" Harry said.

"No. Parker runs a two-bit private eye agency on Eighth Avenue," I told Danny, "two blocks from our old stand. A lot of stringers work for him at bargain wages. Even so, it's gonna add up to money. At this rate we'll be supporting half the dicks in town."

"I can help," Danny said.

"Thanks. I may take you up on that," I said. "Anything on Ranky?" I asked Harry.

"No movement."

"Yeah. Well, I dropped into Elrex this afternoon, chatted with Rifeman and bugged the joint. Remember the guy I caught in Neely's house? He works there. Name's Tony Lynch. Got a phone book handy?"

Harry brought the book. There was one Tony Lynch in Manhattan and three T. Lynches. Harry called, on the off chance that my voice might be recognized, while I listened in on the bedroom extension. One T. Lynch wasn't home. The rest were women. Tony Lynch was the wrong Tony Lynch.

Information gave us the Queens and Brooklyn Lynches. Danny, who did not find the nuts and bolts end of the detective racket very engaging, went home. Harry dialed numbers. I lay on the bed and digested my meal, gazing at the ceiling. The fourth T. Lynch in Queens said he didn't want a subscription to *The New York Times*. Harry, being a polite guy, thanked him anyway and hung up.

"That's our boy," I called.

I rejoined Harry in the other room.

"Something must be wrong," he said. "This is getting too easy."

"Just looks that way," I said. "Better call Parker and give him Lynch, too. At least someone in this racket'll be turning a buck."

"Then what?"

"Then," I said, "we go for a ride, see if we can get Ranky off his ass. He's got to know *something*, right? Or they wouldn't be keeping him on ice. So maybe something will give. Right? Don't answer that."

CHAPTER 45

THE AIR WAS CHILL. NIGHT HUNG OVER YORK AVENUE LIKE A
patchwork quilt, lights both neon and plain carving pieces out
of the darkness. I crossed the street at mid-block. Traffic was
sparse. A foghorn sounded off the East River. The edge of the
world was probably just around the corner.

I went into Lenny's Diner.

There were two customers at the counter, both middle-
aged men. The booths were empty. No gold rush here. I
could see why Lenny might look elsewhere for a living.

The guy behind the counter was a big burly lug in a dirty
white apron. The odor of coffee drifted through the air like
haze. I leaned over the counter.

"Whazzit gonna be?" he asked.

My hand left my pocket; the imitation leather folder was in
it. I flipped it open, giving him a squint at the honorary
sheriff's badge inside. The badge wasn't really mine; it
belonged to Max, but I'd inherited it along with the office.
Back in the thirties the badge and five cents could get you on
the subway.

"I'm looking for a guy," I said. "Maybe you seen him."

"Yeah? Who?"

"Name's Ranky."

"Dunno."

I gave him a description. "That any better?"

"Uh-uh."

"The boss here?"

"Yeah."

The counterman went through a curtained doorway into the kitchen, returning with the short, heavyset, bearded guy Harry had described. He wore a gray sports shirt with the sleeves rolled up. He stepped around the counter.

"What's this about, Officer?"

"You manage this place?"

"Yes sir, at night."

"Ever bump into this guy?" I described Ranky again.

"No, sir."

"He's been seen around here," I said.

"What's he done?"

"Bad things," I said.

"I can't help you."

"His name's Ranky."

He shrugged.

"The rest of this building," I said, "upstairs. Who owns it?"

"Con-Nest Real Estate."

"Here in Yorkville?"

He nodded.

"We'll wanta look up there," I said. "Guy's been spotted in the neighborhood. Back in the morning, pal." I left them, went across the street, got into my car, and drove away.

I huddled in the alley and regretted not taking a blanket with me. That and a campfire might have kept me warm. I had a fine view of my favorite sights: trash cans, back windows, and fire escapes. My Walkman, now that I needed it most, was back at Seventy-seventh Street. I hummed a Bach ditty and tried on Tchaikovsky's Violin Concerto for size as Heifetz played it. I did the snappy three-minute version, using vocal chords for violin strings. It left something to be desired. No moon cast light on my mission, which was beginning to look like a dud. Every few seconds I glanced up to see if Ranky was lamming out the back way. No dice. A merry hour had slid by in this manner and I was seriously considering getting a steady, no-nonsense job as a clerk-typist—maybe for Rifeman, now that I'd made a good impression—when Harry's voice came over the walkie-talkie. "Snap to, kid, our lad just waltzed out the front door. He's got two guys with him."

Ranky's car headed south, then turned west on Eighty-sixth. Harry and I took turns behind it. Otherwise we rode on parallel side streets. Going through Central Park, I was ahead of Ranky and Harry was doing the tailgating.

They went down Seventy-ninth Street. I streamed by on Seventy-seventh, going west, past my building. None of my neighbors were out to cheer me on, but just seeing the place made me feel like a certified hero—a notion so demented that I was ready to sign up for a lobotomy.

"If they're driving to California," Harry said through the walkie-talkie, "I quit."

"You ain't the only one."

We hit Broadway.

"South on Broadway," Harry said.

I slowed. In a moment, Ranky's car pulled even with me on my left. He was in the back seat with a big guy I didn't know. The driver was another stranger.

I fell behind. Harry passed me, grinning. He nodded once, then passed Ranky.

They turned west on Seventy-second Street. I stepped on the gas, and whisked by the Embassy theater, just making the light. Ranky's taillights up ahead blinked at me like the eyes of some giant rodent.

"West on Seventy-second," I said.

"Turning on Seventieth," Harry said. "Is there a future in this?"

"Not in this world," I said.

Ranky's car turned left on West End Avenue. "Coming at

you on West End," I said. I put on some speed, made the turn. The car was gone.

"West on Seventieth," Harry said.

"Jeez," I said, "they're heading for the old Conrail terminal."

"Or the docks," Harry said presently. "Kill your lights. There's no one here but us and them."

I hit Seventieth, turned, left the last traffic light behind. Asphalt became earth under my wheels. I could barely see Harry's car in front of me. It had merged with the night. Two red dots up ahead glittered out of the darkness. The West Side Highway rumbled overhead, blocking out the sky.

Ranky's taillights went dark.

I almost crashed into Harry's rear fender.

I was out of the car in an eyeblink, running; Harry, a couple yards away, had the same idea. The earth underfoot was moist, slippery, absorbing all sound. Darkness poured over us like a black wave. I had a flash in one hand, a gun in the other.

I heard a scream. My flash snapped on.

In the distance, three figures struggled by a parked car. They swayed back and forth, locked in a loveless embrace, as if dancing to unheard music.

"Police!" I bawled. "Hold it!"

Harry raised his gun, fired a shot into the air.

Two figures detached themselves from a third, fallen one. They didn't take cover or shoot back. The pair dived for their car as though convinced that the Hudson was flooding over to drown them. Harry sent another bullet skyward.

The car's engine caught, wheels skidded; it roared off south into the darkness. Hired hands, no doubt. Buy cheap, get cheap.

We slowed to a walk.

"No one," I said, "wants to kill a guy with the cops looking on, do they?"

"Uh-uh," Harry agreed.

"So let's see if they killed him," I said.

"They was gonna choke me!" Ranky wheezed, "choke me t'death!"

"Uh-huh," I said. "And toss you in the drink."

"Yeah," Ranky wailed, "an toss me inna drink."

Harry shook his head. "Some friends you have," he said.

I said, "Can you walk?"

"Yeah."

"This way," I said. "And brush that mud off you."

Harry drove. I sat in back with our passenger. We were on the Henry Hudson Parkway, heading north. City lights winked at us on the right. The Hudson and New Jersey beyond flanked us on the left. Very snug. But not quite a joyride.

"Thisa bust?" Ranky asked.

"No," I said.

"You guys cops?"

"Uh-uh."

"Who are ya?"

"Take a close look."

Ranky peered at my face. No recognition showed in his bleary eyes. "I dunno," he said.

"Right," I said. "And that's how it's gonna stay."

"Whaddaya want?"

"Know a guy called Keller?"

"Keller?"

"Yeah."

"I know him."

"Okay," I said. "You tell us about Keller. You tell us about the guys at Lenny's. You give us the straight goods, we give you a break, put you on a train outta town. Maybe you go on living. You cross us, it's back to Lenny's."

"They'll kill me."

"Yeah," I said.

"I ain't got no dough."

"We'll give you some."

Ranky stared into the darkness. "Sure," he said. "I usta be a baggage handler. That's how come I meets Keller."

"When was this?"

"Four, maybe five years ago."

"Where?"

"At Kennedy."

"What line?"

"Gold Wing. Keller was a cop then. He signed me up."

"For what?"

"Smugglin' coke."

"Just you?"

"Nah. A lotta guys. More'n twenty-five. One guy'd steer him to t'other."

"Just baggage handlers?"

"Cargo too."

"Keller work alone?"

"Him an' this other cop."

"Who?"

"Somethin' like Leech."

"Lynch?"

"Yeah, Lynch."

"Tony Lynch?"

"Yeah, Tony Lynch."

"He there often?"

"Uh-uh. A couple times t'first year."

"Then what?"

"Nothin'."

The coke comes from where?"

"Colombia. Guys in Colombia packs t'coke in marked suitcases, puts 'em inna cargo holds of planes flyin' here. Keller has this guy, Willie, in Gold Wing's control room at Kennedy."

"Willie coordinate ground operations?"

"Yeah. He picks t'crews."

"And the planes carrying coke," I said, "get only Keller's boys?"

"Yeah. We takes t'baggage outta t'holds. Only we leaves t'marked stuff. Them planes is goin' on t'other cities. Still got passengers an' baggage in 'em, see? So after t'inspectors clears 'em, t'plane is moved ta load more passengers. No one nosin' around then, so we picks up t'stuff."

"Then what?"

"We lugs it over ta where Keller's guys is waitin'. They drive it away."

"That's it?"

"Yeah. But I gets canned causa drinkin'. An' Keller gets hisself kicked off'n t'cops. He does somethin' else inna outfit now. I dunno what."

"He kept you on, though?"

"Yeah."

"What's Lenny's?"

"That's where t'stuff goes."

"The restaurant?"

"Upstairs. They gotta couple rooms."

"Which ones?"

"First an' second floor, front. Guy in Lenny's runs it."

"Guy with a beard?"

"Yeah. Him an' Dottie an' Al. They all in it."

"What did you do for Keller?"

"Run errands."

"Like what?"

"See what's goin' down on t'street."

"You in contact with the pushers?"

"Nah. Just keep an eye open sometimes. I gets coffee for t'guys too."

"When were you doing all this?"

"Alla time. Upta last year."

"What happened last year?"

"I gets sick. Keller, he takes care of me."

"Gave you money?"

"Yeah. Then he stopped."

"When?"

"Month ago."

"Why?"

"Dunno."

"What did you do?"

"Holed up with Vinnie."

"Vinnie?"

"Cargo handler. He got canned too."

"How many coke shipments came through the pipeline each year?"

"Five, six."

"When was the last one?"

"Couple months ago."

"When's the next one?"

"Thursday."

"Day after tomorrow?"

"Yeah."

"How do you know?"

"Vinnie."

"He told you?"

"Heard him talkin' on t'phone."

"Which flight?"

"Dunno."

"Who picks up the stuff?"

"Dunno."

"It still end up at Lenny's?"

"Yeah."

We turned back to the city. Ranky knew none of the higher-ups in the outfit and had never heard of Elrex. I asked for names and got some, mostly first names and nicknames. I asked more questions and got more "dunnos." I used my credit card on Broadway and Seventy-third Street at the Apple Bank cash machine, drew out two hundred dollars, gave it to Ranky. Good-bye, sweet dough.

"You're a dead man if you stay in the city," I told him.

"Yeah."

"Go to Penn Station," I said. "Get on the first train outta town."

"This ain't much."

"It's all I can give you," I said.

Ranky went down into the IRT subway. Harry drove me back to my car under the West Side Highway.

"That guy," I said, "used to teach philosophy at City College. Worked on the meaning of life. Found there wasn't any. Now look at him."

"We let him go."

"Why not?"

"He's a witness."

"Some witness. I can just see him on the stand. With a little luck, he might even remember seeing me before."

"He gave us enough," Harry said.

"Yeah. If it pans out."

"What are we going to do?"

"Run with it."

CHAPTER 46

I OPENED MY EYES. THE BLANKET WAS UP OVER MY HEAD. THE
steam was going full blast and I was covered with perspiration. My blue and white pajamas stuck to me as if hoping to
become a part of my body. Chimes were sounding. My door-
bell.

I rolled out of bed. Eight thirty. I staggered out of my
bedroom, through the living room, and over to the door. I
wasn't really in my penthouse but still back in my dream in
midsummer. If the steam had been any hotter, summer would
probably have turned into an oven, with me as the prime
dish. I fumbled for the lock, turned the knob, opened the
door. I was so woozy, I neglected to look through the
peephole. Nothing like giving the opposition a clean swipe at
me. Shaw, generous to the last.

The man standing in my hallway was no hit man. He was
lean, short, about five foot four and in his mid seventies. His
face was oval. A fringe of white hair sprouted on the back of
his head. He had brown eyes, protruding cheekbones, a
pointy chin, and a white, slightly waxed mustache twisted up
at the ends. Underneath his fur-collared tweed topcoat he
wore a three-piece gray pin-striped suit. A two-cornered
white hanky stuck out of his breast pocket. A red silk tie with
yellow polka dots was decorated with a gold tie pin. His black
shoes were polished to a high gloss. Jade cuff links winked on

French cuffs. A white silk scarf was tossed loosely around his neck. He held a pair of black leather gloves and a gray hat in his left hand. The cane and spats that would have been de rigueur with the outfit at the turn of the century were mercifully nowhere in sight.

"Uncle Max!" I said.

"In the flesh," he beamed at me.

Uncle Max, I saw, still had all his own teeth. Too bad genes couldn't be inherited through in-laws.

We embraced. I led him into the living room, where I took his coat, hat, gloves, and scarf and put them in the closet. "Max," I said.

"Yes, Jimmy?"

"What the hell are you doing here?"

"Come to help," he said, "with Hersh. What did you expect?"

"That you'd do the smart thing and keep sunning yourself in Florida."

"Bah! Wrinkles the skin."

I shook my head. "Max, don't be silly."

"At my age, who cares? Also, I miss New York. And you and Danny. And it's time I saw some of my old friends again."

"Max, you've got plenty of friends in Florida."

"New friends. It's not the same, Jimmy. And some of them are older than the old friends. A man drys up if he is only surrounded by old codgers. It's not good."

"You're a faker, Uncle Max. You love Florida," I said. "How did you get in the building?"

"Picked the downstairs lock."

"Jesus, Max. You could've rung the bell."

"Should keep in practice. So what's for breakfast, Jimmy?"

"More coffee, Max?"

"Thank you. Bach, eh?"

"Toccata and Fugue. Loud enough?"

"Yes. Who is playing?"

"Glenn Gould."

"Dead at fifty. If I had died at fifty, Jimmy, I would have died an ignorant man. At twenty, you think you know it all. At fifty, you begin to understand you know nothing."

"And now?"

"I am learning."

"At ninety, you'll be a genius."

"Knock wood," Max said. "Your parents, you know, met in Carnegie Hall, Jimmy. Music runs in the family."

"I know."

"Your father was a great music lover. He played bridge with Heifetz."

"How was Heifetz?"

"Better at the violin. Once your father bought me a record, Heifetz playing Beethoven, an old seventy-eight. We were having guests to the house and someone put it on the radiator."

"Melted, eh?"

"Your father was inconsolable."

"Good old Pop. He buy you another?"

"With what? Those were hard times."

"These ain't no picnic either, Uncle Max, for some of us."

"Not like then. Your father, Jimmy, could have been a rich man. He had the brains."

"The racetrack owners," I said, "got the money."

"No. Even with the horses, he did well. He won."

"Could've fooled me."

"He lost too."

"That I know about."

"Before he married, your father had no problems."

"Lucky guy."

"He worked as a fancy-leather-goods cutter; was active in the union, too."

"Nothing like an honest dollar."

"And spent plenty of time with the ladies."

"I know the story, Max."

"He'd hop a rattler, go from one end of the country to the other, stopping to play cards, play the horses. He carried his shears with him, so if he ran out of money, he could always get a job. That's how your father lived, Jimmy."

"I know, Max."

"The point I am making is that your father was a happy man. You think, Jimmy, he cared about winning?"

"He could take it or leave it, eh?"

"Of course, he wanted to win."

"You had me worried."

"But he loved the game."

"The game."

"That's what counted. So if each day he was happy, why should he worry his head about business? Why should he put away for a rainy day? I said to him often, 'Morris, a man isn't young forever; a man grows old.'"

"You were right there; he wasn't young forever."

"'Morris,' I said, 'what will happen later?'"

"So what happened?"

"He met your mother and got married."

"Those are the breaks."

"No more carefree life, Jimmy, no more cross-country trips."

"He's got my sympathy, Max."

"Your father married late. He was well past forty, and times were already changing. The fancy-leather-goods business wasn't so good anymore. But it was too late for him to go into another trade. So when your father needed money because of the family, it wasn't there."

"But he still went to the track, Max."

"By then he was fixed in his ways."

"By then we were all fixed."

"Why am I telling you this, Jimmy?"

"Why Max?"

"Because I worry about you."

"I worry about me too."

"Make good, Jimmy. Build the agency that I gave you. Now, when you are still young."

"I'm not so young."

"Young enough."

"You're the boss, Max."

Max sighed. "I am also worried about Hersh."

"That why you're here?"

"Something, Jimmy, is wrong."

"Yeah. Even I noticed."

"Danny told me something about this case you have."

"I think it has me," I said. "By the throat."

"Can you give me the details?"

"Sure," I said, "let's go into the living room, shall we?"

We went.

CHAPTER 47

KING'S HIGHWAY IN BROOKLYN IS NO HIGHWAY, AND NO KING ever lived there. It's a wide enough street, though, with a nice mix of private and apartment houses. The neighborhood is mostly Jewish, middle class, but a good deal of ethnic diversity is less than a half mile away. And probably creeping up, as things often do.

I parked my car in front of Hersh's red brick apartment house. Hersh lived on the ground floor. Max rang his bell.

We waited.

"Yes?" Mrs. Hersh.

"It's Max Gabinsky," Max said into the intercom.

Silence. Then, "Go away!"

I grinned at him. "Gotta lot of pull, I see."

"Bah! She's deaf as a stone. Come on."

We left the alcove. Max didn't go very far. He marched over to the first window on the left and wrapped his knuckles against the pane.

"Nothing's happening," I said.

"They're both deaf. Wait."

Max kept using his knuckles. Maybe two minutes went by. Finally the green curtains parted an inch. An eye peered out at us.

Max tipped his hat and smiled.

The curtains parted all the way. A small elderly white-haired woman in a yellow print dress was framed in the window. She seemed astonished.

"You always get that reaction?" I asked.

"Only when they are over seventy," Max said.

The four of us sat in the living room, trying to balance teacups in our laps. The furniture, which was vintage World War II, was dusty. The tan rug, worn in spots, gave off a sweetish-sour odor, which mingled with the odor of old, slightly mildewed books. The bookcase contained a motley collection of Yiddish volumes, classics, and best sellers of bygone years. A framed map of Israel hung on the wall, along with portrait-size photographs of Shalom Aleichem and I. L. Peretz. The pair of Yiddish writers both looked attentive, as if waiting to be filled in on the latest gossip since their demise. Even the TV, an ancient Magnavox, appeared to have been lifted from another world, one where Milton Berle and Sid Caesar still owned the airwaves.

The man who sat facing us wore thick glasses and was almost bald except for a few long strands of white hair combed over his dome. His head was round. He had a double chin, full lips, and a large nose. He was short and overweight and looked as if his major exercise was shuffling from one easy chair to the next. Too bad Danny wasn't here to give him a pep talk. He wore a light green sleeveless sweater over a white shirt. His voice was hoarse, and he puffed for breath as if mentally doing calisthenics while chatting with us.

"You have heard, young man, of the Jewish Emergency Rescue Committee?" Hersh asked.

"He knows," Max said.

"Let him answer for himself," Hersh said.

"Helped Jews escape Europe," I said, "during the war."

Hersh nodded sternly. I had passed the test. I wondered if he was handing out prizes, too.

"We were not very successful," Hersh said. "Do you know that during the war there were more captured German soldiers brought to this country than Jews?"

"Hersh, please," Max said. "No lectures."

"He should know," Hersh said.

"He knows, he knows," Max said.

"The excuse," Hersh said, looking me in the eye as if I were somehow responsible, "was that there were not enough ships to transport the Jews. You hear? Not enough! But for the German war prisoners, they had!"

"Shmuel," Mrs. Hersh said, "stop already." To us, she said, "He thinks wherever he is, there should be a stage."

Hersh sighed. "Liuba Silbert and I were both members of the committee. This was from 'forty-four on. When Poland, in 1939, was occupied by the Germans from one side and the Russians from the other, Liuba was attending an historian's conference in Switzerland. She, of course, never went back. Alex, her husband, perished in Poland, and she, with great hardship, made her way to America. This took more than a whole year to accomplish."

"Silbert, they let in," Max said.

"Liuba Silbert had academic credentials of the highest order," Hersh said. "But even her it was not easy to bring over. The Jewish community had to work miracles."

"Went to bat for her, eh?" I said.

"What didn't we do?" Hersh said. "Anyway, in 'forty-five we were together on the rescue committee. And it was then I first heard of this Rifeman."

"He must have been a kid," I said.

"Nineteen."

"Makes him sixty-five now," I said.

Hersh nodded.

"Guy looks younger," I said.

"He has led an easy life," Hersh said.

"How?" Max asked.

"Born rich," Hersh said. "His parents, they died when he was only sixteen."

"Both?" Max asked.

"In a car crash," Hersh said. "This was in Franco's Spain."

I asked, "What were they doing in Spain?"

Hersh shrugged. "There they had a villa. Also in Italy, in the early thirties."

"They were right-wingers, Hersh?" Max asked.

"Sure. Here in America they made a fortune in the textile business. Lost everything in the crash. Made again a fortune. Always they supported right-wingers. To Father Coughlin, the so-called 'Fighting Priest,' the Rifemans gave thousands."

"Coughlin was anti-Roosevelt and anti-Semitic," Max said to me. "Had a radio program that was heard from coast to coast, and a magazine called *Social Justice*. Pro-Hitler, pro-Mussolini, pro-Franco. A real sweetheart. They got him finally off the air in 1940."

"Their son, the Rifemans' left three million," Hersh said.

"Not bad," I said.

"In the U.S. Army," Hersh said, "he never served."

"How'd he get off?" I asked.

"A bad ear, a bad eye, a bad foot; never was it made clear," Hersh said. "The war, he spent in Spain. At the time this was not known. Only after."

"This kid," I said, "just hung out alone in Spain while the world blew its top?"

"Not alone," Hersh said. "He had a friend, a man fifteen years older. A friend, really, of the parents. His name was Eric Kunst."

"A German?" Max said.

"With the German embassy," Hersh said. "Then a colonel, later a lieutenant general."

I asked, "How close were they?"

"Very."

"Rifeman worked for the Nazis?" I asked.

"This," Hersh said, "would have been a crime."

"So's draft-dodging," I pointed out.

"Never were charges by our government brought against him," Hersh said.

Max said, "You have never heard of a payoff?"

"Gabinsky," Hersh said, "what could he do for the Germans in Spain? There they had better helpers. Kunst was maybe like a father to him and no more. It was later they became partners."

"Partners," I said.

"Yes," Hersh said. "Both men, after the war, disappeared. For Rifeman, no one was looking. With Kunst, though, it was a different story. After Spain he was in Poland. There he became a general. I don't have to tell you, young man, what atrocities occurred in Poland. Because of our work with the committee, Liuba and I became aware of Kunst, and then, later, as we looked deeper, of his friend Rifeman. The committee did not outlive the war, but others took its place, and Liuba and I were active on one or the other. That is how, through the years, we kept hearing of Kunst."

"And Rifeman?"

"No," Hersh said, "about him, we knew nothing more until three months ago. He was not important to us anyway. What was he? A man who knew a war criminal over forty years ago. Even his name we almost did not remember. Then, on the six o'clock news Liuba saw him. His office, which was then on lower Madison Avenue, was firebombed."

"She recognized him," I said, "after all these years?"

"No. It was his name which struck her," Hersh said. "She went the next day to the Archives. There we have a file on Nazi war criminals. And there she looked again at the photographs that show Kunst and Rifeman together. It was, of course, the same man."

"This proves something?" Max asked.

"Wait," Hersh said. "Over the years there were reports that Kunst was in this or that country. All in South America. This we have in the files. And now we knew where Rifeman was and what his business was. So we were able to trace his activities all the way back to the mid sixties."

"That's when he surfaced?" I asked.

"Yes. Before that, nothing. And always after, when he is importing it is from a South American country where Kunst is said to be."

I asked, "Anyone try to nab Kunst?"

"Of course. West Germany, Israel, and Poland all want him," Hersh said. "But he was protected."

"By whom?" I asked.

"The host countries," Max said.

Hersh nodded. "Argentina, Cuba, Nicaragua, Chile. All at one time right-wing dictatorships. And they had living there whole Nazi communities. No one could touch them. Some were even part of the government."

"Comes the revolution," Max said, "they run for their lives. To next door. When Batista in Cuba fell, there was Samoza in Nicaragua."

"Very accommodating," I said.

"Birds of a feather," Max said.

"Any hard evidence," I asked, "that Kunst and Rifeman were partners?"

"In Argentina, in the late sixties," Hersh said, "Kunst lived openly. He was chairman of a business. Dried fruits, they exported."

"Rifeman was the U.S. importer, I bet."

"Yes."

"Not a crime, though."

"No. But it showed they were still together. Also, in Venezuela he had a company in 1971. And with Rifeman he again did business."

"Okay," I said, "they were partners."

"Yes," Hersh said. "Always for a man such as Kunst, there are reports of sightings. But if they are in a country which shields Nazis, what can be done? Also, many turn out to be false. From Colombia for five years now reports have come out that Kunst was seen. Or someone who looked like him. He did not use the name Kunst, but Beckman. And also Müller. And maybe two or three other names."

I asked, "Sure they're all the same guy?"

"No. This Beckman fits the description; his age is correct, and he is in the right business," Hersh said. "But even with him we could not be sure. Not until we found Rifeman.

Beckman is a coffee broker, and it is from a company of which he is an owner that Rifeman imports all his coffee."

I put my empty teacup down on the floor. "Coke comes from Colombia too," I said.

"Yes, young man," Hersh said. "This is absolutely true. Many fugitive Nazis who settled in South America took at once to the drug trade."

"Kunst too?" Max asked.

"Of course. Always there have been such reports about Kunst. This is really how he made his money."

"And Rifeman?" I asked.

"His partner," Hersh said. "Where else is a better market? And who else but a rich businessman who no one would think was a gangster? Now listen. Two years ago, there started reports that this Beckman was coming also here to America. On visits. Where and when we did not know, but once we found out about Rifeman, we had an idea."

"Uh-huh," I said, "and you decided to give Rifeman some attention."

"I myself," Hersh said, "watched his office. My friends too; I asked for help. We followed him from place to place."

I said, "Hoping to bump into Kunst."

"Yes."

"Did you?"

"No."

"Hersh," Max said, "on me you didn't call?"

Hersh shrugged, "You were in Florida."

"Florida is not Siberia," Max said. "This is my kind of business, not yours."

I said, "You put Silbert on Horace Keller."

"That, you know about?" Hersh seemed amazed.

"It is also *his* business," Max said.

Hersh said, "He did not look right. This man who visits Rifeman, I said to myself, is with the underworld."

"Guy used to be a cop," I said.

"Hersh always had a sharp eye," Max said.

"He got it right anyway," I said.

"Liuba moved in where she could watch this man," Hersh said. "Also my friends helped her."

"She wrote you reports," I said. "Why? Afraid to use the phone?"

"Reports? You are also a mind reader? We wanted a written record," Hersh said. "In case."

"In case something happened?"

He nodded, sighing. "About me, they also found out. Of this, I am sure."

"That's why you wouldn't speak to me?" I asked.

"I was afraid," Hersh said. "Every time the phone rings, I cannot breathe."

"Hersh," Max said, "they know where to find you, and yet you *sit* here, waiting?"

"Maybe not where to find me," Hersh said. "Maybe not exactly who I am, but only that I exist. Who knows?"

"Tell me about it," I said.

"What's to tell? When Liuba died, may she rest in peace, I had still not received her weekly report. And in it there might have been some reason why this happened to her. You understand? So I had my nephew, Yossie, go to her place and try to find it. But they caught him. And also me, almost. Thank God he ran away and was able to warn me. Down the block they chased us. If I had, God forbid, tripped, or the car had not started, they could have killed me and Yossie like they did Liuba. Since then, young man, I do not sleep nights."

"Yeah," I said. "We'll need to know everything you found out about Rifeman, down to the last detail. Now. Think you can handle that, Mr. Hersh?"

He nodded. "How is it, young man, you know about Liuba and Keller?"

"Because I was keeping tabs on Keller myself, Mr. Hersh. I was the guy that jumped your nephew and chased you to the car. Rifeman still doesn't know about you. Just me and Max. And both of us are lambs. You've been safe all along, Mr. Hersh; you just didn't know it."

CHAPTER 48

I CALLED TOM PARKER FROM A PAY PHONE.

"Parker," a tired voice said.

"Jim Shaw, Tom."

"How ya doin', Jim?"

"Okay," I said. "Speak to Harry?"

"Yeah, he briefed me last night. At home. In the middle of *Hill Street Blues*. I hate to be bothered in the middle of *Hill Street Blues*, Jim."

"Tom."

"Yeah, Jim?"

"I'm calling from a pay phone."

"Sure," Parker said. "I put my guys on it right away."

"Any results?"

"Overnight?" Parker asked.

"Nothing, eh?"

"I didn't say that, Jim."

"That's nice," I said. "Why do I put up with you, Tom?"

"Because I'm cheap, Jim."

"You're the K Mart of gumshoes, Tom."

"Yeah, the K Mart. And I get the job done."

"Did you get *this* job done?"

"In a manner of speaking."

"Tom."

"Yes, Jim?"

"Why not just come out and say it, whatever it is you want to say?"

"Just because a guy's got the answers at his fingertips doesn't mean he shouldn't get paid for a full job."

"That's your problem?"

"You said I should tell you."

"We pay for a full job when a job's full," I said.

"I'm glad to hear that, Jim."

"There's also a bonus," I said, "for *fast* work."

"You don't say?"

"That goes for fast phone calls, too," I said.

"Hey, great," Parker said. "Listen, I got—oh shit. Hang on. I got a call."

"Tom—"

"I'm puttin' you on hold."

"*Tom—*"

I was left sitting, clutching a dead phone. Sighing, I reached into my pocket for more change. I had a feeling I'd need it. I sat back in the booth, which, if nothing else, beat standing on a cold street corner. I was in an old-fashioned drugstore, a real throwback. The lunch counter served malted milks and ice cream sodas, a sign said. Prescriptions were handled in back next to a large yellowing anatomical poster. The aisles were roomy and the stands were made of wood. There was a lot of polished brown wood showing all over the place and the scent of lavender drifted through the air. The joint had character, even if, like the old guy in the white jacket dispensing drugs or the dame behind the counter, the character was a bit on the seedy side. Seedy, but real.

A mechanical voice in my ear asked for twenty-five cents. I dropped a coin into the slot, was rewarded by a chime and Tom's voice.

"Jim?"

"Back from vacation, eh?"

"Sorry. Business."

"Yeah," I said, "let's get on with ours, shall we?"

"Sure. Tony Lynch."

"Your boys find something?"

"Not really."

"So?"

"Tony Lynch, if it's the same guy, made the papers about three, four years ago. I got it in my files."

"That's Tony Lynch, the cop, we're talking about?"

"Yeah."

"Can't be more than one."

"Right."

"What did he do?"

"Let some drug dealers walk away. A snitch spilled the beans. Lots of trouble. You don't remember?"

"I don't remember what I ate for breakfast yesterday," I said. "He do time?"

"Uh-uh. Didn't have enough on him."

"Bounced from the force?"

"Quit. He coulda stayed, maybe. The PBA came down on his side and his captain backed him. But he quit. Things like that screw up your chances for promotion. Everything you do gets looked at. It's a pain."

"Who's the captain?"

"Rogers. Paul Rogers."

"Uh-huh. Anything on our phony Feds Brady and Blakey?"

"Yeah. They ain't at White Street no more."

I asked, "Where are they?"

"That I dunno, Jim. I sent Sid Hellman there this morning. According to the super, the pair vacated the premises yesterday. Around noon. They didn't say where they were goin'."

"Sid check out the apartment?"

"Yeah. The super let him look around. Clean as a whistle, Jim."

"How long they living there?"

"Blakey, about a year. His pal moved in six weeks ago."

"Any visitors?"

"The super didn't notice. You want Sid should ask the neighbors, Jim?"

"Skip it, Tom. Let's wrap it up."

"Okay, Jim. You satisfied?"

"Yeah. A check'll be in the mail tomorrow. I appreciate the speed, Tom."

"Any time, Jim."

I put the extra change back in my pocket, went back to the car, climbed in.

Max said, "Well?"

I gave him Parker's news.

"Why," Max asked, "didn't you call in comfort from Hersh's?"

"Phone might be bugged."

"You really think so?"

"Who knows? Guy like that playing sleuth, hanging around Rifeman for weeks, could've been spotted easy."

"You told him he was safe."

"Yeah. But just because I told him doesn't make it so, Max. You ought to know that."

CHAPTER 49

WE GOT TO WITHIN TWO BLOCKS OF LENNY'S DINER. A
milling crowd of spectators made further progress impossible.
A thick cloud of black smoke curled skyward in the distance,
sending gray tentacles probing in all directions. I heard
sirens, honking horns, yelling voices.

"Where is this diner of yours?" Max asked.

I nodded toward the tumult. "In there."

"So," Max said.

"Yeah."

I backed up, made a right turn, double-parked on a side
street. Max and I trotted back to the fireworks.

"Look official," I told Max.

I dug Max's honorary sheriff's badge out of a pocket and
flashed it at the first cop barring our way. He let us through.

"You have joined the force in your spare time?" Max said.

"What spare time?" I showed him the buzzer. "Familiar?"

"Brings back memories," Max said.

"How'd you get it?"

"By voting Democratic," Max said, "early and often."

"Bad joke," I said.

"Bad business," Max said.

The sheriff's badge got us within a half block of the diner.
That's about as far as we wanted to go. Any closer would have
meant a hotfoot.

Lenny's was no more.

Flames reached through the door and the shattered plate glass window as if trying to escape the doomed building. Smoke poured from first- and second-story windows. Fire engines had taken over the street, their bright red paint jobs making them first cousins to the flames inside. Black-rubber-garbed firemen trained long hoses on the blaze, scurried up and down the pavement. Cinders filled the air. A wave of heat beat against me, as if enraged by my presence. We were starting to attract attention. Max and I moved back into the crowd. I scanned faces, seeing no one I knew. Beyond the fire engines a block away a second crowd, twin to this one, had gathered. In the front of it a man was waving both arms around, as if trying to take flight. I raised my own arm and waved back at Harry. He pointed right. Right was a side street. Max and I began working our way back through the crowd.

I said, "You remember my uncle Max, our honored founder."

"Mr. Gabinsky," Harry said, "it's good to see you."

More sirens. The sounds of crowd and firefighters carried over the rooftops. There was smoke here, too, but the block was empty.

Max and Harry shook hands.

"You look in good health," Max said.

"Being poor has its advantages," Harry said. "It keeps you lean."

I said, "So?"

"Place went up like a tinderbox," Harry said.

"The cook light one match too many?" I said. "Diners finally fighting back? Or is this what I think it is?"

"It's what you think it is," Harry said. "They must have used explosives."

"Blow up any customers?"

"No. Planted the stuff out back in the alley. There was a

loud *boom.* One of the cooks and a waitress were hurt; an ambulance carried them off. Everyone else piled out on the street. I took a spin around the block but I didn't catch anyone running away. Parked a couple of blocks over and came back to watch the fun. By then the fire was having a field day. And then you showed up."

"Wouldn't have missed it for the world," I said.

Max said, "The coke will not be coming here tomorrow."

"That's for sure," I said.

"Where, then?" Max said.

"Maybe," I said, "I can find out."

A glance through the glass doors showed a couple of folks waiting for elevators. I loitered outside on the corner of Twenty-fourth and Broadway till the lobby was empty, entered it, and made a beeline for the basement door.

I went down a flight of winding stairs. A couple of dim lights near the ceiling kept me from breaking my neck. I had the place all to myself. When I hit bottom, I went straight to the broom closet. It wasn't to mop up. I retrieved my tape recorder from where I had hidden it on the top shelf under a pile of washrags, removed the cassette, installed a new one, returned the recorder to its shelf, and was done.

I went back up the winding staircase, the cassette safely in my pocket. No Brahms or Mozart would come from it. But I figured I'd enjoy it just the same. My tastes were expanding.

I turned a bend in the staircase.

A half inch of shadow spilled across the floor in front of me. No shadow had been there before. Whatever belonged to it was out of my line of vision.

I took the corner in double-time, bent low.

My head plowed into a stomach. A sap came whistling down on my back instead of my noggin. Wasted effort. No damage.

I used both hands to grab the guy's coat front, then fell back toward the stairs, taking my guest with me. My knees went up to my chest. My shoulders hit the stairs. I straightened my legs and the guy flew over my body. He landed five steps away like a stricken bird, crashing into the wall. Chuck Norris never did better.

I twisted around and dived at the guy, putting a right in his face. A fist came at my jaw. I moved my head and it sailed past. I pounded his chin. A foot lashed out at me, caught me in the ribs.

The guy was half up, clawing at his pants pocket as though he'd developed a terrible itch there. His overcoat got in the way. That coat was my pal.

I drove my right into his face, a Mike Tyson special. He bounced against the wall, blocked my left, and tried to kick me in the groin. I took his shoe on my hip. The guy's hand moved to his pocket again. A one-track mind.

His blackjack was on the stairs, near my knee. Enough was enough. I reached out, scooping it up. By then, the guy's gun was halfway out. I swung the sap against his jaw, giving it plenty of muscle. I had to hit him twice more before he lay still.

I sat on the steps and watched J. Edgar Hoover's lookalike, the big-headed guy with the bulldog jaw from Ned Brady's car, sleep it off.

After a while I tried moving, and found that I could. I plucked the guy's gun from his fingers, went through his pockets, found his wallet. A MasterCard told me this was Joe Blakey, Brady's recent roommate. Blakey was wearing a black wool overcoat. I let him keep that but took his pants, wallet, and gun away with me.

I finished my climb up the stairs, left the building, and tossed Blakey's trousers into a trash can. I found a liquor store one block over, bought a pint of cheap booze, and returned to the building. An elevator had just emptied out. When the coast was clear I went back to Blakey. He hadn't moved. I poured the hooch over him and put the gun into his hand. Blakey snored.

Outside, I used a pay phone to call the cops; I told them a flasher carrying a gun was lying dead drunk in the basement of a downtown office building. I gave them the address and hung up.

If that didn't keep Joe Blakey out of my hair for the next couple of days, nothing would.

CHAPTER 50

LYNCH SAID, "SHIT."

Rifeman sighed, or cleared his throat or something.

Lynch said, "We shoulda hit that fucking Brady when we had the chance."

"And start a blood bath?" Rifeman said.

"Whaddaya think we got now?" Lynch said.

"The diner," Rifeman said, "is no great loss."

"It ain't, huh?"

"Once they got their hands on this derelict—"

"Ranky," Lynch said.

"Yes. Once they got him Lenny's ceased to be of importance," Rifeman said.

"Hey George," Lynch said, "you think that's it? They torch your old office, they blow up the diner, they knock off Vinnie and snatch Ranky. You think it's gonna stop there? You think this Brady's just gonna go away?"

"We will deal with him soon enough," Rifeman said.

"Yeah? And what about the others?" Lynch said. "Everyone's linin' up to get a piece of the action."

"Tony—" Rifeman said.

"Listen," Lynch said. "Elrex is comin' unglued. You gotta face that, George."

"Not now, Tony," Rifeman said.

"Half the town is shakin' us down," Lynch said, "and the other half is tryin' to. We gotta cut our losses, pack it in here."

"And start fresh somewhere else?" Rifeman said.

"Yeah," Lynch said, "while we still can."

"Do you know what that would entail?" Rifeman said.

"Hey, George, you're the expert on that," Lynch said. "Don't sell yourself short."

"I appreciate your vote of confidence," Rifeman said, sounding sarcastic, "but I suggest we table this discussion for the time being."

"It's your party," Lynch said.

"Quite true," Rifeman said.

"So where we takin' the stuff?" Lynch said.

"The Springs," Rifeman said.

"Direct?"

"Why not?"

"It's a long way on the open road," Lynch said.

"We will take all the necessary precautions," Rifeman said.

"I call out the boys?" Lynch said.

"Yes. All of them," Rifeman said. "I want a small army at the airport and a convoy guarding the shipment from then on."

"You got it," Lynch said. "Want 'em hangin' around the Springs too?"

"No," Rifeman said. "I shall arrange matters on that end."

"Okay," Lynch said.

A door opened and closed.

I clicked off the tape recorder and sat back in my office chair. Through my windows I could see a couple of hundred offices across the street. People moved in them under neon lights. Some were, no doubt, sitting pretty. But right now I wouldn't have swapped jobs with any of them.

"That's it," I said, "the nugget of gold. The rest is crap, just Elrex business."

"We'll neeed more than this for a bust," Harry said.

"We'll get more."

"What's the Springs?" Harry asked.

294

"Saratoga Springs," Max said. "Rifeman has a home there."

"Hersh dug that up," I said. "It's part of his Rifeman dossier."

"Hersh have anything hot?" Harry asked.

"Only circumstantial," Max said.

"Yeah," I said, "but it'll tell the cops where to dig."

"We ready for the cops?"

"We will be after tomorrow."

"What happens tomorrow?"

"We make our move."

"We do, huh?"

"Yeah," I said. And gave them the game plan.

CHAPTER 51

SARATOGA SPRINGS HAS A DOOZY OF A RACETRACK, A BOOMING summer arts festival that plays host to the Philadelphia Orchestra and the New York City Ballet, and more mineral water cures than a body can stand. There are ritzy eateries like Mrs. Londen's all along the main drag and up the side streets. The Adelphi Hotel looms over Broadway; the joint is almost one hundred fifty years old and as elegant as a Mendelssohn quartet. There's Skidmore College for coed watching, the Yaddo rose garden for the literary set, and the SPAC swimming pool for serious suntan work. For guys like Danny, there are a couple of well-stocked health food stores. For bookworms—also Danny—a neat public library, with one glass wall, to hide out in. Behind it, for just about anyone, a snazzy park with a couple of duck ponds and plenty of kids to give the ducks hell. There's a farmer's market, too, twice a week, which can't be beat for fruits and vegetables fresh from the ground. Half a dozen sportswear shops display their sale items out on the pavement, if you need an extra T-shirt or pair of shorts. And for the addict, a big fifty cents will buy you the early-bird edition of *The New York Times,* which out in the sticks is almost like getting bulletins from another planet. During June, July, and August, Saratoga Springs is jumping. The rest of the year, it's a ghost town.

Harry and I hit town well after midnight. The buildings

lining both sides of Broadway appeared bleached and weathered in the glow of streetlamps. No pedestrians were in sight and mine was the only car on the loose.

"Everyone head for Florida in the winter?" Harry asked.

"They go into hibernation," I said.

"You know this place?"

"Sure. Pop used to come here for the races when I was a kid; took us all along. Max was a regular too."

"Civil War days," Harry said.

"Yeah, lots of changes. But after Mom let me cross the street by myself, I came here for the concerts."

"You were sixty at the time."

"Seventy. Mom didn't take any chances."

"So where are we going?"

"Good question."

I snapped on the overhead light, took a squint at Max's map.

"Nothing to it," I said. "We go straight, make a left, another left, then a right."

"And then?"

"Ask for divine guidance."

Forty minutes and three wrong turns later brought us to a locked metal gate and high stone wall.

"Home," I said.

We cruised on past the gate and up a dirt road that wound through dense woods.

"You sure?"

"Yeah."

"How come?"

"Used to hike here."

"Way back when?"

"Uh-huh. As a kid."

"Got a good memory, I trust."

"This was the old Rothman estate, Harry, almost a landmark. Between the time the Rothman's son died and the place was sold, they used to give tours here."

"Tell me you went on one."

"I went on one."

"What do you remember?"

"A large painting of Venus and a couple of cupids. I can still see them."

"That won't help much," Harry said.

"No, but Max took the tour too. And that guy never forgets."

We hid the car in a clump of trees a half mile beyond the estate and started back on foot. Both of us had backpacks. I carried a canvas bag too. I was dressed in my Midnight Stalker outfit: blue pants, blue shirt, and lined Lee jacket. A black wool scarf was tied around my neck to ward off pneumonia. Harry had on a dark brown windbreaker, black shirt and slacks, and a peaked cap. We both wore running shoes. It was plenty cold. I shone my flashlight close to the ground. We moved fast. By the time Rifeman's stone wall was back in view, we had both worked up a sweat.

Harry got a rope ladder with a pair of aluminum hooks on its end out of his backpack and tossed it over the wall. The hooks caught.

Harry climbed up first, I followed. Harry used the ladder to climb down on the other side. I unhooked it, chucked it to him, then crawled along the top of the wall like some stupid squirrel while he turned his flash on the ground. When he found what looked like a soft spot, I took the leap.

I sat on the ground wondering if I was dead and watched Harry repack the ladder.

"You okay?" he asked.

"No."

He helped me up.

"Next time," I said, "*you* jump."

"Next time we bring a parachute."

Harry and I trudged on to the mansion. We kept our flashes doused this time and stumbled over rocks and shrubbery and into holes. The wind tried to lift us skyward. The moon ducked behind a cloud, making matters worse. The backpack was starting to cut into my shoulders.

"Let's hope," I said, "the coke doesn't get hijacked along the way."

"Or Rifeman doesn't change his plans."

"Don't even think it."

Besides the main house, there were two smaller buildings for servants and a guesthouse down by the lake. No light came from any of them. The entire estate seemed as devoid of life as a crumpled snapshot.

Harry and I made a circle around the mansion, a strong gust of wind hurrying us along. Everything was locked tight.

"I don't think I like it here," Harry said.

"Shows you're not crazy," I said.

We set to work on the coal chute. It was as out of date as a brontosaurus, a relic of days long gone. Hidden behind a jagged tangle of shrubbery, the chute's twin doors were held together by a large rusty lock that looked as if it predated Prohibition. There were easier ways of getting into the building, but none less obtrusive. If you're breaking into some guy's house, you don't want to make a mess.

It took us some twenty minutes before we got the lock to cooperate. By then I'd decided to leave burglary to the experts.

Harry slid down the chute.

I arranged the lock as artfully as I could on its rusted ring on the off chance that someone might come snooping, closed the small, square doors behind me, and shot down into what had once been the coal bin.

"Welcome," Harry said.

I climbed out of the bin and dusted myself off. "Can't say it's a pleasure to be here," I said.

"Wait till the dancing girls arrive."

"Yeah. Or someone."

Our lights showed that a lot of spiders had been busy on their webs. A mouse scurried for cover. The odors of mold and mildew leaked out of walls and ceiling.

"Dracula used to camp here," I said, "but the place scared him."

"Probably moved upstairs," Harry said.

We found the staircase, went up to the first floor. The smell of mildew went with us. The fancy furniture was covered with dust. The place was stuffy, as if someone had pumped out half the air supply. An empty fridge was in the kitchen; a cabinet over the sink held only a few canned goods and a package of spaghetti.

The closets on the second floor were cleaned out except for an old pair of jeans, a straw hat, and a pile of blankets. The beds were stripped down to frame and mattress.

More of the same greeted us on the third floor. A den contained nothing of interest. A makeshift office down the hall held a desk and filing cabinet whose drawers and shelves were as bare as a Vegas stripper.

"Nothing to steal, even," Harry complained.

"Unless we cart off the furniture," I said.

"Not worth the effort."

Our last stop was the attic. Here we found a lot of summer junk: canvas chairs, and loungers, a grill for cookouts, a folding picnic table, two stacks of wooden folding chairs, and five multicolored lawn umbrellas.

"We can have our picnic here," Harry said.

"If we set fire to the roof," I said, "it'll be warm like summer."

"Warmer."

We spent the next hour setting up and testing an elaborate bugging system. Each room got a mike. If Rifeman and his pals went off to a bedroom or chose the den for a private powwow, their words would not be lost to humanity. A couple of state-of-the-art tape recorders in the attic would pick up each syllable, giving it a permanence usually reserved for Bach or Beethoven.

The attic became our headquarters. If someone got the bright idea to visit our hideout, we could always duck behind the folding chairs. And if they looked there too, we could shoot them. Harry had a .357 long-nosed Magnum that would scare an elephant. I had my .38 automatic. A sawed-off shotgun gave us that extra ounce of protection.

We took turns napping away what remained of the night. No one disturbed our rest. We were both up to watch the sunrise through the attic window; the bleak landscape turned golden for a while, which made it look halfway presentable.

Breakfast came out of our backpacks: orange juice, cold cereal and milk, hot coffee from a thermos, and whole wheat raisin muffins as a treat. The empty cartons went back into the backpacks. Cold water was available from a third-floor bathroom sink. We washed up and settled down to wait. Between noting the ills of the world and swapping malicious gossip about our pals, we wiled away the day by listening to our Walkmans. Classical music for me from a pair of local stations and an assortment of other fare, including news, for Harry. We had roast beef on rye for lunch and some dried fruit in honor of our importer host, Rifeman. Our attic window gave us only a limited view of the estate. We relied on our bugs to keep us informed of developments. There were none. We had an early dinner around four: ham on rye and an apple apiece. We killed a second thermos of coffee and made our last trip to the third-floor bathroom. Then we packed our Walkmans, checked our weapons, replaced the canvas-backed lounging chairs, and sat with our backs against a wall. We didn't talk. I could feel the ham on rye knocking around inside me. My back and shoulders began to tense, as though I'd opted to stand off the New York Giants single-handed in the next ten minutes. Harry fidgeted. Gary Cooper always handled these situations better, but then he had a director and camera crew standing by. We took turns eavesdropping on the empty house through the earphones. Dusk darkened the attic.

Our first visitors arrived at five twenty.

A sharp *click*. I heard something that could have been a window being lifted. I nodded to Harry and he put on a second pair of earphones. An instant of silence, and feet began to make noises on a hard floor—more than one pair.

"The kitchen," I whispered.

The feet stopped moving. Someone coughed. A window slid closed.

Harry said,"Can't be Rifeman; he'd use the front door."

"Must be someone else," I said.

"Brilliant," Harry said.

Feet shuffled out of the kitchen, their tread becoming a whisper as they hit the carpeted hallway.

"Think they left traces at the window?" Harry asked.

"Who cares? It's their baby now."

Another cough. A couple of murmurs. Someone banged something against a wall or piece of furniture.

"The living room," Harry said.

"Okay," a voice said, "we park here. We got maybe another hour and a half, but if they connect good, they could be here a lot sooner."

Movement; a few whispers. Then silence. The guests had settled down.

"Put that out," the same voice growled. "Come on, use your fuckin' brains."

"Cigarette," Harry said.

"The death wish, even here."

"Guy has real leadership potential."

"Guy's Horace Keller," I said.

"No joke."

"Can't mistake that voice," I said. "Not through a mike. Hear it in my dreams."

"Must've been fun meeting him."

"Weird. Like meeting Paul Newman, someone you've only seen from a distance. I almost asked for the guy's autograph."

"Now's your chance, kid."

"Later," I said. "Let's leave something to look forward to."

Nothing much happened for another half hour. There were a couple of whispered conversations, some hints of movement, more coughing. Someone needed a cough drop, probably the smoker. Then the kitchen window made noises again. After a moment a voice said, "Here he is. It's like a damn deep freeze out there."

"Stick around," Keller said.

"Shit," another voice said, a familiar one.

Keller said, "Where you been?"

"Fuckin' car wouldn't start," the voice whined. "Took the wrong road. Almost ran outta gas. Went by the damn gate twice before your man flagged me down. What the hell's wrong with him?"

"Nothin'," Keller said. "I told him to be sure."

"Guy need glasses or what?"

"Forget it," Keller said. "Sit down."

"Don't give me orders!"

"Hey, you wanna run this show? Sit down."

Silence.

Harsh coughing.

Keller's voice: "Kill that cigarette!"

"For chrissakes, you think they're creepin' around out there? You think they have guys watchin' the windows? They're miles away yet. What're we gonna do, sit in the dark and look at each other?"

"Just kill it," Keller said.

Silence.

"Must have killed it," Harry said.

"It was him or it," I said.

"Know him?"

"Yeah. That's our beloved client down there," I told him. "Clyde Neely, biggest drip since they invented the faucet."

"You sound bitter."

"I am."

"What's he doing with them?" Harry asked.

"He *is* them."

"You couldn't find a better client?"

"Takes all kinds," I said.

The darkness grew heavy, seeming to pour through the attic window and fill the room. The cold edged through the walls, but I was starting to sweat.

"With the right schedule," I complained, "we could've spent most of the day relaxing in the city."

"And sent the marines instead of us," Harry said.

"*Now* he thinks of it."

A voice down below said, "Headlights on the driveway."

"Okay," Keller said.

"About fuckin' time," Neely said.

"Keep it down," Keller said.

Silence.

"Shit!" Keller said.

Neely cursed.

"Shuddup," Keller said.

Harry moved to the window, peered out.

"So?" I said.

"The guesthouse," he whispered.

Again we waited.

Keller gave the word: "Let's go."

It didn't take them long. They went.

"At least we weren't the only ones to get it wrong," I said.

"It's a learning experience," Harry said.

We went too.

We crept down the staircase, the Magnum and shotgun planted in our hands. We made no noise on the thick carpet, though we could have made all we wanted. The house was empty.

"Shall we?" Harry asked.

"Yeah, let's."

We used the already open kitchen window to make our exit; everyone else had. Chill air dried the perspiration on my face.

Lights were on in the guesthouse. I saw no movement on the grounds, heard no commotion.

"Maybe they all went home," Harry said.

"Dreamer."

Trees far over to the right stretched down to the lake. We wasted no time reaching them and began our trek. Trunks, branches, roots, tangles of dried bushes tried to stop us. Branches snapped at us as if in anger. Holes opened up under our feet. Trees rose before us to block our way. Shifting twigs sent us sprawling. No light guided our progress. By the time we hit the lakefront, I was ready to give up hiking for good.

"Jesus!" I said.

"Let's go back some other way," Harry said.

We headed left toward the guesthouse, crouching as we ran, giving the opposition as small a target to shoot at as possible. The opposition didn't bother. It was nowhere in sight.

We flattened ourselves against the guesthouse, waiting for our breathing to become normal. A lit window was only a few feet away. We crept to it, huddled underneath. Very carefully, I rose until my eyes were level with the pane; I peered inside.

The room held nine men. Keller and Neely sat on a sofa, Rifeman and Lynch in chairs facing them. The rest of the crew were on their feet, scattered around the room, lounging against the walls. No guns were being waved around. It seemed a very peaceable gathering. Except that the guys by the walls all had at least one hand stuck in their pockets. Mouths were moving, those belonging to the sitters. No words reached me.

I nodded to Harry. We moved back a few steps.

"Gotta get closer," I whispered.

"A window?"

"Too chancy."

"The door," Harry said. "Think they locked it after them?"

"No."

"Neither do I."

Rifeman's car was parked near the back of the house, close to the lake. We tried there first, tiptoeing up the wooden steps and onto the porch. My hand turned the knob, inched open the door. I could hear voices. We moved inside, glided down a darkened hall. The shotgun felt heavy in my hands. My palms were sweaty. The voices grew louder. I could see part of a chair through the living room doorway, but no people. We stopped.

"Come on," Keller was saying.

"No," Rifeman said.

"Hey," Keller said, "you ain't got no choice."

"I am open to reasonable suggestion," Rifeman said.

"Guy's a statesman," I whispered.

"Use your fuckin' head," Keller said, "we got you by the balls."

"Ace thinks he's still a cop," Lynch said.

"Delusions of grandeur," I whispered.

"Shit," Neely said.

"Fifty-fifty is absurd," Rifeman said.

"Not any more," Keller said.

"You can't dictate to us," Neely said. "Fuckin' operation's an open book. We can close you down any time we want."

"And what would that get you?" Rifeman asked.

"The poorhouse?" I whispered.

"On welfare," Harry murmured.

"Listen," Keller said. "There's gonna be a deal. Because if there ain't, we all lose."

"There's enough for everyone," Neely said. "More than enough." He was almost whining.

"The racket's okay, George," Keller said, "but it could be a lot bigger."

"You propose that I expand the organization," Rifeman said, "to make room for you?"

"Yeah," Keller said. "That way you keep what you got and we get ours too. In the end, we'll all be makin' more."

"Guy thinks he's GM," I whispered.

"The more we spread out," Rifeman said, "the more vulnerable we become to exposure."

"I can handle that," Neely said.

"You can't handle shit, Clyde," Lynch said; he laughed.

Rifeman sighed. "There are other considerations, limitations on what we can import."

"Yeah?" Keller said, sounding skeptical.

I waited for more. There was none, as if the entire group had suddenly lost control of their vocal chords.

"Easy does it," a voice finally said.

I gave Harry the shotgun, took out my .38, whispered, "Cover me," got down on hands and knees, and crawled toward the doorway. A few feet gave me all the view I needed.

Ned Brady stood on the staircase above the living room, arms on the bannister. He had an Uzi submachine gun in his hands.

"Nice lab you got upstairs," Brady said in his flat voice. "Bet it makes plenty of crack." There was no expression at all on his round face.

No one moved. They were all on their feet now, hands raised in the air.

Another figure came into view. He was carrying a sten gun. Brady's overweight, gray-haired pal from the car.

"Turn," Brady said. "Face the wall. You, too."

The two pair of bargainers didn't argue. They went to the wall, faced it.

Ned Brady made a short speech to their backs. "I asked for a deal," he told them. "I gave you a chance. You wouldn't deal. Now I'm taking the coke. That's a lesson. Lenny's was a lesson. There'll be more. I know who you are, I know how you work. I know where to find you. I know every step in the pipeline from Colombia to the streets. You'll deal with me, or I'll put you out of business."

It was the last speech he ever made.

Three shots and the sound of breaking glass merged into one. Ned Brady, still clutching his Uzi, pitched over the railing.

I could see a cop outside, standing by the shattered window. He had a gun. A second cop was at the other window. He had a gun too.

Behind me a voice said, "Still minding other people's business, Mr. Gordon?"

I looked over my shoulder. The porch door was open. Three men stood in the hallway. They all had guns. Two were state troopers. The third was Detective Danker.

I stood up.

One of the state troopers said, "Drop your gun."

I dropped it.

"Raise your hands."

I looked at Danker. "I'm afraid so," he said.

I raised them.

Harry and I were marched into the living room.

"You never learn, do you, Mr. Gordon?" Danker said.

The two cops from outside had climbed through the window. The nine men by the wall had begun to turn around. Their hands were still up in the air as if together they were trying to balance a giant saucer over their heads.

Neely looked our way. His jaw dropped open like a drawbridge. His eyes seemed to become round like two Ping-Pong balls.

"Hello Clyde," Danker said. And shot him twice.

Neely slid down the wall slowly, leaving a long red smear behind him. His eyes were still on Danker when he hit the floor.

"Resisting arrest," Danker said sadly. His gun swung around toward me. "You too," he said.

Max Gabinsky leaned over the windowsill, a large automatic in his small hand, and put a bullet in Danker's shoulder. It spun him sideways. Another slug knocked Danker's right leg out from under him. He sat down on the floor.

The nine guys at the wall started to move. They stopped.

Cops were leaping over the sill, coming through the front and back hallways, filling the living room. They carried a small arsenal. Max came with them.

"You all right, Jimmy?"

"Uh-huh."

"Harry?"

"Fine, Mr. Gabinsky." Harry seemed a bit dazed. Him and me both.

A tall, beefy, red-faced man with lots of white hair pushed his way through the crush.

"Captain Williams," Max said, "of the Saratoga Police."

Captain Williams grabbed my hand, pumping it up and down as if trying to draw water from a deep well.

"I knew your father," he boomed. "We went to the races together all the time. A real gentleman. And Max, too, of course."

"I know," I said. "That's what I was counting on."

CHAPTER 52

DAPHNE MOVED OVER IN BED, FLUFFING THE PILLOW IN BACK of her head, and smiled at me.

I said, "Rifeman planned it all. His aim was to get everyone into that house and then wipe them out. Sweet and simple. That's why it was such smooth sailing on the grounds. The dope shipment, of course, was the bait."

Daphne said, "Keller knew about the coke."

"Yeah. He ran that part of the operation."

"Brady knew?"

"Sure. He'd been nosing around for months, had the Gold Wing angle figured almost from the start."

"And you?"

"Rifeman hoped I'd show up. And I didn't disappoint him."

From my bedroom windows I could see a good chunk of skyline. It glittered and glowed, as though putting on a special show just for me. Nice to be appreciated. Mozart's Clarinet Quintet was on the tape deck. A touch of real class. It almost made me believe in civilization again.

Daphne had taken notes during my recital of the Rifeman affair. She glanced at them now.

"Tell me about Neely," she said.

"Got wind of the racket and wanted in. When I collected enough names and places, he braced Keller. Keller wanted more of a cut anyway. The guy gambled, was always broke.

The pair teamed up. That's when Keller stopped meeting anyone of importance."

"But Neely still kept you on."

"Sure. I was slated for the fall guy."

"Meaning what?"

"Neely would tip Rifeman that I was a menace. Maybe he'd bump me off himself. Between that and what he knew, he figured to cut himself a deal. Only things got too hot and Neely had to duck."

"Will he live?"

"Touch and go, sweetheart."

"Danker," Daphne said.

"Top dog, along with Rifeman. Neely didn't know it. And neither did Keller."

"Did you?"

"More or less. Either him or Captain Rogers. My story stank, yet they hardly checked me out. *Very* suspicious. And Danker himself showed up when I was in the hospital. Guy had Neely's number, up to a point. He knew I was watching Keller but wasn't sure exactly how I fit in. But until he walked through the guesthouse door, he had me guessing."

"He came with the police."

"Real cops, too. Locals. Rifeman's coke lab was on the estate. He needed protection. The four cops were part of it."

"Max," Daphne said.

"My ace. He and Dad were Saratoga regulars. Max had the right connections, so I sent him ahead by train. The Saratoga law might not believe me, or would take time to convince, but Max Gabinsky was another story. They called in the state troopers, pronto."

"Where were they?"

"On the lake, in boats. About a quarter mile away till dark. Then much closer."

"They showed up," Daphne said, "in the nick of time."

"Sure did."

"A minute later, I would have been deprived of your company."

"Not really. I wore a wire. Max was getting an earful of the whole show, knew just when to pop up. Got it all on tape, too."

"Sneaky."

"Darn right." I kissed her cheek.

She looked at her notes. "The German."

"Kunst. Silbert and Hersh were right on target. Kunst was part of it, ran the South American end. The guy went under lots of names; the last was Saphire."

"Gloria's husband?"

"The same. Mrs. Silbert came into the picture too late. That's why she couldn't find him. Never thought to look in the cemetery. Kunst kicked the bucket. The guy had cancer, came to the States for treatment, and decided to stay. His son by an earlier marriage carried on in Colombia. That's how Ned Brady got into it. He was with Immigration and Naturalization, and their computers are linked with those of other federal agencies. The profile they got on Saphire rang a bell. Brady started digging. By the time he was done, he knew a lot about Elrex. He blew up their old Madison Avenue office because Rifeman wouldn't play ball. Silbert caught it on the evening news and she was off and running. Keller spotted her, sent his boys around for a chat. They got a bit rough. You getting all this?"

She nodded. "They're all such dreadful people, Jim."

"Not Mr. Nice Guys," I said.

"Who left the body in Keller's apartment?"

"Brady. He dropped by trying to recruit Keller, ran into Shorty. They had a tussle. Shorty lost. Keller was away on business and I found the body before he got back."

"The money in the wall?"

"Just wages for the boys. Rifeman's dough. Keller was trying to pull something with those serial numbers. Maybe. I'm not gonna ask him what. No one knows I got the dough."

313

"You're keeping it?"

"Yeah. My fee and bonus for a job well done. Neely sure isn't going to foot the bill, though there's a chance of a federal reward."

"The yellow page in Neely's garbage?"

"A bum steer. Nothing to do with anything. And those three guys who tried to visit Neely before me: one was Lynch, who came back, the pair was Brady and his pal. Another recruitment mission."

"Saphire?"

"Powdered out. The story she told about Keller was bunk. But Keller did meet Kunst during a corporate investigation. So that part, at least, was true. And odds are there *was* bad blood between her and Keller. Had to be about dough, right?"

"What happens to them now, Jim?"

"The suspects?"

"Yes."

"They go to court."

"And prison."

"Maybe," I said.

"Why maybe?"

"A good lawyer could get some of them off. Who knows?"

"From what you've told me, it doesn't sound likely," Daphne said.

"What I've told you is a lot of guesswork. It fits the facts all right, but a jury might see it differently. Even with the tapes."

Daphne shook her head and moved closer to me. "It's over," she said.

"Thank God. This whole case was for the birds. The only good thing to come out of it was you."

"Any complaints?"

"You kidding? That makes it the best case of my life."